Rave Reviews for Barbara Seranella and

UNWANTED COMPANY

NO OFFENSE INTENDED

And the *Los Angeles Times* bestseller
NO HUMAN INVOLVED

Also by Barbara Seranella

NO OFFENSE INTENDED
NO HUMAN INVOLVED

UNWANTED COMPANY

BARBARA SERANELLA

AVON BOOKS
An Imprint of HarperCollinsPublishers

This is a work of fiction. Names, characters, places, and incidents are products of the author's imagination or are used fictitiously and are not to be construed as real. Any resemblance to actual events, locales, organizations, or persons, living or dead, is entirely coincidental.

AVON BOOKS
An Imprint of HarperCollins*Publishers*
10 East 53rd Street
New York, New York 10022-5299

Copyright © 2000 by Barbara Seranella
ISBN: 0-06-109726-8
www.avonbooks.com

First Avon Books paperback printing: May 2001
First HarperCollins hardcover printing: February 2000

Avon Trademark Reg. U.S. Pat. Off. and in Other Countries, Marca Registrada, Hecho en U.S.A.
HarperCollins® is a trademark of HarperCollins Publishers Inc.

Printed in the U.S.A.

10 9 8 7 6 5 4 3 2 1

For Mom and Dad,
Thanks for having me and everything else

ACKNOWLEDGMENTS

My special thanks to the skilled professionals who escorted me through their worlds:

Robert M. Pentz, Neil Ives, and Donald J. Rudy, Ph.D., of The Aerospace Corporation;

retired Rand Corporation consultant Guy Pauker;

Detective Carl Carter with the Riverside County;

private investigators retired LAPD detective Donald Long and his lovely wife Susie Long.

I also owe a great deal to:

the savvy and intelligence of my agent, Sandy Dijkstra, and her fine staff;

the loving professionalism of my editor, Carolyn Marino, publisher, Marjorie Braman, and their assistants, Robin Stamm and Jeffery McGraw;

my wonderful, hardworking publicists Jackie Green, Jim Schneeweis, Randy Sloan, and Michele Lambert;

the unselfish support and enthusiasm of authors like Michael Connelly and T. Jefferson Parker;

the skilled reading by my valued friends Kathleen Tumpane, Diane Ponti, Marie Reindorp, Richard Brewer, and Sandie Herron (A Novel Idea)

Special thanks also to:

my brother, Dr. Larry Shore, who reads and listens carefully and always gives good advice;

my other brother, David Nathan Shore, who keeps me laughing and on track;

and last, I thank my husband, Ron, who always does his very best to stand still while I read him every draft.

UNWANTED COMPANY

PROLOGUE

Christmas, 1983

Artificial green garlands wound around the lampposts topped with aluminum silver stars. Movie-going crowds thronged the wet sidewalks. Colored lights twinkled and Christmas carols played from speakers mounted over the doorways of the shops. The stores were filled with merchandise and still open even though it was almost nine in the evening.

Only in America, he thought.

He'd been in Los Angeles for less than a week and was hungry for diversion. It had been raining most of the week and drizzling off and on all evening. He understood that this was unusual for Los Angeles, even in December. The newscasters blamed it on an El Niño weather front.

He chose an apartment building in Westwood, one of the high-rises on Wilshire. The building had underground parking, keyed electronic gates, and a doorman manning the lobby. Just the sort of place where people relaxed their vigilance.

Westwood was also a college town full of brazen young women who only had eyes, it seemed, for the sculpted torsos and bronzed skin of their contemporaries. He found their overt sexuality offensive. Such decadence usually signaled a civilization's downfall. Didn't they teach history in the universities anymore?

He pushed the button to signal the elevator. He liked to begin at the top of a building and work down, checking for open doors as he went. He was not able to reach the penthouse, lacking the required key for the elevator. His one foible —these crimes, though he hesitated to use such a harsh word, were acts of opportunity. Harmless peeks into the worlds of others. The urges had begun when he was quite young, a boy of ten, confusing as they were irresistible. But what does a boy that age understand of anything?

To satisfy his impulses, he took things from people's homes—worthless things: socks, belts, birth certificates—the majority of which he later discarded. The panties, particularly the pink and blue ones, he kept. And later, alone in his room, the feel of the nylon or cotton or silk against his skin brought a gratifying emission that was both terrifying and splendid. It was as if his body were filled with some volatile churning substance which, while making him more alive than most, also needed periodic venting. By the time he turned sixteen, just the sight of an open window gave him an erection. Though he was disconcerted when sometimes it took many trips through the window before he could achieve the desired release.

As his tastes grew more refined, he discovered and devoured books on sex and crime, reading with great interest the works of Freud and material on subjects of masochism, fetishism, sadism, and flagellation. Not that he needed the famous psychiatrist to tell him that the burglaries were about sex. Or that discretion regarding his taste in entertainment was crucial.

Nearly a decade ago, when he had left home for the university, he had almost been caught. Quick thinking and a few words in the right ears saved him. But from then on he resolved to be a better person and exercise CONTROL. He recognized then the need to change his habits. At the time he believed his activities were probably just a passing phase. He'd even started dating girls, even though he found women quite repulsive. His only requirement was that the woman be quiet —and lie very still—then he was able to get himself into a state where he could perform.

And wasn't rising above one's inhibitions the mark of a great man? A man of consequence? In his second year of studies, he put aside psychology and shifted his focus to history. What better way to achieve greatness than to learn from those singular men who dared to go beyond the boundaries? He had no intention of living his life as a sheep, a mere follower.

The elevator came to a stop. His attention was riveted on the opening doors. He took a deep breath and stepped out. A woman emerged from her apartment just as the doors of his elevator closed behind him. She was dressed in a three-piece knit suit, with simple but expensive jewelry. The look on her face suggested that she neither gave nor asked for any quarter. Not the sort of woman too many men would be attracted to, he supposed. Too strong—too willful. In a way she reminded him of his mother.

He walked over to the stairwell door. In the reflection of the fire extinguisher's glass case, he saw she had spotted him. At least, he thought she had. He was having difficulty concentrating. His head hurt and he'd begun to sweat. He stepped back until the darkness of the hallway's shadows enveloped him. He would have willed himself invisible, but then a powerful anger came over him. Who was this bitch to throw him into such a panic? Did she think she was better than he? He left the dark corner she thought to have boxed him in.

"What?" he asked her.

She acted like she didn't know what he was talking about. He grabbed her arm and shoved her inside. Before she could make a sound, he wrapped his arm around her throat. The pounding of his blood, his juices, drowned out all other sounds, all other considerations. Within a few minutes she was still. He released her. As her body crumpled to the floor, his headache also began to abate.

When he checked his watch again, he saw that over an hour had passed. The woman lay sprawled across the floor of her living room. Her clothes were in shreds, and blood covered much of her body. He ran to the kitchen and fetched a wet towel to wipe her wounds clean.

His mother's voice echoed in his mind. *Clean up your mess, you filthy worthless monkey boy.* She called him many things: stupid, worthless, retarded. She added monkey boy when he began sprouting pubescent hair. Often her exasperation with him was justified. He could be clumsy and thoughtless. Like the time he bent down next to her in the garden to help her weed, and he'd gotten grass stains on his good pants. Slapping his face was the quickest way to get his attention, to teach him right from wrong, she said. But he was on to her little secret. He'd found out for himself on the school yard how good it felt to strike bare flesh, the compensation of release that it brought. Instantaneous. Addicting in its own way. Which was not to say that her other lessons were lost on him.

Cleanliness had its own rewards.

He washed the woman's cuts with soap and hot water, but the blood continued to ooze out. He ran back to the bathroom to look for bandages. He was reaching for the medicine cabinet above the sink when the image of himself in the mirror stayed his hand and nearly stopped his heart. Her blood had sprayed all over him.

Taking a roll of tape from the cabinet, he returned to the woman. He almost hated to admit it, but he felt wonderful— like a new man. As with the little girl-child almost a year ago, whose little body went limp in his hands, this death was not in vain.

"Thank you," he said, bending down to kiss each of the wounds gently before taping them shut. When he finished his ministrations, he placed the woman's cold, bejeweled hand over her heart, hoping to convey his sentiments. Then he returned to the bathroom. Kicking off his shoes, he stepped into the shower and let the water run until the liquid draining away from his black nylon track suit ran clear. He dried himself as best he could, understanding now the reason for the evening's rain, how it was his friend. When he finished, he folded the towels carefully and hung them back up. There was nothing more anyone could do for the woman. The best he could do was save himself. The last thing his career needed was the dark cloud of scandal.

He took the stairs down rather than the elevator. The lobby was full of shoppers, grimly clutching their purchases. He held the door open for an elderly woman carrying a glossy red shopping bag. "Merry Christmas," he said.

She smiled back at him. "Thank you."

That's the spirit, he thought. He also discovered that the wanton appearance of the local women no longer annoyed him. Rather, he felt a benign acceptance. To each his own. Judge not, as they say.

He stepped out onto the sidewalk and took a deep breath. What a city this was, still in its infancy—virginal. Absent, but not missed, were the old-city smells of sewers, subways, and ancient stone. All the buildings here were new—modern monoliths of concrete and glass. So many cars, so many people, and all too busy to notice anything but their own small lives.

The attitude was infectious. Already, he could barely remember the face of the woman upstairs. And why should a stranger mean anything to him after all?

"Ah, me." He sighed contentedly. There was nothing to do but go on; even the strongest of individuals faltered at times. He would not waste a minute beating himself up over what he had no power to change. What was past was past. Los Angeles was a place of new starts. Opportunities were endless. Annals waiting to be written.

CHAPTER 1

June, 1984

"This patient has a history," Munch overheard the receptionist tell the dental hygienist as she handed over Munch's thick file.

She managed a quick smirk.

That had to be the understatement of the century.

Thirty minutes later, after the woman had finished with her scraping and picking, she told Munch to hang tight, that Dr. Moore wanted to have a quick look. How long before that quick look would take place, she didn't say.

Munch glanced at the schoolroom-style clock on the wall above the door. Her appointment for cleaning had been for eleven. It was now almost noon.

She shifted restlessly and adjusted her bib, leaving black smudge marks on the quilted paper. She was wearing her Texaco uniform and greasy shoes, which had also marked up the chair's gray-and-sky-blue-leather upholstery. Even though she had washed her hands before leaving work, black grime encased her cuticles and outlined the numerous small cuts on her knuckles. She longed to get back to the shop and under a hood.

The receptionist ducked her head into the room. "Dr. Moore will be right with you, hon."

"I'd appreciate that," Munch said, but the woman had already gone. Her fingers grazed across one of the dental picks laid out on the tray suspended to her left. The handle was crosshatched for a secure grip; the thin sharp point going off at a ninety-degree angle. It would work well for removing snap rings, Munch thought, or slipping rubber O-rings out of their grooves. Perfect for power-steering pump reseals or any of a dozen other intricate operations. She briefly considered slipping the instrument into her shirt pocket, next to the tire gauge and clip-on combination screwdriver/magnet. The little round mirror that swiveled on the end of its stainless-steel handle raised similar temptations—be good for finding oil leaks in hard-to-get-to places, like the back of intake manifolds. She let the larcenous impulses breeze through her and felt no guilt. Even former president Jimmy Carter had admitted to lusting in his heart.

She thought about the phone call she had received at work just before leaving for this appointment. Speaking of history. The call was from Ellen, newly out of jail, back in Los Angeles, and wanting to hook up. Munch told her to come by later today. She wondered if that had been a mistake, but what else could she do?

Crazy fucking Ellen—with her penchant for country music, Dolly Parton wigs, and the distinctive way she spoke in that exacting Deep South drawl, enunciating each word as if it had special meaning. Funny she should call just before Munch's visit to a dentist. One of Ellen's more successful scams had been her ability to land a straight job—usually in some medical-related field, where the good drugs were. The last of which had been in a dental office. She had lied, of course, made up an outrageous résumé, dressed up in one of her big, curly, redheaded wigs, a tight dress, and gotten herself hired. If she had just stuck to the pharmaceutical cocaine, she probably would have pulled it off. Her downfall had come when her new employer returned early from lunch and found Ellen rolling a tank of nitrous oxide into the parking structure.

"Sorry for the delay," Dr. Moore said, flipping on the bright light over her head. "We had an unexpected emergency."

"Most of them are," Munch said. She leaned back, opened wide, and closed her eyes. She let her thoughts drift as she disassociated from what he was doing inside her mouth.

Robbing banks had been another one of Ellen's bright ideas.

Munch remembered the day Ellen had come up with the plan. The equipment necessary for the great bank heist had been easy enough to come by: panty hose, Superglue, and their disguises. Simplicity, Ellen had assured her, would be the key to their success.

Ellen's plan was to glue the stockings inside the night-deposit drop slots. They would do this at night, after bank hours, and return before the bank opened and reel in their booty.

Jail was full of brain surgeons such as them. It had never gotten that far. Their careers as bank bunglers had been blessedly short. The glue had stuck to their hands. The nylons had stuck to everything but the stainless-steel slots. At the third bank a security guard had discovered them. He'd been alerted, he said, by their giggles. Ellen had convinced him that what they were doing was a harmless sorority prank. On-the-spot improvisation was one of Ellen's strong suits. But then, Ellen was good at anything that involved lying. The rent-a-pig had let them go after they let him cop a feel. Cheap payment indeed. Munch didn't realize until later that bank burglary was a federal beef.

"Open," Dr. Moore said.

"Sorry," Munch mumbled, adjusting the suction hose with her tongue.

"So how's the limo business going?"

Munch started to reach for a business card, but the dentist stopped her. "You gave me one the last time you were in," he said.

He had her rinse and spit. She filled the paper cup and adjusted the suction on the hose. While waiting, she had fiddled with every knob and switch. "Now that prom season is over, we've been enjoying the, uh, slower pace."

"I've heard it's a tough business."

"It's the insurance that kills you," she said.

"At least you don't have to worry about mechanic bills."

"Just parts. But you're right. That's our edge. Plus, with the Olympics coming to L.A. this year, I might have to expand the operation."

"How many cars do you have now?" he asked.

She paused. That was always a tough question. In other words, the truth wasn't the best answer, not if she wanted her business to come off as a going concern. People loved winners. To say she was struggling along with one, previously owned, Cadillac stretch and working out of her house made the wrong impression.

"As many as you need," she said. "Are we all done here?"

"I think we should take some X rays," he said.

How much will that cost? "Maybe next time, I've got to get back to work." She unhooked the alligator clips holding on her bib. The truth was she worked on straight commission, was raising a child on her own, and the limo business—her ticket to easy cash—wasn't panning out.

She thought she had it made when she bought the silver Caddy with its classy, blue-velour interior. Another good feature was that the car had been stretched and outfitted by the reputable Executive Coach Builders, not some half-assed cheapo chop shop that never got the driveshaft right or used enough steel in the reinforcements. The limo had needed some electrical work, but that was no problem. Wire and solder were cheap enough. In fact she had worked all the numbers out, figuring in costs of insurance, advertising, drivers' salaries, and had come up with encouraging results. The limo only had to work twenty hours a month to start earning a profit. After that, everything else was gravy. She worked in Bel Air with all its rich and famous. And weren't those the very people who hired limos to squire them around town?

The reality of the business had been a brutal, depressing lesson in small-business economics. Since starting the business in January and using money earmarked for Asia's education, she had only managed to garner one or two customers who called her with any sort of regularity. And they were mostly sixty-dollar one-way airport runs at inconvenient hours. Then prom season had struck, and she had more business than she could handle and half of those runs had had nightmares attached. The high-school kids sneaked in liquor, threw up on the carpet, or tried to climb out the moon roof while the car was in motion. Once the limo came back with the side windows broken out. Another time the client convinced the driver to bill him for services. Munch was never able to get ahold of the guy. Letters to the address he had given her came back stamped RETURN TO SENDER: ADDRESSEE UNKNOWN.

She caught a glimpse of gold on the dentist's ring finger. "When's your anniversary? We have a special romantic evening package—includes a beautiful silk rose and a bottle of champagne with a three-hour minimum." She didn't mention that both were leftovers from the Valentine's Day special. "You should surprise your wife some night."

"Are your chauffeurs experienced?" he asked.

"And licensed," she said. The dentist would have no way of knowing she was referring to a California driver's license; there was no such thing as a chauffeur's license in California. "I might even drive you myself," she added, trying to sound cheery. "I do that every so often just to stay in touch with that side of the business." She knew she was talking too much. Her bullshit was wearing thin, even to her own ears. It was the first week of June. The opening ceremonies of the 1984 Summer Olympics were still almost two months away. If only she could hold out until then.

When she got back to work, Lou, her new boss and former coworker, was standing in the lube bay and speaking on the extension. After Happy Jack had sold his business to the

Japanese firm that leveled every shop on the intersection to build a twenty-story office building, Lou had bought the mechanical end of a gas station in Bel Air and invited her to come aboard. He even allowed her to install an extra phone line and advertise A&M Limousine Service from the station's upscale location.

In return, she made the limo available for his dates, which were varied and many. Happy Jack used to say that Lou would fuck a snake, whatever that meant. Munch didn't feel she had any room for judgment.

When Lou saw her, he waved her over to him. "She just walked in," he said into the phone as she approached. "Let me see if I can catch her."

He covered the receiver with his hand, and said, "This is that guy with the Vega, the one you put back together with stop leak."

She reached for the phone. "Is it still overheating?"

"No, he wants to rent your limo tonight."

"Great. What was his name?"

"Ward, Raleigh Ward."

She took the phone. "Mr. Ward?"

"Yeah." The man's tense voice conjured up images of his heavy build and nervous eyes. She also remembered the odor of peppermints that had pervaded his car and person, an odor that didn't quite mask the undertones of something alcoholic. "Listen, honey, I know this is short notice—"

"No, that's fine. Let me check our schedule." She waved to Lou to bring her a clipboard. "When do you need the car?"

"Six."

"Uh-huh. And how many in your party?"

"I'm not sure yet. Does that matter?"

"Well, the car seats six comfortably. Eight, if two people don't mind riding in the trunk."

He didn't laugh. "There won't be that many. Maybe three or four, tops."

"And how long do you need the car for? Our minimum on the weekend is three hours."

"Oh, jeez, honey. I don't know. At least until two A.M."

Her heart was pounding now. Six to two in the morning was eight hours. Eight times forty dollars plus the fifteen percent gratuity. . . She forced herself to sound calm. "And will that be cash or charge?"

"Cash."

"We'll need a hundred in advance. Company policy."

"No problem."

"You're in luck, Mr. Ward. I have a car available."

"You sure it's no trouble?"

"Not at all." She took down his address and phone number, hung up the phone, and said a silent prayer of thanks. She heard Lou asking someone if he could help them. By his earnest tone she knew that someone had to be a woman—no doubt a young and attractive one.

"No, thank you, sugar," a woman's voice answered. "I am waiting for that little gal right over there." The woman's cadence was as unmistakable as it was unforgettable.

Munch turned and faced her old friend.

Ellen seemed reasonably healthy. She was blond today. Her clothes fit, and her complexion was clear. She had lost that drawn look, and there seemed to be genuine color on her high cheekbones. Jail does that for some people.

"Hey," Munch said. "Here you are."

"Yep, this is me. Well, don't you look great," Ellen said.

"I was just thinking about you. How are you?"

"I don't know. It is weird, being out in the world. I suppose I will adjust." Ellen spaced each syllable as if it were a separate word.

"You mind tagging along while I work? I've got to get out of here early, and these people are going to want their cars back for the weekend."

"I don't mind a bit," Ellen said, following Munch to her toolbox. "Lord, are all these yours?"

Munch patted her four-foot roll-away Craftsman toolbox with pride. "You'd be surprised how much money sticks to you when you're not spending it on drugs." She let that sink in for a moment while she selected a few wrenches. "Are you getting along all right?"

"You are probably more interested in what I have not been doing."

"Well?"

"Sixteen days of voluntary sobriety." She said "sobriety" like it was four different words. The pride in her tone certainly sounded sincere. Munch had explained in her weekly letters that Ellen should be prepared to change everything about herself—that good habits were the easiest ones to break. After not seeing Ellen for years, Munch had gone to the local woman's prison last Thanksgiving as part of an A.A. panel. Ever since getting sober and off drugs seven years ago, Munch felt it only fitting that she celebrate the holiday by reminding herself that but for the grace of God she would be dead, in jail, or insane.

She had walked into that room of plastic chairs and cold linoleum at the California Institution for Women at Frontera and, lo and behold, there was Ellen. They had to cool their enthusiasm lest the guards think this chance meeting was some sort of conspiracy. And truth be told Munch hadn't been completely at ease with her old friend. Munch had changed so much since getting clean and joining society. Seeing Ellen put her in a momentary quandary. There was an awkward pause while she fought the urge to be hip, slick, cool, and talk the talk or just blast her friend to a safe distance with Program rhetoric.

Then Ellen grinned, and the years between them fell away. Munch felt a surge of relief and wondered why she always had to make such a big deal about things. This was Ellen. The woman with whom she'd spent her formative teenage years. Hadn't the two of them figured out life and men and how the world worked? Hadn't they revealed all to each other as their lives exploded around them? It was suddenly absolutely natural that Munch be the one to guide Ellen through this latest leg of the adventure. Drugs were out. God was in. Grow or go.

Munch spoke about the joy of being self-supporting, and the return of self-esteem, but she had really gotten through when she said, "Ellen, you're almost thirty. You can't tell me you're still having fun." Taking due note of the prison surrounding them and the fact that after the panel Munch was free to leave in her own car, Ellen had been receptive. She even said she was willing to do whatever it took. Munch told her not to bother coming around if she weren't.

"Follow me," Munch said, now walking to the far end of the lot. "I have to put the steering column back together on this Camaro." She stopped at a red Rally Sport and slid into the driver's seat. Ellen came around to the other side of the Chevy, sat in the passenger seat, and watched as Munch pressed the steering wheel back in place over the splined shaft. "What have you been doing?" Munch asked.

"I had to go to one of those halfway houses for a short spell."

"That's where you got your sixteen days?" Munch asked.

Ellen nodded. "They still count."

"Have you been to see your mama yet?"

"Yeah. I stopped by to say hey. It went about as you would expect. A couple of hours is about all I can take of her and all that."

Munch nodded sympathetically. The stepfather was the real problem, but the two of them knew each other well enough to be able to leave certain things unsaid.

"Since I've been back in these parts, I've spent much of my time looking for work. Apparently my résumé is not impressing anyone."

"You got a place?"

Ellen looked out the window on her side. "I am staying with Russ for the moment."

"Roofer Russ?" Russ the roofer lived in Venice. Pushing sixty, he was good for a place to stay and a little spending cash. It was also understood that the price of admission included sharing his bed. He wasn't so bad, if you could get past the smell of tar.

"I am hoping that it will be a temporary arrangement," Ellen said. "Soon as I can get a job I'll get my own place."

Munch was quiet as she hooked up the wires for the horn pad. The Program made all sorts of promises about how your life would improve once you gave up the booze and dope and turned to God. That was true as far as it went. God would put out the fire, but someone still had to run with the hose. "You got a driver's license?" Munch asked. "Any tickets lately?"

"Not lately—not for twenty-eight months, for sure. Why?"

"I've got a limousine service. I could put you on my insurance. It's not full-time work, just weekends mostly. Pays ten bucks an hour plus tips."

Ellen's face grew still, even cautious, as if she wasn't quite sure what she was hearing.

"I'm offering you a job."

Ellen gave off a little squeal of pleasure and squeezed Munch's arm. Lou looked their way.

"You won't get rich," Munch said. "But it's something."

Ellen blinked back tears and wiped a finger carefully under her eye. "Sounds just perfect."

"I've got a run tonight, that's why I've got to hustle." She handed Ellen a business card. "Give me your driver's license number. I'll call the insurance company Monday morning and put you on the policy."

"You will not regret this. I swear."

"Hey, don't worry about it. A lot of people helped me out when I was getting started."

Munch turned back to her work feeling proud and a little nervous. But could Ellen do any worse than the driver that had come back from a high-school homecoming run drunker than the kids?

After Ellen left, Munch finished with the Camaro and two other jobs. She left the shop by four-fifteen and was at her daughter's school by half past the hour. She spotted Asia playing tether ball in the elementary school's still-busy playground. The six-year-old's collar-length brown curls clung close to her head as she spun and slammed her fist into the yellow ball. Asia wanted to work at Sea World when she grew up, training dolphins, or maybe be a ballerina. Munch asked her why not go for both.

"Asia," she yelled as she pulled up to the curb. "C'mon. Let's go."

"Five minutes," Asia yelled back.

"Where's your coat?"

Asia looked down at her torso and shrugged.

Shit, Munch thought, slamming her car into park and shutting off the engine. She got out of her Pontiac and headed for the cloakroom. "We've got to hurry, honey," she said. "We've got a run tonight, and I need to get home and get the car ready."

"Are you driving?" Asia asked, missing the ball.

"No."

"Yippee."

Munch went inside the school building and sifted through a pile of coats until she found Asia's wrinkled down-filled jacket. The front was damp. She shook it out and called for Asia once more.

"Four minutes," Asia implored.

"Now."

Asia slumped her little shoulders and reluctantly left the

playground. Munch threw Asia's lunch box in the backseat and strapped the little girl into her seat.

The first-graders were learning how to read. On the drive home, Asia recited every word she could think of that began with sl and sh. Munch was glad she didn't know them all.

CHAPTER 2

At twenty after five, Munch realized that the driver wasn't going to show. That was the trouble with part-time help: anybody who really had their shit together would have a full-time job. She only had a short list of drivers to call on and none that were any good at responding on short notice. She never dreamed it would be so difficult to find a person with a clean driving record, some semblance of a suit, and a desire to earn some extra cash on mostly weekend nights. Yet the reality was that the limo business brought out all varieties of flakes—drivers and customers included. She'd hoped this latest guy, a wanna-be actor, would be a keeper. Obviously not, especially when he didn't even have the decency to call and offer some feeble excuse.

Now she was left to the all-too-familiar last-minute panic that seemed to be an integral part of the livery business and no time to dwell on Mr. I'm-going-to-be-a-star's lack of a work ethic. All she knew was that if the car wasn't rolling out the driveway in the next five minutes, it wasn't going to make it to the pickup in time. She left Asia in the kitchen eating her McDonald's Happy Meal and called, regrettably, the one person she knew would come right over, her ex-lover, Derek.

"Hi, it's me," Munch said as she laid out her chauffeur costume: black slacks and heels, a white blouse, and thin driving gloves to cover the stains on her hands. She heard the volume of his television being lowered.

"What's up?" he asked.

"I'm in a jam. My driver didn't show up. Could you come over and watch Asia?"

"Tonight?"

"Right now. She's had dinner. I just need you to watch TV with her until bedtime."

"All right."

"Thanks, you're a lifesaver." Now all she had to do was explain to Asia. She clasped a wide red belt around her waist, found Asia planted in front of the television, and explained the situation.

"But why can't Derek drive the run?" Asia asked, watching her mother fit a red-enamel hoop into each ear.

"Don't whine. I told you before. I couldn't put Derek on the insurance because of his driving record. You know I'd rather stay home with you. This is an emergency."

"It's always an emergency."

"No, it's not. I tell you what. After dance class tomorrow, we'll go do something special together. Just you and me."

"Couldn't I just go with you?"

"You'd be bored to death, believe me." She bent down and kissed her. "Be good tonight."

"You, too," Asia said, her large brown eyes solemn. "Remember, let's be careful out there."

Munch laughed. "Silly goose. What could happen?"

Raleigh Ward bolted from his cramped studio apartment, leaving dishes in the sink and dirty clothes on the bathroom floor. Usually he made some attempt to tidy up before going out. Not that he'd be entertaining later. The only female that came around was a marmalade tabby who loved him for his tuna fish. He named her Cassandra and vowed unconvincingly that if she got knocked up, he was putting her out on her ass.

He locked the door before the phone could ring again and foul his mood even further. Although that last call would be tough to match for sheer ball-busting.

As soon as he'd heard the voice of his first ex-wife, he should have known the evening was shot. He should have prepped himself—asked what she wanted now. She only called when she wanted something. Never just to see how he was. And yet the sound of her voice never failed to raise an expectant thrill in his stomach—a feeling he used to identify as love. Now he wasn't sure what to call it.

By the time he'd hung up the phone, he was five hundred dollars poorer. She wouldn't be calling if she didn't have to, she said. The kid needed orthodontia. What choice did he have? Be a prick or a sap? He pulled a tin of Altoids from his pockets and slipped one of the powerful peppermints under his tongue.

It wasn't that money itself was so important to him, but there was a limit. Would there ever be an end to the demands? Or would it be up to him to draw the line?

The source of his well-documented, perpetual state of economic crisis could be summed up in three words: Community Fucking Property.

Even his own dear mother had asked him if he had to marry both of them

What could he say? The stupid truth was that with each marriage he'd had the expectation that she would be the one. And wasn't it amazing that he could maintain that level of optimism despite all? Surely that spoke to something in his character. His unions always ended the same way. Just when his hopes were raised that he was finally getting a handle on things, becoming the winner he always believed he could be, the level of effort required to hold a marriage together would prove too much. He blamed these failures on the calls that always seemed to come in the middle of the night and the absences he was forbidden to explain. Such was the price he paid to serve his country and the agency that employed him.

He still loved his exes, each in her own way, carrying the image of each woman inside him—wraithlike. Lately, though, the burden of their disapproving, disappointed, and disenfranchised talking heads was weighing heavy on him.

There was that.

And then there was the mailing of the two separate alimony checks that reduced his salary each month to a joke. It tended to make a guy bitter, living hand to fucking mouth while all the sleazy fucks like Victor Draicu, the Romanian diplomatic time bomb he was baby-sitting for the evening, grew fat. Especially with everything else he had to cope with— like keeping the world safe from despots. Years of covert operations in Iron Curtain countries had given him glimpses of the world few others in America were privy to. He'd seen firsthand the "threat from the East."

He snorted derisively. Not that Romania was such a threat. One forty-watt bulb per room, fuel rationing, power outages, Securitate agents at every turn. Still, the prevailing wisdom was that it never hurt to develop sources in the enemy's camp. Turning Victor Draicu would be child's play, especially with the man's taste for Western entertainment.

He'd reached the bottom of the stairs and began patting his pockets. The feeling that he'd forgotten something nagged at him.

"Shit," he said out loud, remembering that he hadn't left the window open for Cassandra. He checked his watch, then ran back upstairs to give the little fleabag easy access to his life.

At exactly five minutes to six, Munch pulled in front of the apartment building in Culver City that Raleigh Ward had given as the pickup address. He was already on the sidewalk. She would have rather seen him emerge from one of the apartments. Just in case. She took some comfort in the memory that she had reached him by phone when they had repaired his car, so he couldn't be that much of a flake. If only she could figure out a diplomatic way to collect all the money up front instead of having to wait until she was already out the time and the service.

He didn't wait for her to get out and open the door for him, but waved his hand as if to say, "Don't bother," and climbed into the back with surprising fluidity for his bulk.

"Where to?" she asked.

"The Beverly Wilshire. You got a phone in this thing?"

"It's a dollar a minute," she told him.

"Yeah, fine."

"It's in a compartment in the center armrest," she said. "If you hand it to me, I'll unlock it."

He found the telephone and handed it forward. The coiled cord stretched across the expanse of seats as she zeroed the minute counter and punched in the codes that would enable him to call out.

"All right then, sir," she told him as she handed him back the mobile phone, "we're all set. The buttons over your head operate the moon roof and privacy partition. You'll find ice and mixers in the compartment on the right. Help yourself to a drink."

"Thanks," he said. "After the Beverly Wilshire we need to make a stop in West Hollywood." He handed her a slip of paper with an address on North Gower written on it and a hundred-dollar bill. "Can you find it okay?"

"No problem."

"Great." The privacy partition slid up. As soon as it did, she heard the tape recorder under her seat click and whir. Microphones were strategically placed throughout the passenger section. It probably wasn't legal, but it was her best defense against the teenagers who rented the limo for proms. The tape recorder was activated whenever the thick upholstered panel separated her from her passengers. It had been her experience that whenever teenagers put the partition up they were about to break the no-drinking rule. The mikes fed to the tape recorder under her seat; another led directly to an earpiece.

She slipped the earpiece into her left ear. The system was functioning properly. Raleigh-baby was on the phone.

"Yeah," she heard him say. "We're on the way. All set on your end?" There was a moment of silence, then he said, "You just worry about you."

The Beverly Wilshire Hotel was built in a section of Beverly Hills where no freeways run. To get there, she headed up big Santa Monica Boulevard, past the Mormon Temple, with its golden steeples and acres of perfectly trimmed grass. The lavish expanse of green amidst the teeming streets of West Los Angeles was as impressive a testimony to the sect's wealth as anything else. As she passed the block-long black wrought-iron fence surrounding the grounds, she read the sign posted near the sidewalk. THE CHURCH OF JESUS CHRIST OF LATTER-DAY SAINTS it proclaimed.

Latter-day Saints.

She pictured angels catching the last train to heaven, waiting till the last minute to leave earthly temptations behind. Better latter than never, they were saying.

At Wilshire Boulevard she hung a right, past Wilson's House of Suede on the corner of little Santa Monica and Wilshire. The six-lane thoroughfare was crowded as usual. No matter what time of day it was, the road never seemed wide enough to accommodate the never-ending stream of Jaguars, Mercedes, and Rolls Royces as they headed for the pricey restaurants and the exclusive showrooms of Rodeo Drive.

When they arrived at the entrance of the Beverly Wilshire, with its baroque facade and thick brass railings, Raleigh Ward did wait for the white-gloved valet to open his door. "You going to be okay?" he asked her before he jumped out. "I'll be back in fifteen."

"I'll be here," she said.

The doorman told her she couldn't congest the entrance and would have to circle the block.

"Didn't you see who that was?" she asked.

His cocky expression wavered for an instant.

She made a derisive noise through her teeth and shook her head in disgust. "Only the owner of this hotel."

He studied her for a moment, then moved a cone and let her wait unmolested in the hotel's circular driveway. Ten minutes later, Raleigh returned with a plump, bald man. The second man's polyester pants flared at the hem, and the points of his shirt collar nearly reached his pockets. She was no fashion expert, but she knew which decade it was.

The first words out of Mr. Disco's mouth were, "Where are the whores? You said we'd have broads." He had a European accent—something Slavic.

Raleigh looked pained. "We're going to pick them up now."

The address on North Gower turned out to be an apartment complex. The entrance to the parking lot was blocked by an electronically operated, twelve-foot iron gate. Security cameras were mounted on the complex's light poles. Raleigh had Munch punch the numbers 1–0–3 into a 10-digit keypad. She heard a phone ringing, and then a woman's voice said hello.

"It's us," Raleigh called from the backseat.

"Pull up to the left," the woman said. The gate slid open.

The women who emerged from Apartment 103 were long-legged and buxom. Munch wondered how they managed to move so effortlessly in their four-inch spikes and short, tight skirts. Both women carried tiny purses and no coats.

"Now we'd like to see some nightlife," Raleigh said. He looked over at the bald guy. "Show us the hottest, hippest club in L.A."

"I know just the place," Munch said. She pulled out into the street with one hand on the Thomas Guide, already thumbing to the page that showed the dense grid of streets that make up metropolitan Los Angeles.

Twenty minutes later, they arrived at the Stock Exchange,

a New York–style dance club and bar complete with a tuxedo-clad doorman standing guard under a silk awning. The guy was huge, well over six feet, with a tiny ponytail and a superiority complex. Raleigh's bald friend slipped her a twenty and told her to get them past the velvet rope.

She pulled up in front of the club. When she stopped, she was aware of the people in line trying to see in through the limo's tinted windows. Someone called out, "Hey, my car's here." Like he was the first joker to come up with that line.

She ran a brush through her hair and got out of the car. The doorman raised half an eyebrow. With the twenty folded in her gloved hand, she approached him, stopping short at the edge of the red carpet that extended out onto the sidewalk from the club's door. They leaned toward each other until his lips hovered over her ear.

"How many?" he asked.

"Four," she said as she slipped him the bill. He nodded.

She returned to the limo and opened the door to the passenger compartment. Raleigh and his companions eased themselves out. He patted her arm, and said, "We're going to be a while." He glanced nervously up the street. "Where will you be?"

"I'll keep an eye out for you," she said. "This is my gig. Don't worry. Have a good time."

He answered her with a look that seemed to say she had suggested something ridiculous, then entered the club with his party.

Munch parked the car in the underground parking structure next to the club and climbed into the back of the limo to survey the damage. It wasn't terrible. She washed out the glasses they had used and filled them with fresh cocktail napkins that she folded so as to show off the company logo. The phone was still on. She pushed the recall button and wrote down the phone number he had called. She'd been burned too many times not to take as many precautions as possible. Just last month she'd collected on a deadbeat plumber who owed her two hundred dollars. The run had begun as a two-hour dinner date for which the plumber paid in advance with cash. Then he and his date had started drinking and directing Munch to cruise all over the county. The plumber swore he'd pay her the next day. Multiple calls to the guy's work had produced no results. Then she tried calling the number the guy called from the limo. When she asked for the plumber, the woman said she was the wife and asked what was this about. The wife was not the same woman who'd made nasty with him in the back of the car. Munch made up some quick story about working on the guy's van and needing to talk to him about additional repairs. The wife promised to give the plumber the message. The very next day the guy paid.

After putting the phone back into its niche, she restocked the ice compartment with mixers and wiped down the chrome. Satisfied, she returned to the cab and settled down with a paperback. Two hours later, the book no longer held her interest. In the warm quiet of the car, the day's fatigue was catching up with her. She wondered if they served coffee inside the Stock Exchange. They must. She also needed to use the bathroom. She put down her book, pulled her gloves back on, locked the car, and headed up the garage ramp.

The doorman turned his head halfway in her direction as she approached.

A long line of hopefuls still waited to get into the club. The doorman regarded them with contempt as they smiled gamely at him and hopped from foot to foot, trying to get a peek inside.

The only way to impress Mr. Ponytail, she knew, was with indifference. She leaned against the wall and stared at nothing. The standoff lasted fifteen minutes, then Mr. Ponytail did the only cool thing left. He unhooked his velvet rope and nodded her in. She passed him, acknowledging his graciousness with a slow blink, knowing better than to smile outright. She might need to get in there again sometime.

Inside the club, the walls throbbed with music. Quarter-sized rainbows thrown from a rotating disco ball jiggled across dancers' faces and bodies. Black-and-white Bogart movies played on the twenty-foot walls, providing a backdrop for several go-go dancers who gyrated on catwalks.

When she emerged from the bathroom, she spotted Raleigh-baby leaning against the bar. One of the women they had picked up in Hollywood was dancing pelvis to pelvis with another man. He watched them with pursed lips. Mr. Disco and the other woman leaned over her purse, sniffing coke, it looked like. Raleigh noticed Munch and waved her over.

"What you need, doll?" he asked.

"Coffee."

Raleigh beckoned to the bartender, shouted in his ear, and a cup of coffee appeared on the bar top. Munch sipped gratefully. Raleigh watched his date for another couple of minutes, then turned back to Munch. "Get the car," he said. "We're leaving."

She looked at him uncertainly, wondering if he meant to leave the women behind.

"Get the car," he said.

By the time she had the car positioned at the entrance of the club, Raleigh, the bald guy, and the two women came rolling out. They asked to stop at a liquor store for supplies, then Munch delivered the party back to the address in Hollywood. One of the women jumped out of the back and punched a few numbers on the keypad. The electronic gate slid open. Munch waited until the woman was back in the car, then slowly pulled into the driveway.

"I'll be right back," Raleigh said.

She watched him climb the stairs with the other three. Soon light filled the window of the apartment. Through the thin curtains she could see the four of them walking around.

Raleigh returned to the car minutes later and told her to drive a couple of blocks, then pull over. The privacy partition went up. Over the microphone she heard the tones as he punched another number in the car phone.

"All set," he said. "Later."

She heard him mixing himself a drink: the ice hitting the tumbler, the hiss of a soda bottle opening, the glug of the decanter emptying.

She waited for him to roll down the window that separated them and give her instructions. Instead he made a second call.

"It's me," he said. His voice softened. If his head hadn't been lolling in the corner, near the mike, she would have missed his next words. "Please," he said in a tone that embarrassed her to overhear. "I just want to talk to you." A moment later, the privacy partition rolled down.

"Take me home," he said.

On the drive back to Culver City, he was quiet. She checked on him periodically through the rearview mirror, expecting to see him passed out. But every time she looked, he was staring out the window. When they turned onto his street, he finally spoke.

"I've got a proposition for you," he said.

"What's that?"

"We got a six-hour ticket going. That's what? Two and a half bills?"

"Two hundred and seventy-six plus the phone charges."

"All right. You got a head for numbers. I like that. How 'bout you write me a receipt for . . . How much is eight hours?"

"Three sixty-eight plus the phone charges."

"All right. Make the bill close to four hundred, don't make it an even number. We'll still end now, but I'll give you three bills. I'm talking cash."

"I don't know."

His voice was heavy from the whiskey. She glanced at the liquor decanters and noted that he and his guests had drained all three.

"I'm going to need a car off and on for the rest of the week, maybe longer. Did I mention that?"

She pulled up in front of his building, next to a streetlamp that would give her sufficient light, and pulled out her receipt book. "Do I make this out to you or your company?"

"Just leave that part blank."

She heard the rear door open and wondered if he was going to try to skip out on her. A moment later he was at her passenger door. She cleared her map off the seat just before the door lurched open and he let himself down heavily on the plush velour upholstery. For just an instant his coat lifted up and she saw a leather holster on the back of his belt. Her pen moved quickly across the pad. The sooner this evening ended, the better.

He sighed heavily, filling the compartment with his whiskey breath. She looked over at him, thinking she might make some small joke to lighten the moment.

Instead she found him staring at her in a way that stopped the words forming in her mind. The despair emanating from him staggered her. His head drooped from his shoulders. As he looked over at her, his lower lids sagged open, showing the parts of his eyeballs where they curved under. To call them the whites of his eyes would have been a misnomer. Those orbs of his were completely red, more than she would have believed possible. Beyond tears. He'd have to feel a whole lot better before he could cry.

She knew that because she recognized the place where he was. A person never forgets that place, not if they've ever been there. How it feels when things just keep getting worse and you never seem to die.

The Program called it incomprehensible demoralization; that pretty much summed it up.

She saw that in Raleigh Ward, in the dull gape of his mouth. It was in his eyes, too, that unmistakable expression that was both glazed and naked.

She also knew that there was a safeness in that place, that bottom. If it didn't feel so bad, you could look around and take comfort in the fact that you were invulnerable.

She almost didn't want to take his money. But, hey, they'd made a deal. Whatever was going on with this guy had nothing to do with that. She waited while he stretched awkwardly to reach a hand into his pants pocket. Finally, he pulled out a wad of cash, mumbling something that sounded like, "What they all want." He coughed wetly and jammed two hundred-dollar bills into her hand. She was ashamed when she realized that she had been hoping he'd forgotten about his earlier payment.

She straightened and folded the bills while Raleigh fumbled for the door release, cursing. She got out to help him, but by the time she came around to his side he was already out and heading for the curb.

"I'll phone you about next week," he called over his shoulder.

She watched him stagger off and wondered if he was going home to blow his brains out. *Nah,* she decided, *people don't make plans for the next week if they're going to off themselves. Do they?*

Fuck it, she thought. *It's not my job to save every lost soul in the world. The guy's just drunk.* She got back in the car and started the engine.

So why did she feel like such a jerk for letting him go home to sleep it off?

She put the limo in drive but didn't lift her foot off the brake.

Shit, she thought, *shit shit shit.* She moved the gear selector back to park while she thought. Maybe there was somebody else who knew this guy and would know what to do. She reached back for the car phone and pushed the recall button. A number lit up across the small screen. She pushed SEND. A woman answered by saying, "Go away," then hung up.

Munch tried again but got only a busy signal. She wrote the number down on her copy of the receipt and shut off the phone. What more could she do? Raleigh Ward was in God's hands.

■ ■ ■

It was twelve-thirty by the time Munch pulled into her driveway.

Asia met her at the door, still wearing her school clothes and looking every bit as tired as Munch felt. Derek was asleep on the couch with the television on and one of Asia's Cabbage Patch dolls wrapped in his arms.

"Can I go to bed now?" Asia asked.

Munch scooped her up, carried her into her bedroom, and helped her change into her pajamas.

"I'm really glad Derek came over tonight," Asia said as Munch tucked her into bed and surrounded her with stuffed animals.

"You are?"

"Yeah. I forgot how much I don't like him."

Munch didn't say anything, but she knew what the kid meant.

CHAPTER 3

The call to the police was the least he could do after he dried his own body and did what he could to make the women presentable.

"There's been some killing done," he whispered, partly to disguise his voice, partly to make sure they listened carefully. "Fifteen hundred North Gower, unit 103," he told the operator. Then he left the women's apartment, making certain no one spotted him. He was exhausted physically, but the important part of him—his soul, his spirit—roared with new life.

Earlier, when he had prepared to go out for the evening, he had filled his pockets with everything he thought he would need. The checklist included his own roll of Johnson & Johnson half-inch waterproof tape and a four-inch dagger—his "stinger"—strapped to his shin. Great men needed to be prepared for whatever the world threw at them, and the way he had been feeling lately . . . Well, it was only a matter of time.

How simple the answer had been. How he had fought his natural God-given yearnings. Did birds resist migration? Salmon their spawning? The cold-blooded species their periods of hibernation? The headaches should have clued him in—those stabbing pains were just his body's way of telling him to not question his instincts, to let go and let nature take its course. The truth—seeing it, knowing it, embracing it—set him free.

It was while still in college that he had first read John Locke's lucid work, *An Essay Concerning Human Understanding*. The gist of it was that all thoughts arise from sensory experience. According to Locke, thinking is an entirely involuntary process. There is no free will, no innate concepts. A man can no more control the ideas his mind generates than a mirror can "refuse, alter, or obliterate the image of objects set before it." People are neither "good" nor "bad." One merely does the things that enhance pleasure and avoid those that bring pain.

He knew enough of the secret things that went on inside people's homes to know everyone had their own private ideas of pleasure.

He studied the building's courtyard. The security in the building complex was a joke. It gave the residents a false sense of safety. As if any person with criminal intent would be stupid enough to make himself visible to the cameras mounted so obviously. The joke, of course, was on them—the sheep.

He stepped lightly toward the rear of the compound, savoring the warm afterglow of satiation. He remembered his boyhood credo, particularly his preamble to the Golden Rules for Control, written years ago with a hopeful teenage hand. "I shall endeavor through the application of psychology to adapt myself to the Golden Rules and to attack human nature to my fullest extent." He smiled at the memory of the sweet, naive boy that he had been. With experience and seasoning, he had modified the Rules. He still thirsted for understanding. The human mind still fascinated. Ah, but the rest . . .

He climbed the cinder-block wall that surrounded the building's trash enclosure. Easily vaulting the perimeter fence, he landed lightly on his feet and found himself in a narrow, dark alley. Perfect. He followed the alley to where it joined a small side street and turned so that he was heading toward the neon extravaganza of Sunset Boulevard. As he walked, he threw back his head and laughed.

Why couldn't he run the world? Great men had that choice. Why couldn't he have that same chance? God, it would feel fantastic to have so much power. Money was the key, and soon he would have plenty.

He pulled a bus schedule from his pocket, finding the number of the line that serviced the many cities of Los Angeles's west side. Then he drew a deep breath and pounded a fist on his chest. The bus ride could wait a bit. It was a beautiful night for a walk.

CHAPTER 4

The following morning, Asia woke first and pulled on her light pink tights and rose-colored leotard. Munch was vaguely aware of the sounds of dresser drawers opening and water running in the bathroom. The phone rang only a half tone, then was quiet. No doubt some aborted wrong number where the caller realized his error just as the last digit was pressed but not before a connection had already been made. She pulled the pillow over her head and then heard Asia talking to someone.

"Six and a half," Asia said. A pause, then, "I'll check. I think she's asleep." Munch lifted her head in time to hear Asia yell, "Mom! Telephone."

"All right." Munch reached over to her bedside table, picked up the receiver, and croaked a hello.

"How do you manage to have a kid who is almost seven?" Ellen asked. "I do not remember you being pregnant."

Munch was fully awake now, her heart thumping and wondering if Asia was still on the line. Asia had a general idea about where babies came from. Munch had told her the part about living in the mommy's stomach first. She hadn't told her that sometimes birth mommies die and other lucky mommies find their babies already born.

"Just hold on a minute." She cupped her hand over the phone. "Asia? What are you doing?"

"Eating," came back the muffled reply.

"Did you hang up the phone?"

"All right," Asia yelled back, clearly exasperated. Munch pulled the receiver away from her ear as she heard the extension in the other room ricochet back into its cradle. She spoke back into the phone. "What time is it?"

"Seven. Would you like me to call back at a time that is more convenient?"

"No, that's all right. I needed to get up. Asia has dance class this morning. What's up?"

"I have run into a situation."

"Can you talk?"

"I don't know why not. I am standing on the intersection of Washington and Main with all my worldly possessions scattered at my feet. I will damn well speak until my dimes run out, which should not be happening for another twelve minutes."

"What happened?"

"Russell decided that I was not fulfilling my obligations to him. You want the details?"

Munch lay back in bed, picturing the "personal time" she had spent with Russ and all the guys like him in her other life before she learned she had options. Another point high on her gratitude list: No more having to coax the shriveled white worm of manhood between Russ's spindly legs to brief life. She remembered how when Russ unzipped his tar-encrusted jeans or pulled off his boots, there was always the pervasive undertone of mildew and dried urine. The smell grew nastier as your nose got closer to it. "Couldn't do it anymore, huh?"

"Not sober."

"Welcome to the narrowing road."

"Does this clean-living thing get easier as you go along?"

"Yeah, it just takes a little while to figure out the rules." She didn't say that she herself was still struggling after seven years. Ellen didn't need to hear that right now. What Ellen needed was a safe place to put her next step. "Tell you what, why don't you crash with us for a couple of days? I've got a couch that folds out into a bed. It's not much, but you won't have to share it."

"You are too good."

"You need me to pick you up?"

"No, that won't be necessary. I have your address. I still believe I know how to use my thumb."

"Everything is going to work out," Munch said. "You'll see. Sobriety is easy. You just don't drink or use, and change everything about yourself."

"Is that supposed to be some kind of a joke?" Ellen asked.

"Yeah. The thing that makes it funny is how true it is."

"Any other words of wisdom?"

"We'll have lots of time to talk later. If we're not here, the key is under the mat."

"Thank you."

"Don't worry about it. We've got plenty of ways for you to earn your keep."

After she hung up, Munch pulled on a pair of jeans and a hot pink T-shirt she'd bought at a flea market. She'd paid extra for the black lettering across the front that read, LIFE's TOO SHORT TO DANCE WITH UGLY MEN. She walked out to the kitchen, poured herself a bowl of cereal, and joined Asia in the living room. The two of them watched cartoons until it was time to leave for the little girl's ballet lesson.

Derek was still asleep on the couch, making little popping noises as he exhaled. Munch didn't bother to wake him. If there was one thing Derek knew, it was his own way out. She did write him a short note saying that she was expecting a friend named Ellen, and to make her welcome if she arrived before he left. She propped the note against the coffeepot and ushered Asia out the door.

"An old friend came by my work yesterday," she said as she loaded Asia into the car and waited while the girl fastened her seat belt.

"Man or lady?"

"Lady. Her name's Ellen."

"How old?"

"My age. She's going to drive the limo for us."

"You should have had her drive last night."

"She's not on the policy yet. I invited her to come stay with us for a while."

Asia was quiet as she processed this bit of information. "Does this mean I'll have two mommies?"

Munch felt her throat go dry. "What makes you say that?"

"Some kids have two mommies. One that grows them in their tummy, and one that takes care of them."

Munch wasn't ready for this conversation yet. "Ellen's neither, okay? She's just a friend. If anybody asks you, you tell them you have just one mommy, okay?"

"And we're always going to live together."

"You say that now, but later on you'll change your mind."

"No, never."

"What if you want to get married and have your own kids? Won't you want your own home?"

"I'm not getting married."

"You're sure about that?"

"Me? Live with a boy?" Asia rolled her eyes theatrically. "I don't think so."

"Never say never. Things change."

"Not that much," Asia said with the certainty of the old soul Munch was convinced she was.

Miss Kim's Dance Studio was located in the corner of a single-level minimall on Sepulveda Boulevard. Munch had to park in front of a florist two stores down. As they were getting out of the car, she noticed that Asia's leotard was on inside out. In remedying that situation, Munch discovered a run in Asia's tights.

"Great," she said, twisting the tights around so that the run was along the bottom of Asia's foot. "Let's go. I hear the music starting." They trotted to the entrance of the studio. Asia skipped onto the wooden floor while Munch waited with the other mothers by the door.

Not all the mothers stayed for the class. Munch liked to watch the little girls prance around and was always amazed at the depth of Miss Kim's patience. This morning all the girls were instructed to take a colored scarf from a large cardboard box. That alone took forever, with the little girls arguing over what color they wanted and telling stories about their dogs or their grandpa's car or some other damn thing. Miss Kim took it all in stride. She had to be on something, Munch had decided long ago. Nobody was that mellow, were they?

Asia scratched her knee, and her stocking twisted to reveal the run creeping up her ankle. She appeared not to notice, thank God. Munch sneaked a look at the mothers crowded with her in the small anteroom. She always felt like such an impostor in their company, with her short, black-lined fingernails, lack of stretch marks, and no wedding ring. *Look for the similarities, not the differences,* she told herself.

She was standing next to a tall woman with short hair who she'd noticed drove a diesel Mercedes. They saw each other every week, had a nodding acquaintance, but had never exchanged names.

"Those ballet shoes sure wear out fast, don't they?" Munch said.

"Yes," the woman said. "And last week the stupid maid put them in the washing machine."

"Imagine," Munch said. She couldn't think of anything else to say. The woman checked her diamond-studded watch and left. Munch kept her hands in her pockets. It wasn't that she was ashamed to be a mechanic. She just didn't want anyone to see her hands, not make the connection, and think she was dirty. There was a difference between stained and dirty.

The dance class finished the final exercise. Before the last strains of music had died away, Asia was at her side, pulling her arm, cheeks flushed.

"Remember, you promised," she said.

"I didn't forget," Munch said. She smiled down at Asia. The little girl's clear brown eyes brought a swell of warmth to her chest. What perfect skin she had. "There's nothing I'd rather do in the whole wide world than spend the day with you."

They walked hand in hand back to the car. The day was warm, gently breezy. "How about the park?" Munch asked.

"Yeah!" Asia yelled, leaping high and swiping at something imaginary in the air. They went to the little park on Alla Road near Marina Del Rey. The little girl played on the swing set and made new friends, quickly establishing herself as their tribal leader.

How does she do that? Munch wondered, wishing she'd remembered to bring a set of overalls and a sturdier pair of shoes for Asia. Miss Diesel Mercedes probably had the maid pack a suitcase whenever she went out.

After the park, they went to Uncle John's Pancake House for lunch and had the usual argument over the value of french fries as a vegetable. They compromised on scrambled eggs and hash browns. Munch ordered coffee and finished what Asia left.

They got home at noon. The first thing Asia asked when they turned up the street was also the burning question on Munch's mind.

"Where's the limo?" the girl said.

Munch's first theory was that it had been stolen. The idea following that initial supposition made much more sense. Ellen. Fucking Ellen.

Munch pulled into the driveway and got out. She walked over to the spot where the limo had been parked and noticed puddles ringed with soap suds on the asphalt. Asia let herself out of the car, walked up to Munch, and grabbed her hand.

"Let's go inside and see if anyone left us a note," Munch said, unlocking the front door. Once across the threshold, Munch pointed Asia toward her room, and told her, "Change your clothes."

Seconds later a scream erupted from Asia's room. Munch was there in less than a second. Asia pointed at the line of what appeared to be human heads adorning her dresser. Two wore wigs, the third was bald and on closer inspection turned out to be made of Styrofoam. A suitcase lay open on the floor.

Munch lifted one of the wigs—the blond one—off its form and held it out for Asia's inspection.

"See? Just a wig."

"Whose stuff is this?" Asia asked.

"My friend, the one I was telling you about."

"Where is she?"

"That's what I want to know. Change your clothes. I've got some calls to make."

She sat down at the dinette table that doubled as the limo office. When she reached for the phone, she saw a sheet of limo stationery folded in half. Her name was scrawled across the front. She recognized Ellen's handwriting.

Hi, we got a job. Your honey, Derek, helped me get the limo ready. Is he a hunk or what? Anyway, the guy said he would pay cash and that the two of you had an arrangement. If I am not back by tonight, I'll call in. Thanks again for everything. I will make you proud, E.

CHAPTER 5

Detective Mace St. John of L.A.'s elite Robbery Homicide Division stood at the entryway of the apartment, studying the scene before him. He liked to orient himself for a minute before the first walk-through of a homicide scene.

Detective Tiger Cassiletti loomed behind him, rocking on the balls of his size twelves, seconds away from crashing into his boss and sending them both sprawling through the doorway.

"We've got one in the bathroom and one in the bedroom," Cassiletti said.

"Yeah, I know." Mace had been briefed on the phone. Two victims, both women in their twenties. The first they found in the bathtub, her multiple stab wounds washed free of blood. The second was on the bed in the bedroom. She, too, had been washed, and the twelve puncture wounds in her neck, back, and buttocks covered with white adhesive tape. Neither the tape dispenser nor the weapon had been found at the scene, leading the police to believe that the killer had taken both with him. Later, at the coroner's office, the tape would be removed a strip at a time and the torn edges pieced together. For whatever it was worth, the order in which the pieces of tape were torn would be re-created and cataloged.

The murders had been discovered in the early hours of the morning following a tip from an anonymous male caller. It was the Hollywood Division's jurisdiction, but Parker Center's Robbery Homicide Division (RHD) had been asked to step in. RHD handled high-profile cases: serial murders, celebrity-involved felonies.

The killer's signature mirrored a similar unsolved case that had crossed Mace St. John's desk when he'd first transferred to RHD in December. For a while, the suspect was being called "The Christmas Killer" except by one detective who dubbed their offender "The Maytag Man" because he cleaned up after himself. Mace had been in no mood to joke and had declared that thereafter this murderer would only be referred to as "The Band-Aid Killer."

As with the previous homicide, the killer had washed the victims' bodies postmortem, dressed the wounds, and then positioned their bodies so that their right hands, palms down, rested above their left breasts.

All the women had also been sodomized. At the December homicide scene, the forensic people had collected semen samples and combed pubic hair, looking for whatever part of himself the rapist/murderer might have left behind. The coroner had found no bite marks; their absence again surprised him. Because of the degree of overkill as evidenced by the number of stab wounds, he characterized the murderer as impulsively sadistic. Those kinds were usually biters.

Any communication with the media was to be preapproved by press relations, Captain Earl had cautioned needlessly. Actually, it was almost an insult. As if Mace had ever talked out of school. Like he'd do anything to help a murderer—especially an animal such as this one. But it was a tense time in the city. Mayor Bradley was concentrating every effort to make Los Angeles appear welcoming and safe for the upcoming 1984 Olympics. The bums had been packed up and shipped to a tent city. Commercial traffic now ran in the wee hours of the morning, leaving the freeways as open as Mace had ever seen them. The last thing the city fathers wanted was reports of a maniac killing women inside their own homes.

Still standing in the doorway of the apartment, Mace and Cassiletti each pulled on a pair of latex surgical gloves. Mace studied the front room.

The apartment was filled with inexpensive furniture, much of it dusty. A blue-and-gold silk scarf was draped over the shade of the lamp on the small table trapped in the corner between a couch and an armchair. The cushions weren't dented, he noted. The zipper on the center couch cushion was facing out.

The Scientific Investigation Division photographers arrived and performed their duties in the bathroom and the bedroom. Mace told them to document the living room and kitchenette as well. Mace and Cassiletti waited till the flash stopped popping, then walked into the bathroom. The first thing Mace noticed was how the dead woman in the bathtub had a foot draped languorously over the edge of the tub. Her eyes were open, punctuated by dark smears of mascara under the lower lash lines. *God, she was young.*

"Whose little girl were you?" he asked out loud.

He bent over to study the aftermath of the killer's carnage. There were twelve X's of white tape adhered to the woman's ghostly white torso. He peeled back one of the dressings on her abdomen. Radiating out from the puncture wound he found bruising, indicating that the hilt of the weapon had struck the surface of the skin. He searched her chest, hoping to find a clean kill wound, wondering how many stabs she'd been alive to feel. The medical examiner would check for that and note it in his report.

Mace looked up, following the seashell pattern of wallpaper to where it met the ceiling. Half his brain wondered if this had been her last sight. The analytical half knew something was missing: blood spatter on the walls.

"Don't forget the traps," he told the SID crew. "I want all of them: sink, tub, toilet."

"Kitchen, too?" a tech asked.

"Yeah, kitchen, too," he answered. "Rush the tox reports on the victims," Mace told Cassiletti. "And I want comparisons on the hair and semen."

Cassiletti pulled out his notebook and scribbled. "Anything else?"

"Let's check out the other one."

As they started to leave the room, the phone mounted on the wall next to the toilet rang. Mace lifted the receiver carefully from its cradle, knowing his gloves would not add new prints but not wishing to smudge any that were already there. He answered the phone with a simple, "Hello?"

"Uh, is the lady of the house in?"

"Who is this?"

"A friend of Raleigh Ward's."

"Can I tell her what this is regarding?"

"Um, well, actually I'm trying to track Raleigh down, and I, um . . . Listen, can I give you my name and number, and maybe she could just give me a call, you know, as soon as she can."

"Sounds like a plan," Mace said, pulling out his notepad and a pen. "Go ahead."

"All right, my name's Munch, and the number is—"

"Munch? Munch Mancini?" Mace asked. Cassiletti's head swung around at the sound of the name. Mace pointed at the receiver for the big man's benefit.

"Who is this?" she asked.

"Mace St. John."

"Mace? What are you doing there? How have you been?"

Mace pictured her as he'd last seen her. Was it five years ago? Longer? He had stopped in at the garage where she worked just to say hi, see if she was okay. She was, and it had been gratifying to see. Taking the time to call on her had been his wife Caroline's idea. Caroline, the ultimate social worker, lived by her own idealistic, if naive, credo that in giving you received. It had taken him a few years, but he had finally managed to exhaust her deep wells of compassion.

"Mace?" Munch asked again. "You still there?"

Cassiletti's head was also cocked in question like some six-foot-four puppy dog.

"Yeah, I'm here. What's new with you?" *And what are you doing calling into a homicide scene?* "You still in the Valley?"

"No, I moved back to the west side. Didn't you get my Christmas card?"

"Oh, yeah, that's right. Go ahead and give me your address again." He took down her information, writing with the phone cradled carefully between his ear and shoulder. Cassiletti made a move as if to hold the phone to Mace's ear. Mace frowned and waved him away. Munch also provided her new phone numbers and work address. He looked up into the mirror of the medicine cabinet but saw only the dead girl in the tub behind him.

"So how well do you know the women who live here?" he asked.

"I don't even know their names. Did something happen?"

"What was that name you said when you first called?"

"Raleigh Ward," she said. "He's a customer."

"What kind of customer?"

"I have a limo business. Hey, wait a minute. Are you still working Homicide?"

"How is it that you have this number?" he asked.

"That's a little complicated," Munch said. "Look, I'm just looking for this guy. He, uh, owes me money."

"This Raleigh Ward."

"Yeah."

"Why would you look for him here?"

"I'm just trying all the numbers I have for him."

"When did he rent your limo?"

"Last night. Are you going to tell me what's going on?"

"I want you to write down everything you know about this Raleigh Ward: when you picked him up, where all you took him, and who else was with him. Do it now while it's still fresh. I'm going to be sending out a detective to interview you." She gave him the information he'd requested. "You going to be home for the next couple of hours?"

"You're going to send someone else?"

"I'll send Detective Cassiletti. You remember him, don't you?"

"I remember everything. How's your dad, by the way? Are you still living in that train car? I drive by there every once in a while, but I never see anyone home. What's Mrs. St. John doing?"

"I'm right in the middle of something right now," he said. "I can't talk. We'll make some time later on and catch up, all right?"

"Yeah, sure we will."

Mace rubbed his eyes. He seemed to have a knack for disappointing the women in his life. "No, really, I've been meaning to give you a call," he said.

"Sounds great," she said without enthusiasm, and hung up.

"What was that all about?" Cassiletti asked.

"Just one of those small-world things," Mace said, hoping that was the truth. He peeled off the page with her address on it and handed it to Cassiletti. "When we're finished here, go on over to her house and find out everything she knows with a connection to our deceased." Mace flipped to a fresh page in his notebook. "Let's go check out the one in the bedroom."

The two detectives walked into the second death scene. Again, there was a notable absence of blood. Floodlights illuminated the corpse of the second woman and the odd postmortem field dressings. She was faceup, lying on a queen-size bed with a wrought-iron headboard. The bedspread beneath her was strangely unwrinkled. Her right arm was bent so that her palm was pressed to her chest. Similar white X's of tape crisscrossed her abdomen and chest. *Conscience or trademark?* Mace wondered.

The Band-Aid Killer had evolved. Bringing his own supplies to the scene showed forethought—organization. Whatever else this act signified, it also informed the detectives that these murders had not been a spontaneous act. The killer must have come with a plan. How else could he have subdued two victims with so few signs of disturbance? And where had he done his killing? In the bathtub?

Mace remembered how, back in December, a reporter had asked him to comment on the nature of the brutal Westwood slaying. The guy had asked if the murderer was a serial or a spree killer.

Mace's reply had been picked up by the wire services and broadcast across the country. He'd said then what was still true.

"Call it what you want," he told them. "I'm not interested in the latest pop-psychology term. I don't have college degree upon college degree. I don't know if this guy wet his bed or how he felt about his mother. I do know one thing. He'll kill again."

Mace looked down at the corpse, feeling no satisfaction at the accuracy of his call.

When Raleigh's phone had rung at eight o'clock that morning, he'd answered with a groan. Victor Draicu, code name Gameboy, wanted to drive to Tijuana for the day. Though what the guy expected to find there, Raleigh didn't understand at first. He'd tried to explain that there'd be no mariachi bands greeting them or señoritas in twirling skirts clicking castanets. The border towns were depressing. Nothing but dirt roads and abject poverty. Was he homesick? Tijuana was where one went to buy fireworks, horseshit cigarettes, and cheap pottery. Was he interested in any of those things?

Victor wanted to see a donkey fuck a woman, he said. Take him to one of those places.

Raleigh called in to his supervisor for approval. Document everything he was told, but keep the guy happy. He said, yeah, he knew the drill. Victor was an Eastern Bloc celebrity—a former gold-medal winner and currently a minor bureaucrat in charge of the Romanian Olympic gymnastic team, which gave him mobility and accessibility. Romania alone had had the backbone, or blatant self-interest, depending on how you saw it, to break the Olympic boycott imposed by Mother Russia. The L.A. Olympic Committee was delighted and showed it by giving the Romanians special considerations. Transportation was provided, lodging at the USC village. There were even promises to broadcast television feeds back to Romania.

On the personal front, Victor had some interesting family connections in Bucharest. He would be a useful asset, and Raleigh had orders to bend over backward to make sure that happened. Even if all this effort resulted in merely one defection, it would be a major coup for the people who kept track of that sort of thing—especially in an election year.

At first the operation had seemed like a waste of both his time and talent. Escorting Victor while the man fulfilled adolescent fantasies depressed him no end. It was not an assignment that taxed his considerable abilities, and it made him give serious thought to the wide-open world of freelancing. His Green Beret credentials alone were worth major bucks in the up-and-coming countries. Hell, he could get good work in Africa, Saudi Arabia, or, shit . . . even go back to Eastern Europe. But then, just as Raleigh had almost given way to despair, a remarkable opportunity had opened up. An opportunity that men such as he often dreamed of. A simple defection of some low-level Romanian party boy? No, Raleigh's sights were set much higher.

Victor Draicu had some product he was interested in selling: four kilograms of weapons-grade plutonium "lost" while en route to a conversion facility in Bulgaria that would transform the stuff into reactor-grade plutonium. He came to America hoping to generate an auction among the intelligence-community representatives of competing countries. The information and the means to capitalize on it were going to be Raleigh's ticket out of ex-wife purgatory.

All that said, Victor was still a royal pain. The broads had been hired for the whole night, and the asshole takes a cab back to the hotel in the middle of the night. Was he trying to get Raleigh written up? What if something had happened to the guy? He could have gotten mugged or hit by a car. If the asshole died, that would blow everything.

Mexico. Fucking wonderful.

Raleigh told the limousine dispatcher, a woman with a Southern accent, that he'd need the car for the whole day. When he told her that he wanted to go to Mexico for some shopping, she had laughed.

"Thanks for the warning," she said. "I won't send a blond woman. You know what they think of blondes down there, don't you?"

"Yeah," Raleigh said, "good thinking. Don't send a blonde."

Victor would be wanting to hump her, too, and there were already enough complications. One of Victor's first demands early in the negotiation process had been that before and after the sale of the product, he would have full freedom of movement or no deal. Rules were being bent and broken all across the board on his behalf. Raleigh went along, knowing that ultimately he held the trump card. He knew why Victor could never go back home.

Raleigh opened the drawer of his nightstand and perused his collection of prescription pill bottles. It felt like a two-Benzedrine kind of morning.

When the driver appeared with the limousine, Raleigh was just starting to come to life. The limo company had sent a different driver—a redhead. He rubbed his temples, hoping she wasn't a big talker. She was already almost too much to handle

this early in the day, with her flamboyant hairdo, big hoop earrings, and exposed cleavage. He handed her a hundred-dollar
bill and told her to go to the Beverly Wilshire.

She folded the bill and stuck it in the front pocket of her
tight jeans.

"Where's Munch today?" he asked.

"She took the day off. My name is Ellen. You just sit yourself back and enjoy the ride, sugar."

"Call me Raleigh," he told her. "Did we speak earlier?"

"Yes, we surely did."

"You mind stopping for coffee somewhere first?"

"You are the boss, Raleigh."

He felt the tingling of the amphetamine dissolving in his
bloodstream. A small sigh of appreciation escaped his lips.
Sunshine in a bottle. He moved across the back of the limo,
positioning himself so that he could watch her face. "So how
long you been a chauffeurette?" he asked, taking out his tin of
peppermints.

She hesitated a second, caught his eyes in the rearview
mirror, and said, "Four years."

"Bet you've seen a lot of shit," he said, popping two Altoids
into his mouth and chewing them.

She laughed. "I have had my moments, that is for damn
sure."

He switched over so that he was sitting on the rear-facing
bench seat. He leaned over toward her, his elbow resting on
the sill of the privacy partition. "Where are you from, Ellen?
No, wait a minute, don't tell me. Georgia?"

She opened her mouth wide in amazement, then said,
"Why, you clever thing, you. You are exactly right. Only next
time, put your hand over your heart when you speak of the
South."

"I bet you keep your boyfriend on his toes."

She looked at him warily in the rearview mirror. "I have

had my moments with him also," she said, as they pulled into the parking lot of a small bakery. "Is this all right?" He followed her gesture.

"Yeah, this is great. You want anything? Coffee, pastry, rain check?"

She smiled at the last. "You are not without your charm, Mr. Raleigh Ward. I can see a girl might have to watch herself with you."

The limousine eased to a stop, taking up two spaces, and he jumped out. She didn't know how right she was.

CHAPTER 6

Before Detective Cassiletti arrived, Munch walked across the street with Asia and banged on Derek's door. He answered several minutes later with his shirt off and hair tousled.

"What's up?" he asked.

"My limo is gone," she said.

He scratched his chest and stretched. She supposed the action was his attempt to draw her attention to the well-defined muscles of his tanned torso. She made a note to herself to warn Asia to watch out for men with perfect tans when she reached the dating years.

"Yeah, I know," Derek said, smiling proudly. "I helped Ellen get it ready."

"You know where she went?"

"Somewhere blondes shouldn't go."

"What's that supposed to mean?" she asked.

"I don't know. I just heard her tell the guy on the phone that she wouldn't send a blonde."

"You know who the customer was? Did she tell you a name or anything?"

"No. I knew it was a guy cuz she kept saying, 'Sir.' Is there a problem?"

"Yeah, there's a big problem. She's not on the policy. If anything happens to the limo while she's driving . . . "

"Well, don't get mad at me. I was just trying to help. You didn't even thank me for bailing you out last night."

"I didn't want to wake you."

"And now you're climbing my tree cuz your friend wanted to make you some money."

"Derek, I'm not blaming you for anything." She waited a second instead of blurting out something that would really alienate him like, When are you going to grow a conscience? Or more to the point, Why do you always manage to keep track of every little favor you've ever done for me while conveniently overlooking all the money and effort I've poured down the Derek drain? She fixed what she hoped was a nonaccusatory expression on her face, and asked, "Did she say anything else that you remember? A name, a place, anything?"

"Nope, she just said 'Adios' and split."

"Adios? You mean, she said that literally?"

"Yeah."

"Tell me everything she said, word for word."

"That was about it." He scratched his head. "Oh, yeah, she asked if I wanted her to bring back any fireworks."

Munch felt a surge of adrenaline disrupt her stomach. The blonde thing and the fact that Ellen's note indicated that she expected to be gone all day and possibly longer had already made Munch nervous. Now this last bit of information confirmed it. Ellen had taken the limo to Mexico.

The next call Munch would probably get would be from some Mexican jail asking her to come down and bring cash.

She grabbed Asia's hand and walked back across the street. There was no way she could cover herself without getting Ellen in trouble. She would just have to wait and hope that Ellen didn't do anything extreme. It was a slim hope.

Thirty minutes later, Detective Tiger Cassiletti pulled up in front of her house. He was driving a Chevy Caprice and dressed in a gray suit. She'd forgotten how tall he was. He still ducked his head as he walked.

"Hi," she greeted him from her doorway. "Come on in."

Perhaps he scowled because he was looking into the sun. As he got closer to her, he smiled tentatively, and his eyes lit with recognition. "I hope I'm not keeping you from anything."

"It's good to see you again," she said, smiling. She watched his expression waver, as if trying to choose between being a cop on a mission or exercising the manners his mother had taught him.

"Yeah," he said. "How have you been?"

"Just great," she said, leading him into her house. "I've got over seven years clean and sober. I even quit smoking." She directed him to take a stool at the kitchen counter and stood opposite him so that their eyes were at the same level. "So what's this all about?" she asked.

"We're just trying to fill in some blanks." He pulled a slim notebook out of the inside breast pocket of his suit coat. "How is it that you had the phone number that you called today?"

"My customer last night used my mobile phone. I keep track of the numbers that are called and compare them to my monthly bill."

"And your customers are okay with that?" he asked as he fished out a pen and clicked it open. "You writing down all the numbers they call?"

She felt her eyes shift from his and cursed herself for her lack of poise. Cops were trained to look for stuff like that, even big goofs like Cassiletti. "Yeah, it's never been a problem." She thought about the hidden microphones. What would he think of those?

"And are you often in the habit of calling those numbers?" he asked.

"No, not at all. I sure didn't expect to hear Detective St. John's voice. Or should I say Lieutenant?"

"Detective is right," Cassiletti said. This time his eyes darted away.

"I know he got promoted. I used to see him on the news all the time, giving statements about crimes and investigations. At least I used to. Did something happen? He didn't get in any trouble, did he?"

"He took a downgrade and transferred to Parker Center."

"He was demoted?"

"Not by the brass. He took a cut in rank so he could get back into investigations."

"In other words, you're telling me he didn't want to be a talking head for the department." Cassiletti didn't answer. She watched him wipe the palm of his hand on his pant leg and decided to press. "So you followed him to Parker Center?"

"We're partners," he said.

Was that defensiveness in his tone?

"How's Caroline, Mrs. St. John, with all this?"

"You'd have to ask her," he said.

Munch wondered if it would be possible to resume some kind of relationship with Caroline. It would be easier if Munch could explain why she had distanced herself in the first place. Her friendship with Mace and Caroline had been one of the many sacrifices she had willingly made since Asia came into the picture. Munch had changed the meetings she attended, made new friends, even moved to a new apartment. All this to avoid having to explain the sudden presence in her life of a six-month-old child. A child she was calling her daughter.

"Tell her hi from me when you see her," Munch said, trying to keep her tone offhand. As if Caroline Rhinehart St. John hadn't been one of the most important people in her life. As Munch's former probation officer, Caroline had been the first person to extend hope. Mace St. John came in a close second by absolving Munch of her father's murder. But it was Caroline who had seen beyond Munch's crude bravado and put in a word where it mattered. In this case, to the detective assigned to a homicide that seemed pretty open-and-shut. Caroline had shown Mace St. John, a cop who saw the world in black-and-white, that there were also shades of gray. Her actions and words had saved Munch a certain future in prison. Caroline and Mace had gone on to fall in love and then marry.

Last Christmas Munch had considered penning a long letter to Caroline. In it she would explain how she'd saved the little girl and took her in as her own. The adoption was without benefit of a judge's sanction. Munch had done some investigating into what was involved in a legal adoption. One of the requirements was to track down other relatives and get them to sign off their rights. Munch wasn't prepared to take that risk. As far as she was concerned, any kin of Asia's had relinquished their rights to the kid by not being aware she was being used to transport dope. No court was going to tell her different.

The letter had never been sent or written. Not that she didn't trust Caroline; she just had too much at stake. What if the right and legal thing to do would be to put Asia in foster care until the matter was settled formally?

Cassiletti cleared his throat, pen poised over his open notebook, obviously anxious to get to business. "So why did you call the number you had today?"

"I was hoping to reach a customer I did a run for last night."

"Why?"

"What?" She was afraid he was going to ask that.

"Why did you need to find your customer?" He looked down at his notepad. "Raleigh Ward?"

"Yeah, that's the one. He told me he was going to need the car again, but he forgot to reserve the times."

"So you thought you'd track him down."

"Yeah," she answered reluctantly. He made it sound like she was stalking the guy.

"Have you ever been to Apartment 103 at 1500 North Gower in Hollywood?"

"Is that the building off Sunset?"

"Yes," he said. He was watching her closely now. This must be the question that mattered.

"I was at that building last night, but I didn't go inside any of the apartments. Was that the number I reached you guys at?"

"Why were you there?" he asked. There was an edge to his voice. He had that cop tone that expected, no, demanded unquestioning submission. Obviously he'd learned a thing or two in the seven years since they'd last met.

"My client picked up some women there. We dropped them off later." She let her eyes widen a bit. "Don't tell me they were involved in a murder."

"I really can't comment on that."

"C'mon, who am I going to tell?" she said.

His face dropped all expression, and she knew she wasn't going to budge him. The lines were pretty clear on who was in the club and who wasn't. Cops only let civilians get so close to them.

"Can you recall the exact times you were at the building?" he asked. "I also need the names and descriptions of everyone in your party."

She picked up a sheet of notepaper and handed it to him. "I already wrote it all down for you. Mace asked me to."

He took the paper and read it with poorly disguised surprise. "All right. Uh . . . thanks. This will be a big help." He folded the paper twice and put it in his suit pocket. "Can I look at the limo they used last night?"

"Why?" she asked.

He raised an eyebrow.

She resisted the urge to look out the window. "It's out on a run with one of my drivers," she said.

"When will it be back?"

"That's hard to say right now. Why don't you give me one of your cards, and I'll call you."

Cassiletti called in his report by land line to Mace St. John. Police radio frequencies were easily and constantly monitored by newshounds and thrill seekers. The two men agreed to meet at the Culver City address Munch had given them. When they got to Raleigh Ward's apartment, no one answered their knock. A neighbor who had been home all morning remembered seeing the apartment's occupant leave in a limousine.

"This guy likes to live right," Cassiletti commented.

"I'll meet you back at the office," Mace replied.

The afternoon found both men back at the squad room on the fifth floor of Parker Center. Each concentrated on his respective chores.

Cassiletti perched in front of his typewriter, his large fingers diligently poking at the keys, filling in all the spaces on the Preliminary Investigation Report, and the two separate Death Reports.

Mace sat at one of the scarred empty desks in a windowless corner of the large, open room. A television connected to a video player hung from brackets bolted to the acoustical-tiled ceiling. On it he watched the video footage from the Gower building's surveillance camera while he ate his sandwich from its cellophane wrapper and sipped lukewarm coffee. Actually, he was watching a copy. The original was safely stored in the evidence locker, away from anything with a magnetic field—like a metal detector—and with the write-protect tab broken off. All these precautions were the result of painful lessons.

As soon as they'd gotten to the Gower crime scene, Mace had sent one of the support officers around the neighborhood to seize any videotapes that might have recorded evidence. The building's security cameras were on a two-day recycle schedule. They took eight-second time-lapse photographs but switched to real time whenever the building's keypad was used.

The officer had also recovered the videotape from a camera mounted on the roof of a nearby Bank of America. The cop had correctly noted that the camera's range included the alley running behind the apartment complex. Mace had had two copies made of each tape before returning to Parker Center. It was difficult not to play them immediately, but experience had also taught him that each playing of a tape degraded it—especially tape from a surveillance-camera video system that was constantly recycled.

He began with the apartment-building tapes. A series of stills flashed across the television mounted high in the corner. The time and date showed in white dot-matrix-style print across the bottom right corner of the screen. Later the technicians from the photo lab of the Scientific Investigative Division would develop individual stills off this copy. Pausing the tape or running it in slow motion also caused degradation and loss of data. Later he would have all the time he needed to pore over the individual prints. Indeed, if this was like the last case, those images would be imprinted in negative on the insides of his eyelids. Now he reviewed the footage to make sure nothing that required immediate attention was missed.

Spread before him were several sheets of paper from a yellow legal pad on which he charted a time line of events, beginning with when he'd arrived at the scene and working backward. The anonymous tip had come in at 4:13 A.M. to the Hollywood Division desk. The caller, who had not used 911, had been put on hold while the switchboard routed him through to Homicide. The information, delivered in a whisper, was that there'd been a killing at the address on Gower. The caller did not stay on the line long enough to be questioned further.

A black-and-white unit had been the first to respond. The officers had duly recorded the times they received notification and when they arrived at the scene. Twelve minutes had elapsed. They found the apartment door open. Two minutes later they discovered the two victims and called in a report via land line to their watch sergeant.

The coroner arrived at six-thirty, made small incisions beneath each of the women's rib cages, and inserted his chemical thermometer. He determined from the temperature of their livers and state of rigor that both had died within minutes of each other and no longer than six hours prior. That fixed the time of death between midnight and four that morning, pending any unusual findings when the toxicology reports came in.

What Mace now knew was Munch's limousine had arrived at the apartment complex on Gower at 6:58 P.M. the previous evening. The tape showed the driver's arm, Munch's arm, stretched out from the driver's-side window, reaching for the keypad. The tinted rear window of the limo was rolled halfway down, but the angle from the camera didn't capture the face of any occupant.

He fast-forwarded to 11:29 P.M. One of the victims moved away from the keypad and back inside the limo, which proceeded through the gate. The camera also caught the detail of the open moon roof. At 11:36 the limo left. He clicked through rapidly, stopping at 1:33 A.M. A cab had appeared at the front gate. A few minutes later a bald man was shown letting himself out of the pedestrian gate with a hand raised to the waiting car. The cab's TCP number was plainly visible, as was the bald man's face. He even seemed to smile for the camera. Mace made a note to get a copy of that still to Munch for identification.

He reached for the phone to call Caroline. She'd be interested to hear that he'd spoken to Munch. Munch was one of her great success stories. Caroline had seen something in the little waif that nobody else had. An addict such as Munch, who had so completely turned her life around, was just the sort of thing that made probation officers feel that what they were doing really made a difference. According to Cassiletti, Munch had continued to thrive: She was still working as a mechanic, running a limo business on the side, living in a nicer neighborhood, maintaining her sobriety. Yep, Caroline would love to hear how she'd made a difference.

And besides, he missed the sound of her voice.

He called her at home.

As he listened to the phone ring, a thousand thoughts flitted through his mind. Why did he feel he needed the armor of an excuse? Why didn't he just call her and tell her how empty his life was without her? Because she said she needed her space, that he had wrung her dry.

"Caroline St. John," she answered.

"Hi, it's me," he said.

"Oh. Hi."

"Yeah, I ran into somebody today. Well, I didn't actually see her, but I thought you might be interested." *Oh, God,* he thought, *real smooth. I hate this shit, this groveling.*

"Who?" she asked.

"Munch, Munch Mancini."

"How is she?"

"She's got a limo service. We should throw her some business some night. You know, take in a show downtown—go out to dinner."

He waited for her to jump in, but she said nothing. He wished he could see her face. Was she hopeful? Annoyed? Pleased? Bored?

"So, how are you doing?" he asked. "How's work? I mean."

"Busy. Same as always. Caring too much, getting disappointed a lot."

Was that meant for him?

"Is the car running all right?" he asked.

"The car's fine."

"And you've got everything you need?" he asked.

"I'm fine."

"Good, good," he said. He paused, lowered his voice. "I went to see my dad this weekend."

"How often do you do that?" she asked, her tone gentle.

"When I'm in the neighborhood. I like to put fresh flowers up. You know, make it look like someone cares."

"Mace, he knew you cared. No one could have done more."

"I don't know why he stopped trusting me," Mace said. It was an old debate, but one he'd yet to come to terms with. His dad had died, and his last words uttered could never be erased. *I've got no one.*

"You can't take to heart the things he said. He wasn't thinking clearly. I wish you'd believe that." She paused. "Are you still having those dreams?"

He bit back the familiar heat of irritation that rushed through his chest. If she were with him, she wouldn't have to ask. Big Miss I-give-everyone-a-chance couldn't get past her husband's single infidelity. If you could call going to a hotel room with an old girlfriend only to discover that you'd made a mistake an act of infidelity. He'd gotten as far as unwrapping the condom before he realized there was no way he could go through with it. Technically he hadn't cheated, but he hadn't told Caroline that. She'd already convicted him on the evidence. It was all he could manage now to keep the bitterness out of his tone.

"I've gotta go," he said, looking around the empty room. "Cassiletti's giving me the high sign. You got any message for Munch if I talk to her?"

He heard her click her tongue. She did that when she was exasperated. "Tell her I'm really proud of her for moving on with her life."

"I'll do that." He straightened up in his chair, cleared his throat. "Well, listen then, I'll call you later when we have more time to talk."

"You do that."

He hung up the phone, dropping the receiver into the cradle as if it were too hot to handle. "That went well," he said out loud.

"Sir?" Cassiletti called from the doorway.

Mace spun around to face him. "What you got?" he asked. Cassiletti consulted the yellow legal pad in his trembling hands. He was either nervous or excited, Mace knew. In an effort to build the big man's confidence, Mace encouraged his junior partner to take some initiative. He would die a happy man if he could get Cassiletti to drop the inevitable question mark that punctuated half his statements.

"I ran the name Raleigh Ward through NCIC," Cassiletti said, referring to the National Crime Information Center.

"Anything?"

"No." Cassiletti sounded as if he were apologizing. "So I ran a DMV search?" he said, looking up hopefully. "State of California issued him a driver's license two years ago? We should be getting a copy sometime tomorrow."

"Just two years? Did you try running an address update?" The address update was one of their tricks for backing into a social security number trace.

Cassiletti flipped frantically through his notes, looking for what wasn't there. "I'll be right back."

Mace felt a twinge of impatience as he pulled out the Social Security Index.

Cassiletti returned moments later and handed Mace the nine-digit social security number issued to Raleigh Ward. The first three numbers identified the state of issuance, in this case California. According to the index, the number had been issued prior to 1973.

"Just for fun," Mace said, "let's run him through civil-court records and voter's registration."

Twenty minutes later, the two men compared notes.

"What did you come up with?" Mace asked.

"A lot of blanks. Too many blanks. Then I pulled utility records?"

"And?"

"This is where it gets interesting. The account was opened last year by the diplomatic branch of the State Department, but until six months ago the meters hadn't clocked any usage."

"Six months ago?" Mace asked, thinking of the Westwood murder. "I want to talk to this guy."

He leaned back in his chair and stared at the blank wall. He'd been around long enough to spot a smoke screen. Sounded like this Raleigh Ward was either a protected witness or some kind of spook.

"Write down this number," Mace said, reciting the TCP number on the cab's bumper. "I want to interview this cabbie. We'll have the photo lab make some prints of the bald guy. I'll take one to Munch."

"You're going to go see her?"

"Yeah. I could use the reminder of happier endings."

Cassiletti didn't ask, and Mace didn't explain.

CHAPTER 7

At one o'clock Ellen and her customers reached San Diego. By then they were all on a first-name basis. Victor Draicu announced that he was hungry.

"What are you in the mood for?" Ellen asked.

"Do you really wish an answer to that?" Victor asked. Ellen noticed that he had unbuttoned his shirt almost to his navel and was massaging his chest muscles as he spoke.

"Oh, now, g'wan," she said, gracing him with a giggle. "You know what I'm talking about."

Victor nudged Raleigh and winked at him. "She knows what I speak of also," he said.

Raleigh's mouth tightened. "Take us to a Mexican joint," he said. "Might as well get this show on the road. You'll join us, of course."

"Thank you, Raleigh. Y'all are such gentlemen."

Raleigh snorted. "Oh, yeah, we're the cream of the crop."

Victor laughed and slapped Raleigh's shoulder. "Cream of the crop. I love it."

Ellen looked in the rearview mirror to catch Raleigh's eye and give him some silent sympathy. The venom she saw in his expression made her stifle a gasp of surprise. He looked like he didn't know whether to spit or go blind.

She got off the freeway at Balboa in the small San Diego community of Pacific Beach. After driving three blocks, she spotted a small whitewashed restaurant. Painted above the doorway in the red and green colors of the Mexican flag were the words PAPA GOMEZ's. A cardboard sign in the window promised homemade tamales.

The final selling point of the restaurant was the three empty parking spaces in a row and the lot's two driveways. Driving a limo was like driving any other car, she'd discovered, but you had to pay special attention when you planned to stop somewhere.

The three of them entered the small, dark restaurant. It smelled of beer and fried meat. A dark-haired Hispanic waitress wearing thick eyeliner seated them at a booth. Victor gestured for Ellen to slide in, then quickly took the place next to her. She sneaked a quick glance at Raleigh and saw that this irked him, but by now she'd noticed that everything Victor did seemed to annoy Raleigh. Victor, in turn, seemed oblivious to the other man's disgust. Or maybe he just didn't give a shit.

The busboy, a young man with hair so thick that it stuck straight out from his scalp like a porcupine, set down paper place mats and flatware. He worked without looking up.

"We need menus," Raleigh said.

Without meeting anyone's eyes, the boy pointed at the waitress.

Raleigh pointed at the center of the table and held his hands out as if to show they were empty.

This time the busboy seemed to understand. He held up a finger, hustled off, then returned with a basket of chips and two dishes of sauce. The first dish contained traditional salsa of chopped tomatoes, onions, and cilantro. The sauce in the second dish was soupier and green. The waitress followed with three menus.

Victor attacked the appetizers like a man who hadn't eaten in days. He devoured two large scoops of each sauce before his face changed color. Tears filled his eyes, and sweat broke out on his forehead. He slapped the table with the palm of his hand, then clutched his throat, all the while making small strangled noises.

Raleigh chuckled. "I usually wait until they bring the water," he said, "before I start on the hot sauce."

Ellen waved her napkin to get the busboy's attention. "*Agua, por favor,*" she said when he came over. "*Pronto.*"

The busboy nodded and quickly returned with three glasses of water. Victor took a deep drink and coughed without covering his mouth.

Raleigh grinned, and said to Ellen, "So, you speaka the spic?"

The waitress appeared at the edge of the table. "Have you decided?" she asked.

Oh, yeah, Ellen thought as she looked from Victor to Raleigh, *both of these bad boys are going to pay.* She ran a fingertip over the outline of the folded hundred-dollar bill in her pocket, and thought of the many more to come. Maybe working a straight job wouldn't be so bad after all.

Munch, sitting at her small dining-room table, adjusted the radio to an all-news station, picked up the phone, and pushed REDIAL. It was senseless, she knew, to keep trying to call the limo. Still she had to do something.

The recording came on again, telling her that the mobile-phone customer she was trying to reach was not responding or had left the service provider area. Munch knew the same recording played when the mobile phone wasn't turned on. She also knew there was no way Ellen would know how to use the phone in the car, if she was even aware of its existence. A code had to be entered via the handset before calls could be sent or received. Derek swore he hadn't told her the code. She was too annoyed with him to explain that that would have been the one thing he might have done right even if it was by accident.

Had Ellen ripped her off? she wondered. She had trouble believing that.

Was the limo wrapped around a telephone pole somewhere? Perhaps.

The gnawing truth was that anything was possible with

Ellen. Actually, that was part of her charm. The first time Munch had met Ellen was twelve years ago, when getting high had still been fun. It was at Ellen's coming-out party—Venice Beach style. After serving four months in Juvenile Hall, Ellen was a free woman. The celebration was held at a beer bar on Lincoln Boulevard.

The party had been going for hours when Munch got there. She shared a pitcher of beer with her then-best-friend Deb and then broke away to use the bathroom. While Ellen had been away, Deb had taken up with Ellen's boyfriend. Out of loyalty, Munch was fully prepared to hate the returning bitch. But then she'd opened the toilet-stall door and found Ellen sitting there, tossing reds into the air and catching them in her mouth. Ellen hadn't missed a beat, just invited Munch to join in. The evening had ended with new men for all of them, and fuck any cheating bastard who couldn't take a joke.

Ellen was one of a kind, all right, and not without principles. If she had the choice between taking the easy way out or hurting you, she'd do her utmost to look for other options. In the end she might still sleep with your old man, but she damn sure would give him a hickey. And let him try to explain that. You had to love her.

Even now, when the rules were all different, the thought of Ellen brought a rueful chuckle to her lips. *Fucking Ellen.* Was it just a coincidence that she had come back and craziness had followed?

The news came over the radio again, and Munch turned up the volume. Two people reportedly found dead in a Hollywood apartment. The details were few, as was always true with breaking news. The radio announcer did not know the age or sex of the alleged victims, only that the police were investigating, it was a double homicide, and it had probably occurred in the early-morning hours.

Ellen, she willed, *call me.* Munch wished the radio would give her more details on the victims. Two people were dead.

Was it a man and a woman or the two women? Had they been shot? Were there suspects in custody?

And where the hell was her limo?

To be fair, whatever had happened in the apartment in Hollywood, or how it might concern her customers of last evening, had nothing to do with Ellen. Except—someone had called this morning and booked the limo. Someone, according to Ellen's note, who paid cash and had worked out a special arrangement with Munch. It wasn't as if her client list were so broad or that spur-of-the-moment runs dropped from the heavens every day. That left only Raleigh Ward, the morose drunk from last night. A morose drunk with a gun.

Munch set down the phone when she heard the chimes that preceded the taped message telling her what she already knew. As soon as she hung up, the phone rang, startling her.

"Ellen?" she answered.

"No, it's me again. Mace St. John."

"Hi."

"Are you going to be home in the next half hour?"

"Why?"

"I wanted to swing by and show you some pictures," he said.

"Sure, I'll be here."

"I'd also like to take a look at your limo. The one you took out last night."

"It's the only one I have," she said.

"And it's a silver-gray Cadillac with a charcoal gray vinyl roof?"

"Yes."

"What's the license plate?"

She hesitated for only a moment before she gave it to him. She didn't want him thinking she had anything to hide. Perhaps by the time he got there, the situation with Ellen and the missing limo would be resolved. Yeah, and maybe she'd win the Publishers Clearing House Sweepstakes. "I'll be here," she said.

"See you in a bit, then," he said, and hung up.

Munch cleaned the house nervously while waiting for the phone to ring. She had the same feelings she had felt before when a guy she really liked said that he'd call. She'd spent three insecure hours not daring to tie up the phone in case when he did call, he'd get a busy signal and not try again. Thinking back, she was pretty sure the guy had never remembered his promise.

Fucking Ellen to bring up all this shit.

Twenty minutes later Munch pulled the extension by the front door and went to work trimming the hedge under her front window so she could watch for approaching cars.

Across the street, Derek was mowing his perfect green patch of lawn in the bright sunshine. Lawn care was his claim to fame. When they had lived together, he had leveled, aerated, weeded, fed, watered, and trimmed hers to perfection. She'd once asked him to promise her that he wouldn't turn into one of those old men who sat by his front window and yelled at the neighborhood kids to keep off his grass.

A red bandanna tied around his forehead now caught his honest sweat. His shoulders strained with the effort of pushing the mower. Even those movements seemed deliberate to her. Derek had a way of rolling his shoulders forward one at a time as he walked, his smooth muscles rippling like a panther or some other type of sleek night stalker. Derek's dog, Violet, sat on the front porch watching her master work. Violet was another reason Derek needed to stick close to home. The cocker spaniel had abandonment issues. Derek softened the animal's neurosis with overfeeding. When Violet waddled from her bed to her food bowl, her matted chest hair dragged on the ground. Her only real exercise came when Derek let her hump his leg.

"Why don't you stop her when she does that?" Munch had once asked.

He'd mumbled something about not breaking the animal's spirit, and she had not pursued the issue.

The first time she'd ever laid eyes on him, he'd been standing in the parking lot of the Alano Club—an A.A. clubhouse on Washington and Centinela that held three meetings most days and four on weekends. Derek attended all the noontime meetings at the Alano Club. The members of the fellowship who went to the midday meetings considered themselves the core of the Program—the axis around which the universe of sobriety was able to revolve. Some of them were twenty years sober and still making five and six meetings a week, they'd brag. Munch wondered if maybe they'd missed the point along the way.

"Aren't we all supposed to be rejoining society?" she'd asked her sponsor.

Ruby had replied, "That's the best some folks can do."

The night Munch first spotted Derek, he'd been standing with a small group while the meeting was going on inside. He'd positioned himself against the building with one knee bent, the sole of his tennis shoe resting flat on the wall behind him. He wore faded but clean blue jeans and a short-sleeve sweatshirt. Steam rose from his Styrofoam cup, his mustache just damp as he sipped and watched over the rim with his Robert Redford eyes, waiting for an opening in the conversation. She'd been drawn to his circle, even then wondering if this tall, handsome stranger wasn't the cowboy of her dreams, with his soft Arkansas drawl and easy laugh. It was only later, after he moved in, after they'd done the deed, and Asia got used to seeing him over morning cereal with the woolly buff-colored beast clinging to his calf, that certain things began to leak out.

For one, he was afraid of horses.

And then there was the work thing. He wanted to get his contractor's license, but to qualify he needed two years of experience in his field, which was glazing. He wasn't supposed to work as a glazier, he explained, until he was licensed. "You don't want me to lie on the contractor's license application," he had pointed out, citing the Ten Commandments and the Twelve Steps.

Munch listened sympathetically for a year. He'd had a bad childhood, after all, and he was doing the best he could and he was staying sober and that was the most important thing, wasn't it? Munch finally told him that she, too, had had a bad childhood, but at least hers had ended at some point.

"How do you know whether you should hang in there or when it's time to give up?" she asked her sponsor in one of their weekly chats.

"Honey," Ruby said, "I've been married and divorced four times, and I don't regret a one of them."

Fed up, Munch was determined to split up with Derek on a particularly stormy day in March. Asia was at a friend's, and Munch and Derek had been arguing all morning. Munch finally fled the house in frustration, muttering to herself that she didn't get sober to put up with this kind of shit. She returned midafternoon after doing some serious soul search-ing and reevaluation, only to find him bent over a cardboard box. He'd found a baby bird that had been blown from its nest. Inside the box he'd fashioned a new nest, put in a tin of water, and was trying to get the bird to eat. That bought him another month.

She ended up breaking up with him in April when he managed to rack up three speeding tickets in as many weeks and then miss the deadline for traffic school. The insurance company called him a bad risk.

Munch removed Derek's name from the insurance policy and the mailbox on the same day. That night she requested that he sleep on the couch, but at 3 A.M., he joined her in bed, sobbing.

"Who will take care of me?" he asked.

She found herself in the odd position of being the source of his pain and the provider of his comfort.

Later she told Ruby of the difficult night.

"They're always so surprised," Ruby said with uncharacteristic directness, "when you finally wise up."

Munch's final act of insanity had been to find Derek his job as apartment manager for the building across the street.

She was brought back to the moment when she realized that the man getting out of the car that had just pulled into her driveway was Mace St. John.

"What's so funny?" he asked as he got out of his car.

"Life," she said. "Long story. How about a cup of coffee?"

He looked at his watch. "Maybe a quick one. Where do you keep your limo?"

Munch was framing her reply when Asia burst out the front door, and said, "Mom, I can't find my red shoes."

Mace turned, and asked, "Mom? You have been busy."

Munch smiled weakly, feeling the cold hand of fear grip her heart. It was a fear she'd lived with for six years. A fear and a lie. But what did the whole exact truth really matter? How important was it to anybody that she hadn't actually given birth or gone through legal channels to ratify the adoption? For all intents, Asia was her daughter.

Besides, when is it a good time to tell a kid that both her birth parents are dead? At two? When she's stringing together her first sentences?

Or was the time to deliver the news when Asia was five? When her school did the Thanksgiving play and all the parents had come to see it. Asia had been so proud of her "Pilgroom" outfit with the brown-and-white paper collar and matching hat.

Munch had rehearsed the riff many times about how of all the children in the world, adopted kids were the most special because they were chosen. It was bullshit, but it sounded good. The point was to make the kid feel secure. And she'd always done that. Now Asia was asking questions, starting to figure things out. Munch lived with the fear of what the answers could bring. Always wondering, had Asia said something to a teacher? The crossing guard? Would someone in authority put together the scattered facts and decide the Mancini case should be looked into?

And then what? An investigation from Child Welfare with applications to fill out and social workers to convince? They'd look at Munch's record. Not the one that mattered. Not how she'd raised a happy, healthy kid who made friends easily and wanted to be a ballerina/animal trainer. They'd see a single unmarried woman who worked and wasn't home when school let out. And then they'd dig deeper. Their forms would ask the question, "Have you ever been arrested?" And then they'd give her three lines to explain. As if that would be sufficient to sum up a life story. They'd jump all over the prostitution charges. Like would they be happier if she'd been a thief to support her habit? Would that make her a better parent?

It was with that defiant attitude that Munch turned back to Mace St. John, and said, "I've been real busy. Didn't you say something about some pictures you wanted me to look at?"

"Oh, right." Mace returned to his car. When he ducked through his open window to retrieve a manila envelope, Munch cast one final hopeful look up the street.

It was still empty.

CHAPTER 8

Ellen and her merry band pulled into Tijuana at three o'clock. Raleigh had her drive up a narrow, partially cobbled road. She found a space large enough to accommodate the limo next to an open-air market.

"You two do some shopping," Raleigh said. "I need to pick up a few things."

She followed his gaze to a small whitewashed building. Over the narrow doorway, a sign proclaimed FARMACIA. Obviously he felt he would do fine without her translating skills. Not that she knew more than a few rudimentary commands such as requesting a glass of water, a light, or the lyrical but practical *Dame el dinero primero*, Give me the money first.

Victor grabbed her elbow and steered her toward a vendor selling bullfight posters.

"Now, this is sport," he said.

"Getting a poor little old bull mad and then killing it?" Ellen asked.

"It is the ultimate contest," Victor said. "Good versus evil. The bull gives his blood, his life, to satisfy man's needs."

"Sometimes the bull wins," Ellen said.

"Exactly," Victor said, his eyes excited, searing into hers as if she'd said the very thing he'd been waiting to hear. The intensity in his face made her take a step away from him. He leaned toward her as she moved back. A table full of colorful serapes blocked her escape.

He reached into his pocket and pulled out a wad of bills that was fat enough to make a nun salivate. The shopkeeper had been roaming between the narrow tables that displayed his wares. When Victor's cash appeared, the man hustled to his side.

"Señor." He tipped his head to Ellen. "Señora. How can I help you?"

Victor pointed at a poster depicting fighting cocks and peeled a twenty from his roll. "We're looking for some action. Do you know this place where the donkeys and the women . . ." He finished the sentence with a pumping motion of his hand.

The man rubbed chubby palms together. "Of course."

Ellen saw Raleigh heading their way. He carried a paper sack by its neck and held it up grinning as he got closer. *At least he was smiling now,* she thought. He opened the bag and pulled out a bottle of Del Guzano tequila.

"No trip to TJ is complete," he told Victor as he cracked the bottle open, "without eating the worm."

The shopkeeper took Victor's money, called out to a barefoot boy of perhaps eight, and gave the boy rapid instructions in Spanish while pointing at Victor. The boy listened without looking at any of them, untied and reknotted his rope belt, scratched his ear, then gestured for the three Americans to follow him.

"*Vamanos in el carro,*" Ellen said, making an effort to roll the *rr* in *carro*. Was that even a word? She pointed to the limo, and the boy nodded enthusiastically. "Oh, shit," she said, noticing the naked wheels. The car had been out of her sight for only a few minutes.

"What happened to the hubcaps?" she asked.

Raleigh and Victor passed the bottle back and forth and seemed unconcerned at her distress as they sauntered toward the big Cadillac. Ellen walked around to the driver's side and opened her door. A quick glance down the length of the car confirmed her fear that the thieves had made off with the whole damn set. She reached down and flipped the electronic door locks. The boy climbed into the front seat beside her and pointed off to the right.

"*Alli,*" he said. There.

"Ah-yee is right, kid," she said, wondering what was going

to happen next. One thing for damn sure, somebody was paying for those hubcaps. Ellen thought back to the wad of bills in Victor's pocket. Three questions instantly came to mind. *How big a tipper is this guy? How well does he hold his liquor? And how soundly does he sleep?*

The boy's directions brought them to a street called Avenida Revolución. Bars of every flavor touted their attractions. The Hula Room offered topless girls. The New York Club bragged of live entertainment. The boy urged them forward until they reached the bottom of the block. A flashing neon sign proclaimed THE BLUE FOX. Two sweating locals passed out flyers to a group of American navy men, easily recognized by their short hair and crisply pressed jeans. Fat working girls in short, tight dresses leaned against the windowless walls and smiled at passing traffic. Smoke and tinny-sounding salsa music oozed from the open doorway.

"Perfect," Victor said. Raleigh passed him the tequila bottle, and he took a healthy swig. He offered the bottle to Ellen. She declined.

The Cadillac's thermometer read 100 degrees, and that wasn't even counting the humidity. COLD BEER was painted in white letters above the doorway. *Maybe just one,* she thought, *and only the bottled stuff.*

As the group passed through the flaps of floor-length Naugahyde that served as the doors of the establishment, one of the barkers pushed a flyer into Ellen's hand. The black-and-white photograph was grainy, but she could still make out the heavily made-up fat woman spreading her pussy open and curling her tongue. Large, flabby breasts spilled over the woman's arms.

"When's the show?" Victor asked.

"Twenty dollars," the doorman said. "Each."

Ellen hesitated. "Maybe I'll just wait in the car," she said.

"It's too hot for that," Raleigh said. "Come on in. Don't worry. I won't tell."

"Well," she said, thinking how good just the one beer would taste. "Maybe for just a moment." She deserved that much.

Raleigh followed the two of them inside. The bar smelled of piss and beer. Even with the two fans turning sullenly overhead, the humidity inside the dark bar was thick enough to push him back. Three whores surrounded them instantly, the youngest of whom looked about twelve, even with the makeup. Her Levi cutoffs revealed more than they covered.

"Want a blow job?" she asked. "I do you at the booth. Twelve-fifty."

He pushed past her, taking Ellen's arm and guiding her to the bar. The bartender turned to take their order. Raleigh had a hard time not focusing on what passed as the man's nose. All that remained was a twisted knob of scar tissue above two gaping black nostrils.

"*Bueno,*" the bartender said, pointing the two obscene holes right at Raleigh.

"Tequila," he said, holding up two fingers. "What you want, doll?" he asked Ellen.

"Something cold and wet," she said. "Something that'll fit easily in my hand and make me happy."

Raleigh responded by puffing out his chest. "I think I got just what you need."

"Aren't you going to ask me if I want foreign or domestic?"

"Believe me, doll," he said. "Buy American." He pointed at the cooler behind the bartender. "And one beer. You got that, amigo?"

The bartender wiped his bar rag across his face, then flipped it back over his shoulder and reached for glasses and bottles.

Raleigh turned his back to the man, leaned against the ripped upholstery of the bar top, and assessed the security.

The midday crowd was limited to a dozen sailors, three shabbily dressed dark-skinned local men, and five whores working the room. The wooden stage was bathed in red and blue lights. A blanket covered the large door to the left of the stage.

There wasn't a man or woman in the room he couldn't take. Any one of them he could kill in twenty different ways with his bare hands, or an opportunistic garrote. The cooler of beer held three dozen blunt objects that could easily crush temporal lobes. He took a deep hit of his tequila and sighed, feeling in control and the most relaxed he'd been in days.

CHAPTER 9

Munch invited Mace St. John into her home, motioned for him to take a seat on the couch, and then followed Asia into her bedroom to locate the red shoes.

"I need to talk to this man about some stuff," she told Asia. "You can come in and meet him after you get your shoes on."

"Who is he?" Asia asked.

"He's a policeman. Someone I met before you were born. I haven't seen him in a long time."

"Why is he here?"

"That's what I'm going to find out. Wash your face and hands before you come back."

"Okay."

Munch looked long and hard at Asia, raising her eyebrows and tilting her head. Asia had acquiesced a little too easily.

"I will," Asia said, putting extra emphasis on the second word.

Munch returned to the living room. Mace St. John had spread four photographs across the coffee table. She sat down beside him and looked. Three of the pictures showed her limo from a slightly aerial viewpoint.

"Where were these taken?" she asked.

"Apartment complex security camera."

"Welcome to 1984, Big Brother," she said.

"You recognize this guy?" he asked, pointing at a photograph of Mr. Disco with his hand raised in apparent greeting.

"Yeah," she said, "that's the guy I picked up at the Beverly Wilshire. Raleigh Ward called him Victor."

Mace consulted his notes. "He was the foreigner?"

"Yeah, heavy accent, and he seemed kind of out of sync."

"How so?"

"His clothes were like out of the seventies. And he had a weird way of looking at people, at me, the two floozies."

"Weird how?"

"I don't know, like he'd just arrived on the planet—like he was looking at some kind of zoo species he'd never seen before. Kind of creepy, really."

"What about the two women? The floozies?"

"I don't mean to put them down. They were okay, I guess. Just two party girls out for a good time."

"Pros?" he asked quietly.

"Could be," she said, casting a nervous glance toward Asia's room.

He pulled out two more pictures from the manila envelope. "Are these the women you met last night?"

She looked at the photographs and felt her stomach flip. "Are they dead?" she asked, staring at the open-eyed, slack expressions, already knowing the answer.

He nodded.

"Yeah, these look like the same girls. Was this the case I heard about on the news this morning?"

"After you left the building on Gower, you took Raleigh Ward straight back to his place?"

"Yeah."

"And you left this Victor character with the two women?"

"That's right."

"What was Raleigh Ward's state of mind?"

She thought back to the terrible expression on Raleigh's face, remembered that when he rose up to get the money out of his pocket, she'd seen a gun holstered on his belt. "Were the women shot?" she asked.

"I can't comment on that," he said.

"Raleigh was packing."

"I know, you included that in your report. Was he agitated when you last saw him?"

"More like devastated."

"Go on."

"He made a call on the way home. Some woman, I think. He wanted to go see her, but she turned him down."

"You could hear all this?"

She forced herself not to shift in her seat. "Yeah, I could."

"Then what happened?"

"He paid me and went home. I tried calling back whoever he'd been talking to."

"You did? How?"

"I pushed redial on the phone."

"Why?"

"I was worried about him. He seemed so bummed out, and he was drunk. I was afraid he was going to, I don't know, maybe off himself. I thought maybe whoever it was on the phone might like to help."

"And what happened when you called?"

"She hung up on me. I think she thought it was him calling back."

"And then you left?"

"Yeah."

Asia entered the room. She'd clipped three plastic animal-themed barrettes randomly across her mop of Shirley Temple curls. She'd also changed into this week's favorite outfit: plaid shorts and a bright yellow shirt.

Mace quickly stuffed the pictures of the dead women back into his envelope.

"Asia," Munch said, "this is Detective St. John."

Asia clasped her hands behind her back, crossed her feet, and looked downward. *Well, this is a first,* Munch thought.

"Pleased to meet you, Asia," Mace said.

"Hello," Asia replied, barely audibly.

"Nice shoes," he added.

She looked up then. "Mommy said she met you before I was born."

"How old are you?" he asked.

Munch watched the exchange in incredulous and mounting panic. How was it that the conversation had zeroed in immediately on just the mine field she hoped to avoid? She'd had her dealings with the detective a little over seven years ago. Lord knows, she hadn't been pregnant then.

"Six and a half," Asia said. "I'll be seven in—"

"The limo isn't here," Munch blurted out.

"Where is it?" Mace asked, turning to her.

Asia took a step in front of Munch, placing herself between Mace and her mother. She put a look of resignation on her six-and-a-half-year-old face, an expression that had taken Munch twenty-eight years to earn, and sighed before she said, "Fucking Ellen took it."

Mace made a small choking sound. When he looked over at Munch, his eyes had a twinkle in them. "Who's Ellen?" he asked.

"A friend of mine," Munch said, feeling her eyes bulge as she stared at Asia with a mixture of shock and annoyance.

"Derek told us," Asia said.

"And Derek is?" he asked, addressing Asia.

"My ex," Munch said, louder than necessary, hoping to get everyone's attention back on her.

"Your daddy?" Mace asked Asia.

"No," she assured him. "My daddy is in heaven." She accompanied this statement with a solemn glance skyward.

God, Munch thought, *this kid is good. Scary how good.*

"Derek lives across the street," Munch explained. "He manages the four-unit apartment building. Before that he lived with us and helped run the limo company."

"So you guys broke up and he moved across the street?" Mace asked. "That must be a strain."

"Actually, I helped get him the job," Munch said.

"That was nice of you."

"I don't hate the guy," she said. "I just didn't want to live with him anymore."

"He never got out of bed," Asia added.

Munch blushed. Unbelievable what those little eyes and ears picked up.

"So are you saying this Ellen took the limo without your permission?" Mace asked.

"Apparently when Asia and I were out this morning, Ellen took a call. Derek helped her wash the car and stock it with ice and drinks."

"When will she be back?" Mace asked.

"She didn't say," Munch said.

"Where did she go? Who was her customer?"

"Look," Munch said, exhaling with defeat, "here's the thing. I don't know for certain. Some guy called. Ellen said something to him about not sending a blonde because of what they thought of blondes down there. When she left, she asked Derek if he wanted her to bring back any fireworks. I've tried to call her on the mobile phone in the limo, but she either doesn't have it on or she's out of range."

"Is that why you called the apartment on Gower?" he asked. "To try to track her down? You think she's with Raleigh Ward?"

"Let's just say business hasn't exactly been booming. Since prom season died down, I've had about three calls. Raleigh Ward told me last night that he was going to be needing the car off and on all week."

"To entertain this Victor guy?" Mace asked, pointing at the photograph.

"Possibly." She showed Mace the note from Ellen. "I think they might have gone to Mexico."

A beeping noise interrupted their conversation. Mace looked down at the device attached to his belt.

"Mind if I use your phone?" he asked, tilting his head toward the phone on the table.

"Help yourself," Munch said. Taking Asia by the hand, she led the girl back to her room, and asked her, "Haven't we talked about not using certain words no matter where you hear them?"

In response to the page, Mace called Parker Center. While he waited to be put through to Cassiletti's extension, he checked out his surroundings. There was a bulletin board mounted on the wall next to him. On it was a map of the city and a list of phone numbers for the major airlines. Checks addressed to Munch filled the left edge of the board. Each was stamped with either INSUFFICIENT FUNDS, ACCOUNT CLOSED, or PAYMENT STOPPED in red ink across the face. *Assholes,* he thought.

Cassiletti answered his phone. Mace identified himself and asked what was up.

"I showed the picture of our witness to the concierge at the Beverly Wilshire," Cassiletti said. "I've got a name to go with the face: Victor Draicu."

"That checks with what I have," Mace said. "What else you got?"

"Draicu is a Romanian diplomat. He's connected with the Olympics."

Mace made a note to himself. That connection bore some looking into. "Any luck with the cabbie who picked him up?" he asked.

"Yeah, I tracked the guy down. He remembered the call. Said he took Draicu to titty bars by the airport and dropped him off. I asked the hotel personnel when Draicu got in, but nobody remembers seeing him until this morning, when a limo picked him up."

"What make and color?" Mace asked.

"Gray Cadillac?" Cassiletti said.

"All right, good work," Mace said, wishing the big man had half the confidence of Munch's daughter. "I need you to call Border Patrol. You got a pen and paper?"

"Just a minute."

Mace glanced skyward while he heard Cassiletti fumble for writing utensils.

"All right," Cassiletti said. "I'm ready."

Mace read off the license number of Munch's limo. "Find out if this vehicle has passed the checkpoint today and, if so, when." If the limo had gone to Mexico, that would be a break, Mace knew. The American Border Patrol had increased security because of the upcoming Olympics. All commercial vehicles entering as well as exiting the country were being noted and entered into the agency's database.

"You want them to stop the car?" Cassiletti asked.

"That would be the idea," Mace said, trying to stifle his impatience.

"What should I tell them?"

"That the vehicle is physical evidence in a homicide investigation, and that the driver and passengers are needed for questioning. Tell them to proceed with caution."

"What are you going to do?" Cassiletti asked.

"I'm going to head back to downtown. I've got a meeting with Steve Brown."

"OCID?" Cassiletti asked, referring to the Organized Crime Intelligence Division.

"Yeah, he said he might have some answers for me." And given Steve's line of work, Mace knew anything he had worth listening to wouldn't be said over the phone.

CHAPTER 10

He felt restless. The fluids coursing through him screamed for release. The woman driver who had been tantalizing him the entire evening drank like a man, he noted with disdain. Who did she think she was? And she was noisy. The woman was unbearably full of herself.

The hot liquid of his own juices bubbled within him, the pressure of it building. He could feel the vessels behind his eyes dilating, threatening to split his skull apart. It didn't stop there, this distention of his fluids. The swelling reached even to the marrow of his bones. He knew his cycles well. The force of it both awed and—yes, he was man enough to admit it—at times the power frightened him. What if he did nothing to answer this call? Would the noodle-shaped pieces of his own precious brain spill out in red, oozing gobs?

He tapped his fingers on the rim of his glass, staring in the rippled mirror behind the cash register, and visualized the pulsing organs of the loud, brash woman seated at the end of the bar. He knew a lot about anatomy. Even as a child he'd studied the miracle of the circulatory and digestive systems. Often he'd been late to school, enthralled by the sight of dead animals on the roadway, with their insides squished out into the open, the tread of a tire imprinted on their fur and intestines, the milky look of their open eyes. His mother thought him lazy. Lazy, filthy monkey boy. But she had been wrong about him. Very wrong. He realized he had an erection.

He had to do something soon.

■ ■ ■

Mace drove to the headquarters of the Organized Crime Intelligence Division. The OCID made its home in a windowless three-story building across the street from the Greyhound bus station on the edge of downtown. Cops in the know referred to the headquarters as Fort Davis, in homage to the former chief, Ed Davis.

Mace had called ahead. If he hadn't, the flashing of his detective's shield would not have been enough to get him inside the ultrasecret fortress. He only knew of its existence through his friendship with Steve Brown. Detectives working under the auspices of the OCID not only never made the news, but also never made arrests. Their duties were only to gather intelligence. They weren't choosy about their methods—a fact that never held up well in a court of law. If the odd crime was observed, OCID investigators passed the information along. Sometimes they used the anonymous WETIP line. But Steve fed his intelligence directly to Mace.

He greeted Mace at the doorway. A lean, handsome man, Steve stood a shade under six feet and had a touch of gray at his temples. He looked more like a TV anchorman than the spy Mace knew him to be.

"Let's take a walk," he said to Mace.

"So what did Tommy Lasorda have for lunch today?" Mace asked.

"The usual," Steve answered, not rising to the bait. The duties of the OCID, despite its name, had little to do with investigating organized crime. OCID investigators were divided into teams that covered politicians, entertainers, athletes, team owners—anybody who was anybody. Information was gathered and stored in private facilities throughout Los Angeles, giving the chief of police Hoover-like power over the Who's Who of the city.

"You've got a name for me?" Steve asked.

"Raleigh Ward." Mace slipped his friend a piece of paper.

"Here's his address and everything else we could find out, which was damn little. I can't even get a photograph out of the DMV."

Steve slipped the paper into his pocket. "You think this guy is a spook?"

"He's something."

"Preparing for the Olympics has brought all kinds of shit to town. I've worked double shifts for a month. Fucking spooks think they can do anything they want, like the rules don't apply to them."

Mace coughed into his hand. If that wasn't the pot calling the kettle . . .

"I've got an unusual signature on the D.B.'s," Mace said. He described the washing of the bodies, the placement of the victims' hands, and the white crosses of tape covering the wounds. He knew that OCID shared information with organizations similar to their own in other countries. He also appreciated the lack of bureaucracy involved. So much time was saved when cops didn't have to mess around with rules of conduct, protocol, and giving rights to those who deserved none.

"It's a big world," Steve said. "Anywhere in particular you think this guy might have operated?"

"I filed a report with Interpol six months ago, after the December homicide, just in case the suspect was a tourist." He'd been grasping at straws, but there were no other leads to follow. All the victim's family and acquaintances had checked out. He could find no motive. The victim's jewelry had not been stolen. She had no enemies, according to everyone he interviewed. It was the worst kind of murder to try to solve: murder by stranger. "But that doesn't mean the Eastern Bloc countries are cooperating. I also need you to keep an ear out to Mexico. I have information that my guy might be there."

"I'll see what I can find out," Steve said.

"One other thing," Mace said. "My homicide victims"—he

wrote down the women's names and address—"had their rent paid by Southern Air Transport. I didn't find any record of either one of the women's employment there."

"I know the company," Steve said.

"You do?" Mace asked.

"Government op. They fly DC-3s and DC-4s in and out of Central America. Good cargo planes, I understand, and able to operate on short runways."

Ellen woke up cold, vaguely aware of the sound of rushing water. Rocks and branches poked her back. She sat up. Her pants were pulled down to her knees; her shirt was on inside out and full of foxtails. A quick check confirmed that she'd recently had sex. She had a vague recollection of getting friendly with one of the American sailors at the bar.

She pulled her pants up and checked her front pocket. The money was still there. Thank God. For a moment she had been really worried.

She continued to take inventory. In a back pocket she found a cache of capsules wrapped in coarse toilet paper. Where had those come from? She had a vague recollection of arranging a trade with one of the local working girls. The pills were chloral hydrates—a tasteless tranquilizer that dissolved quickly in liquor. She didn't know what their medical use was, but they made great Mickey Finns.

Judging from the position of the moon, now high overhead, it had to be close to midnight. *What else happened during the missing hours between one-drink-won't-hurt and waking up in these nasty old bushes?*

The last thing she remembered was sitting in the bar. The navy boys were lining up shooters. Raleigh got all pissed off when she told the one sweet-faced fella that she was from North Carolina.

"I thought you said Georgia," he said.

She didn't remind him that Georgia had been his idea, and she had just gone along to be agreeable. Men like to feel like they know something—that they're smart. You can just see them preen their feathers when you tell them what they want to hear. And what was the big deal anyhow? Georgia was right next to North Carolina, wasn't it? Maybe she grew up on the border or something. What harm was there if she told a lonely sailor boy—a member of the Armed Services of these United States—that they hailed from the same neck of the woods?

Still, she thought, zipping her jeans shut, you would have thought sweet-faced North Carolina would have had the manners to pull her pants back up.

She heard shouting from farther down the embankment and realized that these noises were what had wakened her. Angry male voices raised in argument, and in the background was the sound of rushing water. She recognized Spanish swear words. *Pinche* this and *cabron* that.

She stumbled down the bank toward the source of the commotion. It was Raleigh and Victor, she saw, with two Mexican men. The Mexican doing most of the shouting was young, maybe twenty. The other man was thicker in the chest, old enough to be the youth's father. They all stood beneath a bridge that spanned a muddy river. With the palm of his hand Victor pushed the younger Mexican. The man staggered back, sending out a stream of invectives and pointing at Raleigh.

She caught the Spanish words for "sister" and "brother" and something that sounded like "mortar." The man's voice broke as he shouted. His hysterical tone made her instinctively crouch under the cover of a bush.

Victor charged the slighter man and thumped his fist into that man's chest. As Ellen watched, the young Mexican performed a strange, slow-motion pirouette. His knees buckled and he sank to the sandy ground. Victor pulled his hand back, and there was a flash of silver. He had a knife. Everything made a horrible sort of sense then: the look of shock on the older Mexican's face, the spreading dark stain on the stricken man's loose-fitting white-cotton shirt.

Raleigh disarmed Victor with startling efficiency—one quick, fluid move, and he was holding the knife. Victor just stood there, looking bewildered. The whole scene was made even more surreal by the absolute silence in which everything that followed seemed to be happening. It was as if the world needed a moment to catch its breath after this rash, irreversible act. Then Raleigh's hand struck out again and grabbed the older Mexican by his hair. Before she could blink, the man was spun around and his head pulled back. Raleigh looked once more at the body on the ground, then ran the knife blade across the helpless man's throat. The next sound she heard was a sickening gurgle. By the light of the moon, she could see the man's lips move uselessly above his slashed neck.

At some point in the seconds it took for the gruesome scene to be enacted, Ellen's fist found its way into her mouth. She bit down on her finger until she felt the flesh break, but she couldn't stop herself. She dared not make a sound.

Raleigh and Victor rolled the two bodies into the river. The corpses made a slow progress with the current. They were both facedown, the backs of their shirts billowing with trapped air. Eventually the shirts wilted and the bodies sank. Raleigh pulled a gun from his belt and the wallet from his pocket and threw them both on the sandy bank. He then jumped into the water. Victor also threw his billfold onto the shore and waded thigh-deep into the river.

While the two men washed the evidence of their deeds from their clothes and skin, she took the opportunity to scramble back up the bank. She forced herself to move slower than her racing blood demanded, picking each footstep so that no rock was dislodged or dry twig snapped.

She found the limo parked at the top of the hill with one front tire in a ditch. She tried the driver's door but found it locked. She searched her pockets with shaking hands, already knowing she didn't have the keys.

How far is the town? she wondered. *And where the fuck are the* federales *when you need them?* A fifth of tequila rested against the windshield, balanced on the wiper blades. Three fingers of liquor remained. She heard Raleigh and Victor stumbling up the riverbank. She grabbed the bottle, popped open the capsules, and dumped the powdered drug into it.

When the two men emerged at the top of the hill, Ellen was sitting on the hood. She smiled drunkenly and held out the bottle. "Where the fuck have you two been?" she asked. "The party is just getting started."

CHAPTER 11

Saturday night, Asia pulled out a jigsaw puzzle, and asked, "Can we?"

"Yeah, sure," Munch said, clearing the coffee table. She brought the phone over and set it on the floor beside them.

Asia dumped out the box and went to work on the edges. The picture on the box depicted two puppies under an umbrella in the rain. While Asia constructed the frame, Munch gathered all the pieces that made up the dogs' faces. Twenty minutes later, Asia had linked all the edges. Then, instead of working on the umbrella, or a puddle, or even the tree limb lying on the ground in front of the puppies, Asia had to start messing with some of the dog pieces.

Every time she reached across the table, her arm caught the edge of the puzzle and sent it askew.

"Stop moving everything," Munch finally said, "and keep away from the dog stuff. That's mine."

Asia didn't say anything. She didn't have to. Munch had heard herself. "All right," she said. "You can touch anything you want on the puzzle."

Asia responded by taking her index finger and touching every piece in front of Munch. Munch watched Asia's face out of the corner of her eye, then laughed. She was up to the test, and Asia was one smart kid. That's what counted, that and spunk. It was okay to be fair and kind and share with others, just so long as you kept your eyes and ears open.

"So, Mom, I've been thinking."

"Oh, yeah?"

"I don't think it would hurt my dad's feelings if we found another daddy here on earth."

Munch choked on her coffee. "What?" She shouldn't have been surprised. Asia had been on the daddy riff a lot lately—asking questions about her real dad. Munch told Asia as much as she could. That John Garillo had a great smile, that Asia had his same dark eyes. John was part-Mexican, making Asia about an eighth; maybe there was even an Inca princess somewhere in the mix if they went back far enough. Munch told Asia that her daddy used to give her baths when she was a baby. He died when she was six months old, although Asia swore she could remember lying on his chest and him smiling down on her.

"You and me are good cuddlebugs," Asia said. "I just wish I had a daddy, too. Then he could come to school on career day and talk about what he does."

"What about me being a mechanic?" Munch asked. "Isn't that interesting?"

"Yeah, but all the kids know that already."

"Is that the only reason you want a daddy?"

"No. If we had a daddy, we could all walk down the street together. I could hold both your hands and you could swing me up."

"And we'd always be smiling?" Munch asked.

"Yeah," Asia said. "Because we'd be at Disneyland."

"Oh, I see. Maybe we should look for some guy who works at Disneyland."

"Or Sea World," Asia said, brown eyes sparkling. "Good idea."

"But not a redhead," Munch said.

"Not like Justin," Asia agreed. She'd often complained about the annoying boy in her class with the red hair and freckles. Some days he was all she could talk about.

"When should we begin this search?"

"Oh, I already started. My friend Scott doesn't have a mom. Him and his dad know all about you. He asked me what kind of music you liked."

"Your friend?"

"No," Asia said, a little exasperated. "Eric, his dad. I told him you liked that Aerosmith song. 'Big Ten Inch.'"

Munch felt her face flush. "You didn't."

"Well, you're always singing along real loud when it comes on the radio."

Munch covered her eyes with her hand, feeling the heat of her cheeks. Then she looked over at the kitchen clock.

"You know what? It's bedtime."

"Ten more minutes."

"Five."

"And three more pieces."

"One each, then you brush your teeth and put on your jammies."

They worked for a moment in silence, then Munch said, "I don't think your real daddy would mind either." And was her real mommy also smiling down on them? Munch liked to think so.

After Asia went to bed, Munch worked the puzzle long into the night and again the next morning. When Asia woke up, they finished. Asia, of course, popped in the final piece.

The phone didn't ring until nine o'clock. It was Mace St. John.

"Border Patrol reports that your limo crossed the checkpoint at two o'clock yesterday afternoon," he said. "They don't have any record of its coming back across."

"So it's still down there," Munch said.

"Most likely. You didn't hear anything?"

"No. How about Raleigh Ward? Have you found him?"

"No. As far as I know, he hasn't returned to his apartment. I'm still trying to get a photo of him. I'll bring it by when I do."

"All right."

"How long have you known Ellen?" he asked.

"Over ten years."

"That long?" he asked. She heard papers rustle. "So you knew her from partying?"

"Yeah, we partied some."

"Did you two always get along?"

"What are you saying?"

"Maybe she just ripped you off," he said. "Have you thought of that?"

"You don't know her. She wouldn't do that, not without a reason."

"People make up their own reasons, especially dopers."

"Look, I don't expect you to understand." Munch picked up the phone and walked into the kitchen, out of Asia's earshot. "I'm not saying she's a saint, but she has her principles. She's got no reason to rip me off."

He didn't say anything for a long moment, then, "I hope I get a chance to meet her."

She didn't like his tone or his pauses. It made her think of someone who had bad news for you and was waiting for a good time to break it. "There's more, right?" she asked. It was always best to get all the bad shit out in the open; then you could deal with it.

"Yeah. The Judicial Police in Tijuana have found the bodies of three people."

"That probably happens a lot down there," she said. "Why did they call you? Were the dead people American?"

Mace took a while before he answered. She knew there were things in an ongoing case that cops didn't tell, details they didn't give out.

"Two of the victims were local men," he finally said, "stabbed, slashed, and found floating in the river. The other was a woman. They haven't been able to identify her."

"Was she young, old, white?"

"The only information I have is that she is a young female. She was found nude and wearing a red wig."

Munch thought of the wigs lined up in Asia's room. There was a blond one and a brunette, but no red. "My friend Ellen wears wigs."

"I know. Your boy Derek told Detective Cassiletti."

"Are you going down there?" she asked.

"Yes."

"I want to come, too," she said. "If that body is Ellen, I can identify her."

"I can take a Polaroid," he said. "Might be easier for you."

"I can also identify Raleigh Ward," she reminded him.

He paused again, obviously weighing the merits of involving her. "What about your kid?"

"Derek can watch her. That's the least he can do."

"All right. I'll pick you up in twenty minutes."

Munch called Derek and told him what she needed of him.

"Damn," he said, on hearing the latest developments. "You think it's her?"

"Right now I'm trying real hard not to think anything until I know."

"Yeah," he said. "That's probably best."

"I thought you might understand," she said. Waiting for problems to solve themselves was one of Derek's specialties.

After hanging up with Derek, Munch dressed Asia. She insisted on wearing her dress with the yellow daisies when she understood they were to have another visit from Detective St. John.

For herself, Munch selected a pair of Levi's, a thick white T-shirt, and tennis shoes.

"Aren't you going to put on some makeup?" Asia asked.

"I wasn't planning on it," Munch said. "Why?"

"Makes you prettier."

"This isn't a date, honey. Besides, Detective St. John is already married to a really nice lady."

"Oh," Asia said, clearly deflated.

Munch was just tying her laces when Derek arrived. He let himself in without knocking. She heard the refrigerator door open.

"Asia's in the bathroom," she called to him. "I'll call in every couple of hours to see if you've heard from Ellen. So stay close, okay?"

"You're out of milk," he said.

"Shit," she said. "I was going to go marketing yesterday. Go on out and get something to eat, but then stick close to the phone, all right?"

"No problem," he said.

She heard a car door slam out front, and said, "That's probably him now."

The bathroom door opened and Asia emerged, preceded by a haze of floral perfume. Was that blush on her cheeks? Munch wondered. Where did this kid get all her girlie-girl instincts? And would the phase pass? Munch was constantly trying to puzzle out how much of the girl's personality was genetic and how much was environmental. She once went to a meeting about adoption. The joke among the adoptive parents was that any bad traits seen in the children were attributed to the birth parents, and consequently all good characteristics were a result of upbringing. One thing for certain, this kid was very much her own person and always had been.

Munch heard the gate latch jingle and opened the door. Mace had parked on the street and was walking up her front steps.

"I'm all set," she said.

"Good, good." He glanced down the street. "Can I use your phone real quick?"

"Of course," she said. "Come in. You want some coffee or anything?" She shooed Derek and Asia back from the doorway.

"No, just need to make a call." He nodded hello to Derek

and gave Asia a smile. She did her newfound shy number, tucking her chin down to her chest and batting her eyes.

Mace crossed the room to the phone. "Is this the only extension?"

"You need privacy?" Munch asked.

"Uh, no, this'll be fine."

Munch took Asia's hand and led her outside, giving Derek the high sign to follow. Asia's eyes remained focused on Mace St. John, even though it meant walking with her head swiveled backward. On the front porch, Munch reached into her wallet and pulled out a twenty. She handed the bill to Derek. "I'll call you guys in a couple of hours and let you know what's going on."

"Okay," Asia said absently, poking her head around Derek's legs as she tried to get a last look at the detective in her living room.

"Eat something healthy," Munch admonished, wondering which of the two she had a better chance of reaching. It was close.

She came back in the house in time to hear Mace say, "Hi, it's me." There was a pause while he inclined his head and put a finger over his free ear. "Something's come up. I have to go down to Mexico."

He closed his eyes as he listened.

"The Band-Aid thing. Can you feed the dogs? Maybe throw the ball for Nicky?"

He seemed to be holding his breath, then his shoulders slumped. "I know you know."

He nodded. "I'm at her house now. She's got a nice place, almost in the Marina."

Munch had been heading for her bedroom, but slowed her steps as soon as she knew she was out of his line of vision.

"No, she looks good. She's got a kid."

She breathed slowly and stood very still.

"A girl." He dropped his voice. Munch leaned closer from her position around the corner.

"Almost seven," he said. Now his voice was barely audible. "I thought so, too. I'll try to find out." She heard him inhale, saw the reflection of his body straightening in the window. "Thanks for taking care of the dogs."

His next response came quickly.

"I know I don't. That's not the point. I want to let you know I appreciate you. I'll call you later?"

A second, maybe two passed, then he said, "Bye. Take care," and hung up.

Munch walked back to the bedroom door and closed it.

"All set?" he called to her.

"I hope so," she said. Before walking out the door, she grabbed the spare set of keys for the limo and her leather coat.

The Sunday traffic was heavy in West Los Angeles. St. John spent much of the time on the radio, speaking in cryptic, clipped sentences full of numbers and letters. She heard none of the emotion that had weighted his voice earlier.

"So how did Asia's father die?" Mace asked. "Natural causes?"

"You could say that," Munch said. "He got on the wrong end of a methamphetamine deal with the Gypsy Jokers."

"Loser," Mace said.

"More than you know," she said.

They drove against traffic inland to catch the San Diego freeway southbound. It, too, was crowded. They made some small talk about people spending hours in smoggy traffic on their day off for the privilege of paying five dollars to sit on hot, tarry sand and then fight the traffic again to get back home.

An hour and a half later, the freeways merged north of San Clemente. The wind took on a sudden freshness, and then they were on the Coast Highway. The ocean to their right was blue, dotted with sailboats. Flocks of seagulls, their wings white chevrons against the cloudless sky, circled above. Sitting inside the hot car with the scent of the crisp salt air in her nose, it was hard to argue with the wisdom of the throng of beachgoers parked along the shoulder.

Munch knew a woman who considered the ocean her Higher Power, claiming that the shifting enormity of the Pacific Ocean was a lot easier to believe in than some bearded entity on high.

"You ever pray?" she asked Mace.

"Isn't the first question, 'Do you believe in God?'"

"Do you?"

"Only when I'm really desperate," he said. "How about you?"

"When I first got sober," she said, "it was like every time I turned a corner some kind of miracle was happening. Big things, coming just in time to save my butt. Back then everything was a miracle: correct change at the market, finding a short in a wiring harness, parking places opening up when I needed them. Everything was like, 'Wow, you mean getting loaded had to do with this, too?'"

"And now?" he asked.

"Things have been going along pretty evenly. Work, meetings, shuttling Asia to all her different activities. God doesn't come into the picture too much until the shit hits the fan."

"He must be used to that."

She smiled at the ocean, liking the idea of God understanding human nature and not holding a grudge. Then she turned back toward Mace so she could watch his face for the first sign of a lie. "How's Caroline?" she asked.

"She's, uh," he said as he rubbed his hand over the stubble on his chin, "probably happier."

"Probably?"

"We separated. We've agreed to disagree," he said, his voice dripping with sarcasm.

"I'm sorry."

"Yeah, well . . ." He sped up to pass the Buick in front of him, cutting back into the lane just inches in front of the other car. She gripped the armrest.

"What happened?"

He looked out the window. She saw the muscles in his jaw flex. "You hungry?" he asked.

"Not really."

"We'll stop in San Diego. I need to check in with a buddy of mine at the San Diego PD."

"Yeah, okay." They crossed over a bridge. A train trestle ran parallel to them. She thought about his train car, the one he was always fixing up. The 1927 office car was parked on a siding of track on Olympic Boulevard. She passed it Wednesday nights when she went to an A.A. meeting held at a women's recovery house. It was a beautiful piece of engineering and craftsmanship inside and out. He'd taken her on a tour once, shown her the lush interior created for railroad executives and lovingly restored by him. The exterior was painted Pullman green and still had the original leaded-glass windows, though Mace had covered them with grating. Like a ship, she had a name: Bella Donna. It was stenciled along her side in gold-leaf script. Mace told her once that one day he and his dad were going to hire an Amtrak engine to tow them up the coast. She had thought that sounded so cool, especially when he told her there were tracks that ran through parts of the country unspoiled by any other symptoms of civilization. Crystal blue lakes stocked with noncancerous fish, virgin forest. Just you and your portable self-contained armored car.

"How's your dad?" she asked.

"He . . ." Mace St. John blew out his breath, looked to his left, then straight ahead. "We lost him."

"Oh, I'm sorry. I didn't know. Was it a stroke?"

"Nothing that clean. Six months ago he just started to slip

away. He wouldn't eat unless you ground the food up in the blender, and then only a couple of bites."

"That must have been rough."

"I fucked that one up, too," Mace said.

"How did you fuck up?" she asked, realizing now that for all the anger he exhibited, the majority he reserved for himself. "He was old, right?"

"Yeah, right."

She knew she had gone too far. The temperature inside the car seemed to drop thirty degrees. His whole body was rigid, from the hands gripping the steering wheel to the taut muscles in his forearms. Even his head angled forward awkwardly as he watched the traffic.

"Look at this asshole," he said, climbing up behind the black Chrysler in the lane ahead of him. The Chrysler peeled off into a slower lane. Mace muttered, "Fucking jerk," and glared at the driver as they passed.

They drove several miles in silence. She wondered if cops ever listened to music when they were on the job. The silence in the car was setting her teeth on edge.

"What about the dogs?" she asked. "Didn't you have a couple of dogs?"

His face relaxed then. His lips puckered in a kissing motion. "My babies," he said.

"I'm glad you still have the dogs," she said, knowing for a fact how kids and dogs had a way of keeping your heart alive.

He looked at his watch, and said, "We'll reach San Diego around noon."

She rubbed her eyes and yawned. "You mind if I take a little nap? I didn't get much sleep last night."

"Yeah, you do that," he said.

She closed her eyes, but only pretended to sleep.

CHAPTER 12

Munch and Mace arrived at the San Diego police station ten minutes after twelve. Mace flashed his badge to the uniformed cop guarding the entrance to the parking lot and was directed to take any available space.

After they parked, Mace reached into the backseat and retrieved a large manila envelope. They entered the building. Mace again showed his police identification at the front desk. He was given a plastic badge to clip onto the collar of his shirt. Munch was issued a sticker badge that read, VISITOR. The day's date was stamped across the bottom. SAN DIEGO POLICE DEPARTMENT was printed in blue across the top.

Mace asked the cop on duty how to get to Enrique Chacón's office.

"Narcotics," the cop said. "Third floor, left as you exit the elevator."

Mace thanked the guy and told Munch to follow him. As they waited for the elevator, police of all sizes, sexes, and colors walked past them. Munch realized that she would have had trouble making over half of them as cops. Maybe it was how they smiled when she made eye contact. She looked down at the pass pasted to her shirt and decided it was much better to be a visitor than a guest.

They took the elevator to the third floor and turned left. The hallway was full of cardboard file boxes. A sign with an arrow directed them to the Narcotics Division. Mace led the way, the manila envelope full of morbid pictures tucked under his arm.

They entered the open door of a room with NARCOTICS stenciled on the opaque glass inset of the door. Smooth rough wire mesh, she thought to herself as she ran her hand over the multifaceted surface. Six months with a glazier filled your head with all sorts of useful information like that.

Desks lined the walls of the narrow office. In the corner, a gang member in starched khaki pants traded jokes with a seated detective. When the boy turned, she saw the police badge hanging from a chain around his neck.

Damn, she thought, *he's good. He even has tattoos.*

Another Hispanic cop was on the phone with his back to them. He swiveled in his chair, and his face opened in a broad smile when he saw Mace. He held up a finger to say just a minute.

Mace waved for him to take his time.

The seated cop finished his call, stood, and extended his hand to Mace. "Mace St. John," he said. "How are you?"

"Chacón, this is my friend Munch Mancini."

"Call me Rico."

Munch shook hands with Mace's friend. The narcotics cop's hand was warm and his manner friendly. She wondered if he saw her old needle marks. Would that chill him out?

"So what brings you to town?" Chacón asked.

"Munch has a limousine that crossed the border yesterday. We were hoping to track it down," Mace said.

"Officially?" Chacón asked.

"We really don't have that kind of time," Mace said. He had explained to Munch on the ride over that relations between the two countries' law-enforcement factions were not good. In fact, he'd said, the Mexican *federales* were downright hostile to American lawmen. Asking for permission would only invite trouble. The two of them would get much more cooperation just going in as civilians.

All that she understood. But why wasn't Mace telling his friend about the murder investigation?

The other two cops left the room.

"I need a silver bullet," Mace said.

"I figured there was more," Chacón said, looking in the direction of the departing officers.

Mace opened his manila envelope and pulled out some photographs. Munch recognized them as the same pictures he'd shown her earlier. "I think this guy is operating in TJ," Mace said. "I got a tip that another victim showed up this morning. She might have been driving the missing limousine."

Chacón looked at Munch sympathetically. "Friend of yours?"

Munch nodded and blinked back tears. She had to remind herself that she wasn't going to make any assumptions until she knew for sure.

"I want to go see without raising any flags," Mace continued. "You still got your connections down there?"

"I'll call my mother," Chacón said.

While Chacón dialed, Mace leaned over to Munch. "His family knows the family who owns funeral homes all through Baja. They have a contract with the city to handle murder victims. Rico helped them out of some trouble last year."

Chacón finished his conversation and wrote down directions. "Just tell the girl you know me."

"Thanks," Mace said.

"What are you driving?" Chacón asked.

"An unmarked unit. A Caprice."

Chacón opened his desk drawer and threw Mace a set of keys. "Yellow Pontiac station wagon," he said. "The plate number is on that white tag. You buy your own gas."

"We'll be back in a couple hours," Mace said.

"Good luck," Chacón said. He spoke the words like he really meant them.

Mace and Munch took the elevator back down but exited the building through a side door that took them to the parking lot. They found the lemon-colored station wagon. While Munch checked the oil and water, Mace locked his badge, ID, beeper, and gun in the trunk of his Caprice.

Within minutes they were back on the freeway and headed south.

"What was the trouble?" Munch asked.

"Huh?"

"At the mortuary. You said Rico helped the people out."

"Oh, yeah," Mace said. "They do autopsies there. Turns out that a couple of their customers weren't all the way dead."

"Great," she said. "And a silver bullet is. . . ?"

He shrugged. "A favor. A free pass."

In San Ysidro, Mace exited the freeway and pulled into the driveway of a Carl's Jr.

"What are we doing?" Munch asked.

"I need some coffee," Mace said as he stopped at the drive-thru speaker phone.

"Make that two," Munch said.

Five minutes later, they were back on the southbound freeway. The line of cars waiting to cross the border stretched eight lanes wide and half a mile long. After they entered Tijuana, they maneuvered through a maze of one-way streets. Every other building seemed to be a pharmacy or a body shop. Men stood on the street waving rolls of window tinting or the flat, round hammers they used for pounding out dents. Horns honked constantly. The smell of raw rich exhaust gave her a headache.

Mace urged the big yellow station wagon forward. A man carrying bundles of brightly painted miniature guitars knocked on Munch's window and held up his wares. For a brief instant she thought of Asia, wondering if this would be something she'd like. She was careful to keep her eyes blank so as not to encourage the man.

They drove until they reached the funeral home. A large truck was parked in front of the entrance. Two men unloaded caskets of all hues: purple, pink, glossy white. There was even a chrome one. Mace circled the block and parked around the side, squeezing between a green taxi and a Monte Carlo with no license plates and the darkest tinted windows Munch had ever seen. She got out of the car, locking the door behind her. She tried to see inside the Monte Carlo, but even the windshield was blackened.

Before they turned the corner, a thin, dark boy of perhaps thirteen crossed the street to catch up with them. He carried a plastic grocery bag and held his hand out for Mace's coffee cup.

Mace turned from the boy, and said, "No." The boy persisted, mutely holding his hand out for the paper cup, his fingers curled as if already holding it. Mace finally shook his head in defeat and handed over the cup. The boy took it and immediately brought it to his lips.

What sort of place was this, she wondered, *where children begged for lukewarm coffee?* She handed him hers also. He clutched it close to his body with his other hand and slunk away.

Mace and Munch walked around to the front of the building and pushed through the glass doors. The reception area smelled of mildew. A glass curio case exhibited box-shaped urns made of stone and polished metal. She wondered what you were supposed to do with it once it was filled. Did you display it on the mantel? Make it into a lamp?

The woman behind the reception desk looked them over, then greeted them in English.

"We are here to identify a family member," Mace said. "Enrique Chacón told us that you received the body of a woman this morning. We think we might know her."

The receptionist grabbed a ring of keys and came out from behind the counter. She wore a short black dress and three-inch spike high heels that brought a slight definition to her plump calves.

"Hector," she called into the anteroom on the other side of the entrance.

A man came out. She held up the keys, pointed at Mace and Munch, and fired off a string of Spanish. Then she turned back to the waiting gringos. "Follow me," she said.

They walked through a viewing room, between rows of upholstered benches covered in the same sort of thick plastic that people staple to their carpet to protect high-traffic areas. Large gilt crucifixes adorned the walls. The woman led them to a door to the right of the viewing platform and down a hallway. To their right, the wide doors of a service elevator gaped open.

"This way," the woman said.

Mace and Munch followed her until they came to a room with a double sink. Hoses fitted to the faucet connected to an embalming pump. The louvered windows above the sink were open, letting in flies and sounds from the street. Munch was glad the steel gurney in front of the sink was empty. She noted the blood smears near the center and the used bandages lying on the floor next to the drain.

"Not here," the woman said, and led them to a second room. She genuflected before opening the door. "Come back out front when you're through."

The hum of refrigeration pumps filled the dank room. Three bodies awaited service, their feet poking out from under plastic tarps. The dead girl was laid out on a table in the center of the room. What appeared to be a shower curtain covered her. It was too opaque to make out the facial details, but it was clear that the dead woman was naked. Munch stopped at the doorway.

"You all right?" Mace asked. His hand wrapped around her elbow. The simple gesture made her want to cry.

"Just give me a second," she said, feeling in no hurry to enter the hot, rancid room. "It smells like someone forgot to empty the outhouses."

"That's not what you're smelling," he said.

"I guess I knew that," she said. "I'm ready when you are."

"Let's do it."

They approached the body on the table together, still linked by his hand on her elbow.

Mace reached forward and grabbed the top corner of the tarp. Slowly, he pulled the veil of plastic back so that the face was exposed.

Munch sank to her knees, suddenly too weak to stand. "That's not her," she said, surprised at the tears streaming down her face. "It's not Ellen."

He knelt down beside her. "You okay? You feel sick? Faint?"

She steadied herself against his strong arm and pulled herself up. "No, I'm fine. Just relieved, but still . . ." She stared at the slender prepubescent body before them.

"Sorry?"

"Exactly." She looked at him with new respect. There was only one way he could know how she was feeling. "I don't know who this girl was," Munch said, "but she's too young to be so dead and naked and alone. She looks thirteen, fourteen."

"Yeah," he said. "They're getting younger."

"Who are? The victims of that Band-Aid guy?"

He looked at her sharply.

"I heard you on the phone," she said. "It doesn't matter. I'm not dumb. I figured there was some connection." She looked again at the dead body. "You're going to get this guy, right? I don't like the idea of him living in the same world as me."

Mace pulled the sheet back to reveal the rest of the corpse. Half-inch strips of white surgical tape were pasted over much of her torso. Each strip overlapped another, forming crisscrosses. Mace peeled back the edge of one of the crosses, and Munch saw at its center a knitting-needle-size puncture parting the girl's skin.

"Can you handle this?" he asked.

"What am I looking at?" she asked.

"Hold this," he said, indicating the edge of the plastic tarp. "I want to get a picture of the wound."

She held back the tarp while he peeled off the crosses one at a time and placed them inside a thick plastic evidence envelope. After removing each makeshift bandage, he lifted the Polaroid camera hanging from his neck and took pictures. Then he took a second camera, a 35mm, from his pocket and shot another series.

"Okay," he said. "That should do it."

He walked over to the other two bodies. "These must be the two from the river," he said.

"You still need me?" she asked.

"No," he said. "But I'm going to be a while."

"I'm going to find a phone," she told him.

"Okay," he said without looking up.

She needed to hear Asia's voice.

CHAPTER 13

Ellen was exhausted, hungover, and pissed off. Her feet hurt. She had two hundred dollars in her pocket, and she was hungry. She needed to find a phone, food, and something for her hangover. Not necessarily in that order.

She rubbed her burning eyes and thought about the terror she had felt when Raleigh and Victor climbed up that hill.

"Where have you been?" Raleigh had asked, no, he'd demanded—the son of a bitch. *Like who died and made him King Kong?* His lips were a tight line as he waited for her answer. Victor's mouth had hung open, like he had nothing left to pump up his jaw. Victor's gaze was unfocused at first, but then when it came to rest on the area just above her forehead, he seemed to come back to life. It was then she became aware of the emptiness there.

She reached up and felt the top of her head. It was naked, exposed, empty. Her wig was gone. All that was left was the knob of her own dishwater blond hair, tied up in a cheap red rubber band. She spread her fingers, but the gesture was useless. There was no hiding. All she could think to do was cover her eyes. She felt the heat of her face. *God, what did I do to deserve this night?*

"We've been looking all over for you," Raleigh said.

She uncovered her eyes and looked at him. Should she ask them why they were wet? If she didn't notice, wouldn't they think that odd? Something tickled her arm. Thinking it was an insect, she swatted it. Then she looked down and realized that what she had felt was a knotted thread dangling from the embroidery of her shirt. Well, the shirt she was wearing anyway. It wasn't the same one she'd begun the day with.

"Drink," she said, passing Victor the bottle. He tipped the tequila back and took a long slug. She watched the worm float down to the neck of the bottle, wincing as it drifted closer to his open mouth. "Hey, hey," she said. "Leave a little for the rest of us."

She took the bottle back and passed it to Raleigh. He had not moved or smiled since asking his questions. She saw a hardness to his eyes that hadn't been there before. She leered at him. "Hey, baby, looks like we saved you the worm."

He took the bottle from her and tilted it back, letting the final contents drain down his throat. The big fat white worm—big as a potato slug—was the last to go. She watched, fascinated, as it funneled down into his waiting mouth.

"Oh, my God," she said. This had to rank with one of the most disgusting acts she'd ever witnessed.

Raleigh threw aside the empty bottle. Grinning, he swallowed.

They were parked next to a field of some sort of grain that had been allowed to run wild. She slid down from the hood, lifting her arms above her head and howling at the moon as if she hadn't a care in the world. She landed in a furrowed row and stepped into the moonlit meadow. The loam gave way easily beneath her shoes. She saw dried puddles of cow shit, and thought about bullfights. She remembered how Victor's eyes had glowed when he spoke of them—of that immortal contest between good and evil. And she had said something dumb about how sometimes the bull wins. Oh, Lordy, but she'd fixed herself good this time.

Fuck the wig, where are the keys? How am I going to get back to civilization and away from these crazy assholes and those bodies floating down the muddy river? And speaking of murder, Munch is going to kill me when she sees the limo. Ellen reached down and ran her fingers over the indentation in the driver's door. Had that dent always been there? And what had happened to the hood ornament and the antennae?

"We need more booze," she said. "If no one's got the keys, it looks like we're walking." She headed off toward the faint yellow light she saw winking in the distance.

"I've got the keys," Raleigh said, dangling them from his fingertips. "You left them in the ignition."

She stopped. She had no reason not to stop, to turn around, to head back toward them, even though that was the last thing she wanted to do.

"I'll drive," he said.

She thought about the barbiturates already at work in his bloodstream. "No, darling, 'fraid not," she said. "It's against company policy."

"Company policy?" Victor asked. He slugged Raleigh's arm with the back of his knuckles. "She is company?"

Raleigh looked from them to the keys to the limo. He never looked at the river, none of them did. Will they notice, she wondered, that I'm not looking at the river? What she needed was a distraction. She turned her back to the men and peeled off the borrowed shirt, giving them a quick flash of her white breasts in the moonlight.

"Let's go swimming," she said, heading for the riverbank.

"No," Raleigh said. "You're right. We're out of booze. Let's head back to town."

She kept her sigh of relief silent and pulled the shirt back on. "But I drive," she said, holding out her hand for the keys.

Victor spoke up, "Yes, by all means, give her the keys. You and I will stretch out in the back."

Raleigh seemed to see the sense of this suggestion and dropped the keys onto her waiting palm. She quickly unlocked the driver's door and flipped the master lock control. Resuming her role as chauffeurette, she held the door open for them as they clambered back into the car, then took her place behind the wheel.

How long before the effects of the Mickey take hold? she wondered. She found herself praying, that same hopeful, close-your-eyes-real-tight-and-wish kind of praying she'd learned as a child.

She hoped, as she had hoped then, that wanting something really bad would make the difference. But wishing never changed things. Not then, not with her mother's new husband. He had always come back. As soon as Mama slipped into her nightly Valium-induced stupor, old Dwayne baby would come to Ellen's door. Finally, she'd screwed up the courage to take action. She spent her salary from the coffee shop and a whole afternoon installing a hasp and lock on her bedroom door, sneaking drills and screwdrivers from Dwayne's store of tools in the garage. The man at the hardware store said the case-hardened padlock offered the best security.

The next day she came home from school and found her door resting against the hallway wall. Dwayne had even removed the hinges. Later her mother had confronted her in the kitchen. She'd grabbed Ellen's arms just below the shoulders with her sweaty hands. Mama's bleary eyes—darting right to left, twitching in their sockets—had searched her own. "You'd never run away, would you?" Mama asked.

That was the closest thing to an answer Ellen had ever gotten from God. If you wanted something in this life, she knew, you had to make it happen.

"Y'all set back there?" she asked through the rearview mirror.

"Let's go," Victor answered. His words came out as if he were speaking from underwater. His lips had to be getting numb.

She started the car. The privacy partition went up. *How rude,* she thought. Not that she wanted to keep looking at them. But who did they think they were to shut her out like that?

She grew aware of her hair again, how flat it was, how dirty and thin and awful. *Why does it matter now?* she wondered. *What difference does it make what these two assholes see or think? What any of them think?*

She revved the engine and popped the car into reverse. The sudden shift sent a jolt through the long car, and then the engine stalled.

"Shit," she muttered, and turned the key again. Nothing happened. She switched it off and tried again. Nothing. A fist hammered against the privacy partition followed by muffled complaints. *Do they think I'm doing this on purpose?* She looked down and saw that she was still in reverse. She shifted back to neutral, and this time the car started immediately. She took a deep breath and then noticed the gas gauge. The indicator was on empty. Great. *How far will a car this size run on empty?*

She goosed the accelerator carefully this time and cranked the wheel to the right. The narrow, rutted road was more dirt than asphalt. Working the gas, brakes, and steering wheel, she maneuvered a three-point U-turn. The tires sank into the soft ground and spun uselessly for an endless second before finally taking hold. She allowed herself a thin wedge of hope.

The light up ahead looked like it came from a small house. Another ten minutes of driving brought her close enough to make out the details of a darkened gas station with a small store attached. The sign in the window announced, CERRADO, "closed." But what really caught her attention was the pay phone. She had told Munch in her note that she would call. Hopefully, Munch wasn't too worried.

Victor and Raleigh had to be out by now. On the control panel over her head were two toggle switches. One was labeled PRIVACY PARTITION. She toggled, and the panel separating them slid down. Victor and Raleigh were slumped against each other sound asleep. She put the partition back up, pulled up to the gas island, parked, and came around to the back.

She opened the door. Raleigh was closest and snoring. She clapped her hands next to his ear. His eyes never flickered. The same was true with Victor when she poked him.

Gently she pushed them apart from each other and went

through their pockets. She took the cash first, then continued
to search. When she found the white surgical tape, she wondered what the hell he was doing with that. Strapped to the
same guy's shin was some kind of short, weird knife in a black
scabbard. The angle of his leg prevented her from unbuckling
it, not that she wanted it bad enough to keep trying.

Raleigh's wallet was difficult to pry out of his back pocket.
She pushed his deadweight, rolling him more on his stomach.
Victor slid into the spot Raleigh vacated, but she still managed
to wedge her hand down between the two of them and slide
the wallet out. He didn't have much cash, and only one credit
card, which she wasn't interested in. Using one of the limo
napkins so as not to leave her fingerprints, she took his gun
and threw it into the bushes. Then she dragged the two men
one at a time out of the car and left them faceup by the side of
the road.

Change spilled out of Raleigh's pocket. Ellen was
reminded once more of the phone booth. She picked quar-
ters and dimes out of the dirt. She had every intention of calling Munch and letting her know what was going on, but then
one of the men groaned.

The hell with it, she thought. Munch had waited this long;
no point in waking her up just to deliver bad news.

Ellen pocketed the money, climbed back into the limo,
and pointed the car for the good old U.S. of A. With any luck,
she'd be explaining the whole situation in person in a couple
of hours. Five miles later, the fumes in the gas tank played out,
forcing her to coast to a stop by the side of the dark highway.
She searched the trunk, hoping that Munch kept some spare
gas there, but all she found was more minibar supplies, the
spare tire, some tools, and a blanket. She grabbed the blanket
and a screwdriver with a long blade. Before she hiked off into
the darkness, she realized she still had the mysterious roll of
surgical tape. *You never know,* she thought to herself. *Something*

like this might come in real handy. She tucked the tape into her waistband, next to the screwdriver.

The moon was long gone. It was dark, and she was tired. She hoped that the light of day would bring some solutions. As she dropped off to sleep, cuddled in a small cave, she resolved to call Munch at the first opportunity.

Now it was morning. She hiked all the way back to the gas station, hoping that when Raleigh and Victor had come to that they headed back for town on a different road. Just in case, she stayed off the open road, clutching her screwdriver like a dagger. When she finally reached the Pemex station, her heart fell. Not only were her customers still there, but they were talking to the Mexican police. She hid in the bushes and watched. The voices of the men carried to her.

She heard Victor demand to be taken to the Romanian embassy, heard him say, "Fucking bitch," as he pulled on the white fabric of his inside-out pants pocket. The "fucking bitch" would, of course, be herself.

The one who worried her was Raleigh. She watched as he walked up the road, studying the ground. He pulled one of the *federales* over, showed him something, and then pointed exactly the way she had left. *Shit,* she thought. *That Raleigh is on to my scent.*

If she hadn't looked so raggedy-ass, she might have just tried walking on out there and taken her chances. But you never knew which direction those *federales* would fall. Only fools believed that the truth alone protected you.

CHAPTER 14

Munch and Mace walked the short distance from the funeral home to the police station. The relief Munch had felt at the morgue was short-lived when she learned that Ellen still hadn't checked in. She was still mulling that over when Mace asked, "So what's the deal with your friend and her wigs? Something wrong with her real hair?"

"No, that's not it," she said.

He waited for her to elaborate.

"It's more like she needs the extra layer between who she really is and what you get to see. She puts up a lot of fronts. It's all part of the life, makes her feel more protected."

"Wearing a wig makes her feel safer?" he asked.

"Or different, like she's playing a part."

"Why does she need to be somebody else?"

Munch shook her head and decided on a different approach. "You've worn a uniform before, right?"

"Yeah," he said, "but how is that the same?"

"It gives you an identity. You go out and be a cop or a soldier or whatever all day. You talk and walk and do things, but it's the soldier doing his thing. You go home at night and take off the outfit, who are you? Just another guy trying to crack his nut. But when you're out there in the war zone, you want to feel bigger than life."

"So she puts on her wigs to go on patrol."

"Yeah," Munch said. "That's about right. I've been trying to get through to her that the war is over. We were just about there, and then all this shit had to happen."

"This is it," Mace said, stopping before a building sporting the Mexican flag. "Just let me do the talking."

"Fine," she said.

The Tijuana headquarters for the Judicial Police of Mexico was a two-story building in the center of town. The walls of the ground floor were brick and painted an orangey shade of red. An air-conditioning unit hung out a window on the second floor, supported by an unpainted two-by-four.

Munch and Mace entered the smoke-filled reception area. Flies circled in lazy formations. A potted palm sat dying by the door. They walked up to the counter and stood under a sign that read: ACCIDENT REPORTS.

Mace waited for the woman seated on the stool across from him to acknowledge his presence. She finally turned tired eyes on him.

"Do you speak English?" he asked.

She slid him a form printed in English.

"My friend's car was stolen," he said.

"*Aiii*," she said, "*robar*." She pointed at an adjacent room.

Mace thanked her and gestured for Munch to follow him. They entered a whitewashed room where four desks were spaced haphazardly. Old-fashioned black rotary phones sat on each desk next to stacks of yellowed paperwork. Munch saw no typewriters, teletype machines, or even radio equipment.

At a table in the corner four *federales* played dominoes. The pearl handles of their holstered pistols peeked out from beneath the square edges of their embroidered shirts. One of the *federales* said something and looked at Munch. If she had been wearing a button-down blouse, she would have secured the top button. She resisted the urge to cross her arms across her chest.

One of the telephones began ringing. No one jumped up to answer it. Finally, after some discussion, the cop nearest the phone slid his chair back, stood, and ambled over to the offending instrument.

"*Bueno*," he said. Munch could see the glint of his gold dental work.

"Who's in charge here?" Mace asked.

The stares that turned on him were blank, giving away nothing. A yellow, short-haired mongrel ran into the room. Like most of the dogs they'd seen on the drive through town, this one had no collar. The dog ran over to one of the desks, lifted his leg, and let out a stream of urine.

The seated *federales* rose in unison, shouting at the dog and clapping their hands.

Munch leaned over to Mace, and said out of the side of her mouth, "I guess you know what you have to do around here to get some attention."

Mace cracked a small smile. Munch was amazed at the transformation that the small shift of his lips brought to his face. She could see how other females found him attractive. He had that tough but tragic air about him that a lot of women went for. Derek had cured her of that wanting-to-be-needed syndrome. Now she was only interested in men who needed nothing, which narrowed the field considerably.

"Amigo," Mace said, addressing the cop who'd just hung up the phone. He'd shed his pissed-off look and now wore a broad smile. Munch fought to rein in her surprise at this second metamorphosis. Mace walked over to the *federale* and extended his hand. "Mace St. John," he said.

The Mexican cop accepted the handshake. "Gilbert Ruiz," he said. "What can I do for you, Señor?"

"My lady friend here is looking for her car," Mace said.

Munch nodded in agreement, keeping her expression neutral.

"What kind of car?" Ruiz asked.

"A limousine," Mace said. "Silver Cadillac. Came across the border yesterday but never returned."

The other *federales* stopped their play and looked up.

They smell money, Munch thought.

"We have such a car in impound," Ruiz said.

"Where is it?" Munch asked. "And the lady driver?"

They were interrupted by a woman who entered the police station, crying hysterically. She went at Ruiz with clenched fists, screaming in Spanish. The *federale* deflected her blows, but managed to do so gently. The woman sank to her knees, beating her chest and sobbing.

"What's wrong?" Munch asked.

Ruiz pulled a chair over for the woman to sit in and told one of the other cops in Spanish to get some water. He patted the woman's shoulder.

"Her husband and son suffered a tragic. . . accident," Ruiz told Munch. "Their bodies were fished from the river just this morning."

"*Mi niña, tambien,*" the woman said.

"No," Ruiz said.

The woman choked out another rapid string of words, interrupted by moans and sharp cries of pain. Munch distinctly heard "*gavacho,*" the Mexican slang for white man, used several times.

"*¿Es verdad?*" Ruiz asked, anger and surprise clouding his face. He fired back another round of words. Munch watched as well as listened. Occasionally a word would be used that was the same in both languages, such as "television" and "radio." When Ruiz spoke to the woman, his face was kind, almost pleading. The woman shook her head as she replied, obviously not buying whatever he was selling. A second *federale* helped the woman gently from her chair and led her outside.

Ruiz finally looked up at Munch and Mace. "She has just come from the morgue. They did not tell her that her daughter was also dead. I tried to explain that there was no identification on the body of the woman—the girl. No one knew it was her *niña.*"

Mace placed a hand on Munch's shoulder and gave her a quick squeeze. She didn't need his prompt to tell her to keep her mouth shut. She stared at the poor woman, wondering how anyone could endure the sight of their child laid out on a mortician's slab.

"I can see you are all very busy," Mace said. "Do you have any idea where we might find the passengers and driver of my friend's limousine?"

"After you pay the impound charges," Ruiz said, "you may take the car. We, too, are looking for the driver. She robbed her passengers and left them by the side of the road. They have filed complaints."

Munch dug her nails into Mace's arm. She hoped he'd get her message. If Ellen had ripped off her customers, she must have had a good reason.

"How is it that you have the car and not the driver?" Mace asked, looking genuinely puzzled.

"The limousine was found abandoned eight kilometers north from the two men," Ruiz said.

"Two men?" Munch asked.

Ruiz smiled at her, flashing his gold front tooth. "The victims. The passengers. We believe the car might have developed mechanical difficulties. An unlucky break for our thief."

"So you had to tow it?" Munch asked.

"No," Ruiz said. "The car remains where it was found. Without keys."

Munch wanted to ask why she had to pay an impound charge if there had been no towing or storage involved.

"Can I use your rest room?" Munch asked.

Ruiz pointed at a wooden door in the corner. "Thanks," she said. "I'll be right back."

She pushed open the door and stepped onto the wet cement floor. The bathroom smelled of urine. When she closed the door, it was almost too dark to make out the fixtures. By reluctant feel she found her way to the toilet and sink. The seat was up, so she put it down. She turned on the faucet and ran her fingers under the dribble that leaked out.

Then she opened her purse and removed her wallet. Her money was all together in the side fold, and that wouldn't do at all. She left two twenties and three ones in the bill compartment of her wallet; then she separated the remaining twenties, folding them and distributing them in different pockets of her jeans. She still had the hundreds that Raleigh had given her. One she stashed under her driver's license; the rest she tucked in her socks. Then she flushed the toilet and reemerged.

"How much do we owe you for your trouble, Señor?" Mace asked Ruiz.

She watched the man's eye calculate. Without waiting for his answer, she opened her wallet and pulled out the two twenties.

Ruiz shook his head. "Your limousine was operating without a Mexican permit. We'll need to let the judge decide."

Munch put the twenties back and dug out the hundred.

Ruiz reached his hand out. "There is also the impound charge."

With a sigh she pulled the twenties back out and added them to the hundred on his outstretched palm.

"I'll draw you a map," he said. He didn't offer her a receipt.

"Maybe we should go talk to your customers," Mace said to Munch. "Sounds like they had a rough night."

"I believe they made other arrangements to return to Los Angeles," Ruiz said.

Munch will just have to understand, Ellen thought. *I'll make it up to her someday, but I have to survive if that someday is ever to come around. Besides, didn't Munch say something about having insurance? Shit, if she works it right, she can come out pretty sweet on the whole deal.*

Ellen walked along the poorly paved highway, ducking into the bushes when she heard cars. Finally she arrived at a small town and risked contact with other human beings to buy much-needed supplies.

The door of the small market stood partially ajar. Flies buzzed at her face as she entered, and she swatted at them angrily. The woman behind the cash register regarded her with only small interest. Ellen found that reassuring.

A rotating stand by the front door was filled with cowboy hats. Ellen selected one made of black felt and tried it on. She studied her reflection in the small four-inch mirror embedded in the hat stand. Not quite satisfied, she went to the display of sunglasses next to the hats. She chose a pair of mirrored aviator glasses and felt pleasantly incognito when she viewed the results.

She walked to the back of the store, accompanied by salsa music piped out of AM transistor speakers. The handle of the screwdriver pressed against her spine. Munch's blanket was folded over her arm. She grabbed a bag of Fritos, comforted by the familiar orange wrapper, and then proceeded to the unlit cooler humming noisily against the back wall.

As soon as her hand grasped the handle, she knew that she was going to have a beer. She'd already broken her sobriety, so what was the big deal? Besides, *cervesa* was the only cold beverage the market offered. Surely, nobody expected her to swallow warm Pepsi this early in the day.

She passed her money to the cashier and received pesos in change. She had no idea if she was being ripped off, but at this point that was the least of her worries. Pocketing her change, she left the market to find a secluded spot where she could consume her breakfast and form some kind of plan.

She walked with her face averted to the street, ignoring the kissing noises directed toward her by the local men. *Did that ever work for them?* she wondered.

She ripped open the bag of corn chips, ate a handful, and chased it down with a healthy chug of the cold beer.

"Ahh," she said out loud, feeling halfway human again. She continued to walk, passing an array of small shops, private homes, and an old church with a whitewashed marquee entrance. A picture of the Virgin Mary kneeling in prayer before a gory, crucified Christ was enshrined behind a glass signboard. Ellen lifted her bottle in a toast.

Beyond the church was a line of warehouses. She headed for them.

A loud squeal of brakes nearly made her drop her breakfast. The ground beneath her feet rumbled; then the shadow of a large truck overtook her. She turned around. The first thing she noticed was the stack of bug-spattered license plates on the truck's grille. She took a deep breath, threw back her shoulders, and smiled her biggest and brightest.

The truck stopped. The driver stuck his head out the window. The brim of his cowboy hat cast a shadow over most of his face, but Ellen didn't care. She was in no position to be choosy.

"Hey, Texas," she said in her best Lone Star drawl. "Y'all taking any passengers?"

CHAPTER 15

He had never felt so violated. The woman had left them on the side of the road like garbage. And if that wasn't bad enough, she had touched his body while he had no means by which to defend himself, no conscious choice in the matter at all.

He thought of his mother pulling down his pants, making him lie across her lap as she slapped his bare bottom. She managed to double the castigation by scorning the emergence of his pubic hair, all the while taking advantage of his helpless nakedness.

You think you're a man? Whack. *Stupid, sloppy monkey boy.* Whack.

Whatever minor infraction of his mother's impossible rules the punishment had been for was long forgotten. But the humiliation of her treatment still made his face burn. And now another woman had evoked all those same feelings of outrage. He knew of only one way to alleviate his angst.

She was probably laughing at him still. That was intolerable.

Her second mistake had been to leave them with a credit card. Perhaps he would incorporate the sharp plastic edges in her punishment. It was her fault; he had no sympathy for her. She was the one who had made it so personal. Before, he'd merely disapproved of her brashness. Now, he hated her more than he'd ever hated any woman, and that was saying a lot. She'd brought this on herself. She would pay.

Once more he studied the automobile registration card in his hand, reading again the name and address printed on it. His mind filled with the fantasies of what he'd do to the woman, how her eyes would reflect her fear. He chuckled. She'd probably wet herself.

"What's so funny?" his companion asked, intruding on his daydream.

He turned to the other man, feeling a kinship. He smiled and shook his head as if to say, never mind. He'd never had many friends. Maybe he should work to cultivate relationships with others who shared his interests. After he'd dealt with the woman, this Ellen, he might very well pursue that next and see where it took him.

"Let's go find a car-rental agency that takes MasterCard," he said.

"Yes, we've had enough fun here," his companion said.

Munch followed the road signs pointing to Tecate. She found her battered limousine just where the *federales'* crudely drawn map said it would be, on the shoulder of the highway.

"X marks the spot," she said to Mace, as they pulled up alongside the mud-spattered stretch. Her casual remark belied what she was really feeling. Was Ellen also lying in some muddy ditch, broken and battered?

Munch walked around her ravaged limo and did a silent calculation of the damage. The spoke hubcaps cost a hundred dollars each if she went to the dealer. No doubt she could buy back her own from some curbside booth in town. The antennae were another matter. The little cellular-telephone antenna was no big deal, but the car's radio antenna would set her back another bill. Add another twenty for the Cadillac hood ornament. The dent on the driver's door really pissed her off. It would have to be pulled out, feathered with Bondo, and repainted. Besides being costly, the process would put the car out of commission for a week, and they'd never get an exact match on the color.

She walked around to the passenger side and studied the broken window. She could buy new glass for forty bucks and install it herself. The small blessing there was that the front windows weren't tinted, so she was saved that hassle and expense.

"Anything missing inside?" Mace asked.

"You mean besides the people?" She looked in through the hole where the window had been and saw the open glove compartment. "Someone went through the glove box."

He grabbed the handle of the rear door on the passenger side, pushing the button in with his thumb. "Locked," he said.

She saw that the privacy partition was up. Maybe she still had a television and a sound system in the back.

"I wonder why the crooks didn't just unlock the back doors with the power switch," Mace said.

Munch shrugged. "Maybe they got scared off before they got that far." She walked back around to the driver's door and opened it with her key. The first thing she noticed was that the dome light didn't go on. She reached down and flipped the door lock switch. Nothing happened. "The battery's dead," she said.

"Great," Mace said. "I'll see if there are any jumper cables in the Pontiac."

"We might not need them," Munch said. She reached down and pulled the hood release. The hood popped up an inch. She selected a small key on the ring of keys she'd brought with her and came around to the front of the car. Working by feel, she found the chain and lock protecting the contents of the engine compartment. She slid the small key into the lock and opened the hood.

Mace came over and stood next to her. She checked the oil, inspecting not only the level but looking and smelling for signs of coolant or fuel contamination. Next she checked the radiator level and found it full. Mace stuck his finger in the green fluid, then wiped it on his pants. She wondered what that test was supposed to prove as she replaced the radiator cap. She pointed out the limo's second battery.

"The limo has a lot of extra electrical accessories," she

explained. "When it's running with two blower motors going, the TV on, headlights, whatever, that draws a lot of juice from the system and really puts a strain on the charging system. The factory puts in a hundred-amp alternator, but they still burn out quickly. By running two batteries in sequence, the alternator doesn't have to work as hard."

Mace nodded like he was understanding her. Most men did that, feeling they should automatically know anything automotive. "So does that mean both batteries are dead?" he asked, standing in front of the engine with his hands on his hips.

"Not necessarily. If the battery ran down because something was left on after the engine was shut off, only the primary battery will be dead. I can jump the car off the auxiliary battery." She pushed him gently aside and pointed at the Ford starter solenoid mounted on the fan shroud. "That's what this is for." He stuck his hand out and touched the solenoid. She handed him the keys. "Turn the ignition on, and I'll crank it from out here."

"Okay," he said.

She waited until he was seated behind the wheel; then, using a small pocket screwdriver, she jumped the solenoid connections. The engine cranked but didn't start. She saw the accelerator linkage move back and forth and stopped cranking the motor. "You don't have to work the gas," she said. "This car is fuel-injected."

"Oh, right," he said. "You want me to just sit here and look pretty?"

She grinned. "You're getting the idea now." She opened the cap covering a fuel fitting on the fuel rail. Using the small screwdriver again, she depressed the spring-loaded shraeder valve. The fuel rail should have been full of pressurized gas, but when she held the valve open, only air escaped. "I think we're out of gas," she said.

She came around to the driver's side and flipped a lever by

the floorboard.

"Don't tell me," Mace said. "Auxiliary fuel tank?"

"That's right," she said.

"What other tricks do you have?" he asked.

"A few." She thought about the tape recorder under the seat. Before she played the tape for him, she hoped to get an opportunity to listen to it privately. She went back under the hood and cranked the engine again. This time it caught. He got out from behind the wheel and came around front to watch the engine run.

"You all through under here?" he asked, hands on the hood.

"Yeah."

He slammed the hood shut and dusted off his hands.

She went back to the car, unlocked the back doors, and rolled down the privacy partition.

Mace came around to the passenger side and spoke to her through the broken window. "Don't go back there," he said. "I don't want any contamination of evidence. We're going to want to go over the whole area to collect prints and trace evidence."

"How long will that take?" she asked. She leaned across the seat and pushed the yellow button in the glove compartment that released the trunk latch. There was a clunk as the lid popped open a few inches, then settled down. The boomerang-shaped television antenna bolted to the trunk lid bounced outside the small rear window.

"A day or two," he said. "Anything else missing?"

"That's what I'm trying to figure out." She got up from the driver's seat and walked around to the trunk. Mace met her at the rear of the car. She lifted the lid and looked in. "I kept a blanket in here," she said. "It's gone." She rummaged around, trying to figure out what else was missing.

"Hold it," Mace ordered. "I told you not to touch anything."

"You said in the back, not in the trunk."

"Leave everything as you found it."

"Okay, I'm sorry. Jeez."

"Before we cross the border," he said, "I need to call Cassiletti and have him cancel the APB I put out on your limo."

"You're welcome to use my mobile phone, but it probably won't work out here. Especially without an antenna."

"I'll use the pay phone at the gas station back down the road. Follow me over there."

"Yeah, okay," she said. They got back in their separate vehicles. She was glad they didn't have to drive back to Los Angeles together. His attitude was starting to get to her. He started the station wagon and waited while she turned the limo around. They drove the short distance back to the Pemex station, where he pulled up by the pay phone.

"You want to get gas here?" he asked.

"Not really," she said, not trusting the contents of the tanks in the ancient, run-down gas station. She watched him head off to the pay phone, then resumed her inventory of the glove box. "Why would somebody take the registration?" she asked out loud. As soon as the words were out, the chilling truth hit her.

She jumped out of the car and ran after him. "I've got to call my house," she said. "Whoever went through the glove box took the registration. My home address is on it."

Mace handed her the phone and stepped aside.

She dialed the operator, and asked, "Do you speak English?"

"Uno momento," came the reply.

A second operator came on the line, and said, "Hello?"

"I have to make a collect call," Munch told her. She gave the operator her name and number. When the call finally went through, she heard her own voice on the answering machine's outgoing tape.

"I'll guess you'll have to try again later," the operator said. "There's no one home to accept charges."

"Can I charge the call to my home number and leave a message?"

"Is there anyone at your home phone number to verify payment?"

"No," Munch said. That was the problem.

"You'll just have to try again later, ma'am," the operator said.

"But this is an emergency," Munch said.

"I'm sorry," the operator said. "But I cannot put your call through at this time."

"Wait," Munch said, hearing the desperation in her voice. "I'd like to try another number." She gave the operator Derek's number, but there was no answer there either. She hung up in frustration and turned to Mace.

He picked up the phone, and said, "Don't worry, I'll call Cassiletti and have him send out a patrol unit to the house. Nothing's going to happen to your kid."

Ellen watched as all the trucks and buses leaving Tijuana were funneled into the far right lane. Billboards and lit signboards flashed the word *Bienvenido*. Welcome. Open booths lined the side of the road, selling every kind of kitschy bright-colored thing known to man. Electric yellow ceramic Tweety birds vied for space under Aztec plates and fluttering piñatas. A plaster of Paris life-size Jesus with blood dripping from his side wound rested in the arms of a blue-robed Virgin Mary.

"Just what I want in the middle of my patio," Ellen said.

"*¿Que?*" Paco the driver asked.

"Nothing," Ellen said. "*Nada.*" It was going to be a long ride.

Stick-legged brown girls with long braids reaching to the waistbands of their dresses darted among the cars. Their heads just barely poked above the fenders as they sold individually wrapped candies out of small cardboard boxes.

The speed of exiting traffic picked up. Ellen noticed that Paco kept buttoning and unbuttoning his shirt cuff. Occasionally he licked his lips and looked from side to side. As they drew nearer to the border, his tics increased.

Four car lengths from the kiosk, a boy of perhaps ten beat together two flare-sized sticks and sang a song in Spanish. His mouth contorted to enunciate the words that he shouted more than sang. As they grew even with the boy, Paco rolled down his window and held out a handful of coins.

"Buenos días," the boy mumbled, allowing the coins to be dropped into his hand. His eyes stayed focused on the departing traffic.

The truck inched forward. Between the turnstiles old withered women in long skirts held waxed paper cups and begged for change. They had young children with them. Surely, Ellen thought, the kids were grandchildren. The women watched the rows of cars like wary birds. Paco reached into his pocket and pulled out another handful of change.

The flow of traffic urged them on.

"Noña," Paco called out. Ellen twisted in her seat to watch. The woman wasn't responding. The bus behind them honked. Paco flung the change behind him. Ellen heard it ricochet cruelly off the metal stanchions.

They pulled up to the booth. The border guard was a white man.

"Citizenship?" he asked.

"U.S.," Paco said.

"U.S.," Ellen echoed.

"What are you hauling?" the guard asked.

"I have no cargo," Paco said.

This must have been one of the sentences they missed, Ellen thought, when they exhausted their mutual vocabulary fifteen seconds after meeting. Paco started fiddling with his button again. She saw a fine trickle of sweat run past his ear.

"Anything to declare?" the guard asked.

Ellen leaned forward and grinned. "We're just glad to be going home."

The guard waved them forward.

Paco wove the truck through the array of cement barriers arranged so as to prevent speedy getaways. A yellow sign depicted a man, a woman, and a child in black silhouette. Their hands were linked, and they were running. The message of the sign was obvious: Beware of fleeing families crossing the highway.

"Are you okay?" Ellen asked.

Paco didn't answer. His eyes were still glued to the rearview mirror. Finally, he exhaled. She wondered how long he had been holding his breath.

He reached down under the seat and retrieved a bottle of orange-flavored Fanta. Cracking it open, he offered it to her.

"No, thanks," she said. The sun beating in through the windshield made her realize how tired she was. "I'm just going to shut my eyes for a second," she said. She didn't care if he understood or not. He'd get the message soon enough. She put the screwdriver on the seat between them and made the blanket into a pillow. Pulling the brim of her cowboy hat over her eyes, she snuggled down for a nap.

Upon arriving back in Los Angeles, Raleigh moved Victor to another hotel. Victor demanded that housecleaning come and change his linen. Raleigh had been through this drill before with the guy. Victor had a thing about germs. He even traveled with his own pillow. Actually, Raleigh couldn't fault the guy that. He had his own quirks when venturing to foreign places.

It took an hour before Victor was finally settled in. Raleigh told him to stay put. "Can you do that for me?" he asked.

"Sure, sure," Victor said. "I will take a hot bath, change my clothes. Tonight we will go out and have a big steak. My treat."

"My people are growing impatient, Victor. It's time to wrap things up."

"Are you going to report what happened on our trip?" Victor asked.

"I haven't decided yet," Raleigh said. "Let me deal with one mess at a time."

When Ellen woke up, the truck was parked in the shade. It was obvious by the look of the tree-lined street that she was in some upper-middle-class suburb. Paco was gone. The keys dangled from the ignition, not that they'd do her any good. Her street education didn't include driving eighteen-wheelers with fifteen-gear transmissions. Besides, maybe ol' Paco was coming back.

She was definitely in Ozzie and Harriet land. The houses all had gingerbread trim, flower gardens, even some white picket fences. Her mouth was dry, and she had to pee. She cracked open the heavy door of the semi and climbed down the corrugated chrome step in search of a spigot and maybe a bush. Hopefully, she wouldn't freak out some citizen in the process. She blinked at the brightness of the day, trying to figure out what time it was. She saw a fat edition of the morning paper leaning against someone's garage door. After she got a drink and relieved herself, she might just borrow it and try to get a fix on where she was.

She stepped onto the easement. The grass there was thick and green and perfectly trimmed. There wasn't even dog shit anywhere. She rubbed the sleep from her eyes and started looking for the green coil of an unattended hose.

The cop pulled up out of nowhere. One moment she had the street to herself, the next he was there with lights blinking and radio muted. He was riding solo. She watched him get out of his car. He had that prissy, pursed-lip kind of look cops get—like he just knew you were shit, didn't belong there, and was up to no good. She hated judgmental bastards like him. Who was he to make such on-the-spot assessments of her?

Where was his humanity? The pig, son of a bitch. What ever happened to the old "to serve and protect" motto?

She looked at his blue-and-white patrol car. According to the door he was part of the La Jolla Police Department. She was in worse trouble than she first thought. Cops who worked nice neighborhoods never had any play in them. The biggest crimes they interrupted were dogs off their leashes. She doubted he'd have much trouble finding some code she'd broken; it would be the bust he bragged about all year. He'd probably come unglued if he ever had to work East L.A. or Venice Beach—this Andy Mayberry of La Jolla.

"How's it going?" he said with that false cheeriness. He ran a hand over his trim little cop mustache and smiled to reveal straight white teeth. His hand swaggered to the butt of his gun. He probably felt like he was totally on top of the situation—in absolute control. There wasn't a damn thing she could do to oppose him, and he knew it.

"You got some ID?" he asked. He stood at parade rest, all six feet of him. His posture was perfect.

She reached to her back pocket, knowing it was empty, but smiling at him all the while. And not that sniveling con smile that said she'd roll over and let him do whatever he wanted. She wore her innocent look, followed immediately by her surprised look. "Well, I'll be," she said, turning so he could watch her pat the empty pocket of her tight jeans. "Maybe I left it in the truck."

"Is this your truck?" he asked.

Like he even thought that was a possibility. "Why, no," she said, eyes going wide again. "I just hitched a ride." She thought about all the times she'd used that line as part of her defense. And now here it was true. Wasn't life just full of its little ironies?

"Where's the driver?" the cop asked.

"You know," she said, "I was just wondering the same damn thing. I just woke up a little bit ago, and he was gone."

"So you probably didn't even know the truck was stolen."

There he goes again, being sarcastic. And here I go, she thought, feeling her eyes widen again, but this time in genuine surprise. "Honest to God?" she asked. "Well, as I live and breathe. Wait till I tell my mama."

"Step over here," the cop said, indicating a spot on the sidewalk near his patrol car.

She refrained from assuming the position. That was always a dead giveaway.

The cop pulled out a pen and what she recognized as a field identification card. "What's your name?" he asked.

"Susan," she said. "Susan Scott."

He asked for her address, and she quickly rattled off the first combination of number and street that came to mind, only realizing afterward that it was Russell's address in Venice.

"Phone number?" he asked.

"Oh, you," she said, finding a giggle in her bag of tricks.

The cop smiled, and she gave him Russell's number. Hell, Russ had done nothing wrong, so he had nothing to worry about.

"Do you know your driver's license number?" he asked.

"No, sir," she said. "Sorry, numbers were never my strong suit."

The cop walked back to his car and radioed in the name she'd given him. Three minutes later, the report came back. Susan Scott had been arrested for forgery, prostitution, and armed burglary. Shit. The woman had a worse record than Ellen.

"That's not me," she said. "Did you get my middle name?"

The cop's expression never changed as he called his dispatcher back and asked for scriptors. The crackly voice came back saying, "African-American, five feet ten inches, one hundred and eighty pounds. Currently in custody."

Well, all right then, Ellen thought. *It's about time for a little luck.*

A couple in a Buick drove by, slowing down to look at them. The man driving was wearing a black suit; the woman beside him wore a hat. They both stared. She wanted to yell, What the fuck are you looking at?

Instead she took advantage of the distraction. "Is it dangerous being a cop?" she asked.

"You never know," he said.

She watched his chest puff out. "Can you give me a ride to the nearest bus station?" she asked. "I need to get home. I know I look a fright. You wouldn't believe what I've been through."

"Try me," the cop said.

She took a deep breath, feeling her mouth begin to quiver and letting tears fill her eyes. "My . . ." She paused to fight for control, swallowed and began again, "My fiancé left me at the altar." She looked down at her clothes. "Well, maybe not exactly at the altar. The skunk ran off with some bimbo from his bachelor party. I guess I had too much to drink, and now I just want to get home."

She felt his hand on her shoulder and threw in a few heaving sobs. The tears she shed were real enough. She needed some dope.

CHAPTER 16

Mace gave Cassiletti a list of orders, starting with the dispatching of a unit to Munch's house and ending with the cancellation of the border alert.

"What do you want to do with the kid?" Cassiletti asked. "Protective services?"

Mace looked over at Munch. "No," he said. "When they locate the kid, have her taken over to Caroline—she's at my dad's house. Bring the boyfriend, too. Tell Caroline I'm on my way and that I'll explain everything."

"Where are you now?" Cassiletti asked.

"Down south," Mace said.

"The captain's been trying to reach you. He's called three times already. Steve Brown's called twice. He said he's got some information for you."

"Give me an hour," Mace said, "and I'll be back in radio contact."

Throughout the entire conversation Munch had been pacing alongside the phone booth. She stopped in mid-step and tugged on Mace's arm. "What time is it?"

He checked his watch. "Half past one."

"I know where Derek might be," she said. "There's an A.A. clubhouse on Washington, across from Royal Market. I bet he went to the midday meeting."

Mace turned back to the phone and asked Cassiletti, "Did you get that? A.A. clubhouse on Washington and Centinela in Mar Vista." He turned back to Munch, and asked, "What's he driving?"

"A '63 blue Chevy pickup," she said loudly, then pulled the

phone away from Mace and spoke directly to Cassiletti. "You can't miss it. It has a wooden A-frame glass rack in the bed."

Mace took the phone back. "I'll call when I'm back in my unit." He hung up and turned to Munch. "Let's get out of here. But for God's sake, stay within the speed limit. You get pulled over down here without your registration, and they'll take the car."

"I don't care about the car. I just want to get back home."

"I know that. Don't worry. We're on top of it. I need you to keep your head." He also needed the limo back in Los Angeles, where the crime-scene techs could vacuum the upholstery for fibers and the fingerprint crew could collect latents.

"Get in the right lane at the border," Mace said. "And have five bucks ready. They'll funnel us ahead of the other traffic."

"Let's go," Munch said.

While they waited for their turn to pass through the border check, Munch reached under her seat and pulled out the tape recorder. She ejected the tape and saw that it was nearly at the end of the reel. She slid the tape into the limo's built-in cassette player and pushed the rewind button. A little girl, no older than eight, came to Munch's window with a box of candy. Munch dug into her pocket and handed the kid her change, but waved away the candy. The tape player clicked to a stop, indicating that the tape had rewound. Munch hit play.

The first voice she heard was Raleigh's. She recognized the same half of the telephone conversation she had overheard when she first picked him up on Friday night. He had not closed the privacy partition again until after they had dropped Victor off at the Hollywood apartment. The hidden microphones recorded several minutes of dead air. Expecting this, since she had listened simultaneously through her earpiece, she pushed the fast-forward button in small bursts until she again heard Raleigh's portion of his telephone conversation.

"All set," he said. Followed by, "Later."

Munch pushed the fast-forward again. Raleigh had made one other call that night.

Munch assumed that the recipient of that last call had been some sort of love interest. She listened once more to Raleigh's entreaties for the person at the other end of the line to talk to him.

Traffic inched forward ahead of her. She stayed behind Mace's car, refusing to let other cars merge between them. They reached a Y of traffic lanes. A uniformed guard approached Mace. While the guard gestured with one hand, his other snaked in the open window to receive his payoff. The guard then directed Mace to a faster lane. Mace pointed back at Munch.

She had her bill folded and ready. The guard took it without looking at her and motioned for her to follow Mace. Sounds from the tape came out of her speakers: heavy breathing. Munch reached over and turned up the volume. She heard Victor's accented voice.

"Do you think she saw anything?"

And then the reply from Raleigh.

"You're just wondering that now?"

"What should we do? I will only be of use to you if I stay free."

"Don't you think we know that?"

"Shit."

"Don't worry."

"By the way, I was meaning to tell you. Pakistan has come in at three hundred and twenty thousand. I think we can push Iran to three thirty."

A minute passed where neither of them spoke, then Munch heard Victor's accented voice once again.

"I was always meant for bigger things. From the time I was a small boy, I was singled out in sports and academics."

"Me, too. Top of my class. Destined for greatness."

Munch noticed the voices were changing, growing slurred. It was getting hard to distinguish which man was talking.

"Rules developed to govern a society cannot apply to every individual."

"Of course not."

She turned up the volume. With each sentence their voices grew fainter.

"All the great men through history have had their idiosyncrasies."

"Thas right."

Silence followed, but Munch didn't touch the buttons of the tape recorder. The "she" had to be Ellen. What was the thing they were worried she'd witnessed? The murders? Had they killed her, too?

Now the only sounds coming from the tape were the vibration hums of the limo and the rustling of the passengers shifting in their seats. Several minutes passed. The drone of the limo stopped. This could only mean that the engine had shut off. Munch heard a pounding sound and one of the two men shouting, "Why have we stopped?" The humming resumed. *Had the limo stalled?* Munch wondered. That would tie in with the mechanical problems. The limo restarted. Another minute passed and new sounds began, snoring. The humming changed tempo, as if the limo had come to a stop but the engine was still running. Munch heard the car door opening, muffled noises, a woman's soft grunt of exertion. According to the Mexican cop, Ellen had robbed her customers and left them unconscious by the side of the road. Was this what Munch was hearing? No jury in the world could extrapolate that, could they? The fact that the men had passed out simultaneously in the rear of the limo made Munch wonder if they'd been drugged. That wasn't beyond Ellen's capabilities. Sounded like she had good reason.

Munch rewound and ejected the tape, then slipped it into her coat pocket.

∎ ∎ ∎

At two-fifteen, Mace and Munch arrived at the San Diego PD parking lot. The same cop was still on duty at the desk and issued them passes. They went directly to Rico Chacón's office, where Mace paged Cassiletti, punching in Chacón's number after the beep. Two minutes later, the phone rang.

Chacón answered, "Narcotics. Cassiletti? Hold on." He handed the phone to Mace.

"We got the kid," Cassiletti said first thing. "Found her and the boyfriend at that A.A. meeting just like Munch said."

Mace turned to Munch, and said, "Your kid is fine."

She let out her breath in a huge sigh and sank onto one of the chairs lining the wall.

"You better call the captain," Cassiletti said.

"Did you take the little girl to Caroline?" Mace asked.

"Yeah, that's all handled."

"Where are you?" Mace asked.

"The office."

"Anything new on—"

"Sir?" Cassiletti interrupted. "Captain Earl is very anxious to speak with you."

"He can wait another minute."

"He said code two," Cassiletti said, using LAPD shorthand for ASAP.

"All right, so hang up." Mace shrugged at Rico, then redialed the phone and asked to be connected to the command center. The receptionist asked for his name.

Captain Earl came on the line within thirty seconds. "Where the fuck have you been?" he asked.

Why is it, Mace wondered, *that no matter who the guy is, once he puts on the brass, he becomes an asshole?* Even Earl the pearl, who'd been a good investigator and a stand-up guy when he was a D3, was a shining example of this phenomenon. "You wanted to talk to me, Captain?"

"You still working the double in Hollywood?"

"Yes, sir. I believe it's the work of the Band-Aid Killer."

"You haven't spoken to the press?"

Mace's hand tightened on the receiver. "No, sir. On your orders."

"Why haven't I been apprised of your progress?"

"I'll file a report this evening," Mace said, wondering what the real problem was.

"Do you have any solid suspects?" Earl asked.

The use of the word "solid" put Mace on guard. "I have some possible witnesses I've been trying to locate."

"Come in," Earl said. "Do you understand me? Come directly back to Parker Center. Do nothing else. Am I clear?"

"Yes, sir. I'm en route now." Mace waited a second, then called Cassiletti back. "What's up with the captain?"

"I don't know," Cassiletti said. "He wanted all my case notes. We must have stumbled into something."

"I'm on my way," Mace said.

"What did Steve Brown want?" Cassiletti asked.

"I haven't had a chance to call him. I'll see you in a couple of hours."

Mace hung up the phone and turned to Munch. "I need to go back to Parker Center. We'll leave the limo at the crime lab, then I'll take you to your little girl. I just have to make one more call." He looked at Chacón. "Do you mind?"

"Help yourself, *compadre*," Chacón said. He turned to Munch while Mace looked up Steve Brown's beeper number. "Did you find your friend?"

"No, it wasn't her after all," Munch said.

"You must be very relieved."

"I'd be more relieved if I knew where she was," she said.

The phone rang. This time Mace answered, "Narcotics."

"This is Steve Brown, anybody there page me?"

"Yeah, Steve. Mace here. Cassiletti said you called."

"We have to talk," Steve said.

"You're going to have to stand in line," Mace said.

"Yeah," Steve said, "I imagine you're feeling some heat just about now."

"Where are you going to be later?"

"Page me," Steve said. "We'll work something out."

"All right," Mace said, and hung up. He turned to Munch, "You ready?"

"Yeah."

He shook hands with Chacón, saying, "I owe you."

Munch and Chacón shook hands and exchanged "nice to meet yous."

As they walked down the hallway on the way to the elevator, Munch held up a cassette. "You got a tape player in your car?" she asked.

"No. What is that?"

"It would be easier if I showed you."

Raleigh called the number he'd committed to memory. The voice on the other end of the line answered the call, saying, "Four one three eight."

"Two bravo echo six," Raleigh replied.

"Confirmed."

"Gameboy deviated from the program," Raleigh said.

"Any problems?"

"Some wet work was involved."

"Is the situation contained?"

"Actually, better than contained. This is going to work out to our advantage," Raleigh said. A hot belch erupted deep in his throat, leaving the burning aftertaste of bile. He wondered if his duodenal ulcer was acting up again.

"So we're still on schedule?" the voice asked.

"Yeah, Gameboy's in our pocket."

"Excellent."

"There is one loose end," Raleigh said, popping his sixth Altoid in an hour.

"Go on."

"First name: Ellen. Caucasian female, mid-twenties, five feet six inches, one hundred and thirty pounds. Green eyes, light brown hair, but wears wigs. She works for A&M Limousine."

"Recommendation?"

"Silence her," Raleigh said.

CHAPTER 17

Ellen's ride dropped her off in front of Farmer's ground-floor apartment on the corner of Brooks and Main in Venice. Farmer had lived there for twelve years. The landlord had given up hope of ever raising the rent as long as Farmer chose to stay there. The only windows in the narrow, dungeonlike apartment faced Main Street. A twelve-year build-up of grime provided the privacy and darkness Farmer craved. He'd also nailed thick wire mesh between the wood sashes to further ensure his security.

Somehow, even though all his cash went to drugs, Farmer still managed to own a '69 Panhead, which he parked inside his apartment. The Harley-Davidson oil spot on his carpet was a source of pride.

Ellen rapped on his door, and called out, "Farmer," so he wouldn't think she was the cops. She knew Farmer was a night person. His displeasure at being disturbed would not last, not when she flashed her cash in front of him.

"The fuck you want?" he called out.

"Open up." She looked nervously up and down the street while she waited for him to undo the multiple locks on his door. "C'mon," she said.

At last the door opened, and Farmer stood before her, squinting at the bright light of day and looking like Willie Nelson after a two-week bender. He wore a dirty white T-shirt and grimy jeans. The skin of his bare feet was white. "The fuck you want?" he asked again.

She slid past him. "Shut the door," she said. "You holding?"

"You got money?"

"Yes."

"How much you want?" he asked.

"A dime," she said.

He lit a cigarette and appraised her. "Only a dime?"

"I've been clean a while," she explained.

He nodded. "When did you get out?"

"A couple weeks ago. You holding or not?" she asked.

His apartment smelled of raw gasoline, dirty socks, and decaying produce. Farmer told her once that a man could live very easily on what markets threw away. Obviously he was still making the Dumpster circuit. She wondered if he ever washed his clothes or just wore them until they fell apart. The sheets on his unmade bed showed the imprint of his body like some greaser's version of the Shroud of Turin.

"I'm out of pocket right now," he told her. "Donna Dumb Cunt has D's, but she only sells three for a quarter."

She knew he was referring to Dilaudids, a pill form of synthetic morphine. One of the drug's prized features was that it was water soluble and easily rendered into injectable liquid. Donna Dumb Cunt had a lucrative business forging prescriptions and filling them at select pharmacies. No one called her anything but Donna to her face, especially when she was holding.

"Are they the yellow ones?" Ellen asked. Dilaudids came in three different milligram dosages. The yellow were ten milligrams and the strongest.

"Yeah, of course," Farmer said. He scratched a scab on his arm. "You want me to cop for you?"

"I know Donna. I can go over there myself."

"Yeah, but she don't like foot traffic, and she won't let you fix there."

Ellen didn't see that she had many options left, not if she wanted to medicate her hangover. "All right. Take me over there, let me use your works, and I'll split the dope with you."

Farmer snuffed out his cigarette on the badly scarred carpet and pulled on his boots. She stood aside while he straddled his bike and kick-started it. The sound of the Harley roaring to life reverberated off the walls of the apartment. Ellen held the door open while Farmer wheeled the motorcycle out to the sidewalk, leaving behind a spotted trail of dark oil. She pulled the apartment door shut and jumped on the back of the Harley. Farmer took off toward the canals by the board-walk. At the top of Dudley Way, he shut off the engine and rolled down the alley.

There was a carport behind Donna's building. Farmer secured the bike with a heavy chain and padlock to one of the support columns, then he and Ellen climbed down through a cement planter and knocked on Donna's kitchen door. After what seemed an interminable pause, Donna came shuffling to the door. Donna had been around Venice forever. She had dropped acid with Jimmy Morrison and had smoked dope with Janis Joplin. She still wore her dry, frizzy gray hair long down her back, like the beatnik she had been too many years ago.

She peered at them through her thick, smudged glasses, tilting back her head so she could see under her bangs. "Yeah?" she asked. The pupils of her gray eyes were the size of pinpricks, indicating that she had recently partaken of her own goods. Constant drool had left chapped trails on either side of her mouth. Her teeth were yellowed.

"Hey, Donna," Ellen said. "How have you been?"

Donna laughed her throaty "Ha, ha." The same imbecilic chuckle that had helped her earn her nickname. "Well, I'm fatter," Donna said.

"Oh, no, you're not," Ellen said immediately, even though that was the first thing she'd noticed. The flowing kaftan Donna wore couldn't disguise the width of her hips. "You look great."

Donna regarded them both suspiciously. "I'm not fronting you."

"I've got money," Ellen said.

Donna turned from them and lumbered back into her cluttered apartment. "How much you want?"

"Three," Ellen said. She felt the anticipation building inside her. There was no stopping now. The thought of getting down had carried her since waking up in La Jolla. How she was going to handle the rest of her life was all safely on hold. Everything but the dope was secondary.

Donna poked absentmindedly through her junky collection of bottles and books, opening each one and mumbling all the while, "Now where did I hide it?"

Ellen and Farmer exchanged looks. They'd been through this before with her. Donna said the neighbors noticed if there was a lot of in and out traffic, so she slowed things up with this game of hers. Ellen knew better than to volunteer to help search. Donna might be a dumb cunt, but she was smart enough to know that a dope fiend would keep searching long after they'd already pocketed your stash. An alcoholic would rip you off, too, but when they sobered up the next day they'd come back crying and beg forgiveness. An addict would rip you off, help you look for your stuff, and vow on their mama's grave to get the dog who did you dirty.

Donna was standing on a stool, going through the foodstuffs stacked on the open shelves in her kitchen.

Waiting for Donna to finish her ritual torture was giving Ellen too much time to think. With thinking, came worrying. Just being here, consorting with known drug users, was enough to violate her parole. And what about Munch, who had only tried to help her? What was she going to tell her? Even worse than the thinking and worrying, Ellen realized, were the feelings. Either the hangover was making her oversensitive, or she had forgotten how bad it felt to grovel.

"How can you not remember where you stashed your dope?" she asked.

"Everybody's always in a hurry," Donna mumbled, and climbed down from the stool. Farmer held out a hand to help her down and frowned at Ellen. Hurrying Donna always had the opposite desired effect.

"Here they are," Donna said finally, producing a vial of pills from her pocket. "They were here all along." She laughed again, and Ellen wanted to punch her, but you never had that luxury with the connection. There was no saying, "Fuck you," and stomping off. Everybody understood this.

Ellen reached in her pocket for the cash.

"Is this the best you can do?" The question entered Ellen's mind unbidden. She hadn't meant to even say it out loud. An unexpected tear trickled down her face. She wiped it away with the back of her hand.

"Three for a quarter," Donna said, answering the question as if it had been directed to her. "That's a good deal."

Ellen couldn't speak as she counted out the money. Donna dropped the three little yellow pills into Ellen's palm. Farmer slipped the cellophane off his pack of Marlboros and handed it to her. The volume of tears rolling down her cheeks surprised her.

"What's the matter with you?" Donna asked.

"It's been a long time," Ellen said.

She rolled the cellophane around the pills and held the package in her hand for the short trip back to Farmer's. Farmer and Donna exchanged shrugs, unable to fathom her strange reaction. For them, it was all business as usual. But she understood. Her new life had already failed. And coming back to where you've left is always the end of the road.

Mace and Munch listened to the tape together. The first time, Munch said nothing. Then she rewound it and Mace paid close attention as she explained what she thought they were hearing.

"What's Ellen's last name?" he asked.

"You're not going to arrest her, are you?" Munch asked.

"Do you want to press charges?"

"No, of course not."

"I need her full name for my report," he said, not telling Munch that he planned to issue an APB. It was as much for Ellen's safety as anything else, but he didn't want to spook Munch.

"It's Summers," she said. "Ellen Summers."

He had her wait in his car while he booked the limo into evidence and explained to the Parker Center criminalists that he wanted the back of the limo searched for evidence. Mace secured another visitor's badge for Munch, took her upstairs, and had her wait at his desk.

"I shouldn't be too long," he said.

His desk was in the corner by the window with a view that encompassed the Federal Building and the massive office complex of Immigration Services. Pictures of various crime scenes and mug shots of career criminals were spread across his desk.

"Don't mind the mess," he said, shuffling to the bottom of the pile a death-scene shot of an elderly woman who had been shot in her sleep and bled out on her white pillowcase.

Munch pointed to the photograph now on the top. "Hey," she said, picking up a picture of someone's living room. "I've got the same hide-a-bed."

Mace took the picture from her. "What are you talking about?"

"This sofa," she said, pointing. "I've got the same one."

Mace studied the photograph and again noticed the turned-around cushion. Now it took on a whole new meaning.

Cassiletti came through the doorway, relief evident on his face when he saw Mace. The big man nodded a hello to Munch, then said, "Captain Earl is waiting for us."

Mace showed him the photograph. "This is a hide-a-bed. Let's call the SID crew and get them back over there."

"The captain?" Cassiletti asked.

"What are you? My conscience? Just make the call. I'll deal with Earl."

"He's waiting?" Cassiletti said.

"All right, forget SID. I'll stop over there myself." Mace looked down at the seated Munch, and said, "I'll try to be quick." He turned back to Cassiletti, extending his hand toward the doorway as if he were an usher, and said, "Lead the way."

They walked down the hallway to the captain's office. Earl's secretary, Brenda, stopped typing and pushed the intercom button. "Sir?" she said. "Detectives St. John and Cassiletti are here."

"Finally," came the reply.

She let go of the button and smiled only at Mace. "He'll see you now."

"Thanks, Brenda," he said. "Don't you ever get any time off?"

Her smile grew bigger. A touch of pink highlighted her cheeks. "Seems that way. I haven't even had lunch, and I don't know what I'm doing for dinner."

"He doesn't pay you enough," Mace said, letting the opening slide. He and Cassiletti entered the spacious office. "You wanted to see me, sir?" Mace asked.

Earl was seated behind his desk and didn't rise when the two men entered. He was wearing a polo shirt and chinos, as if his day off had been interrupted. "It's come to my attention that you've been requesting information on a Raleigh Ward."

"Yes, sir."

"You're looking in the wrong place," Captain Earl said. "He is not a viable suspect."

"I'm not ready to rule him out, sir."

"This isn't open for discussion. I don't want you going to this man's home, making any more inquiries, or conducting surveillance of any type."

"Who is this guy?" Mace asked.

"That's strictly need-to-know," Earl said, looking out the window at his own view of the federal court building. "Let's just say he's covered at a high level."

So that's it, Mace thought, *the feds are involved.* "I don't care if he works for God himself. If this guy did those girls, I'm bringing him down."

The captain looked only at Mace. "I'm giving you a direct order. You are to cease all inquiries regarding this man. Look elsewhere. Am I making myself clear?"

Mace knew he'd come as close to the line as Earl would tolerate. Now he flirted with serious insubordination. But he was pissed, and he hoped that somewhere in Earl's brass-studded little heart he was feeling it, too. Almost nothing felt worse than caving in to the feds. The only feeling that surpassed it was letting a murderer go.

"Anything else, sir?" Mace asked through gritted teeth.

"I want your case notes."

"I haven't typed them up yet," Mace said.

"Give me what you've got, then," Captain Earl said.

"It's all in my head, sir," Mace said, knowing there was no argument for that. He thought of the roll of film in his pocket, the tape of Munch's, and the limousine parked in the back lot of the sheriff's crime lab. "But as soon as I get the chance, I'll type them up for you."

"How do you plan to proceed with your investigation?" Captain Earl asked.

"Just good old honest police work, Captain." Mace was gratified to see a small wince cross Earl's countenance.

Munch spent her time at Mace's desk idly reading whatever reports were visible. Then she saw her own handwriting on a Xeroxed sheet of paper under the picture of the hide-a-bed. This was the report she had written for Mace. Someone had made notes in the margin with a red ink pen. She casually slid the paper out to where she could read the addenda. Next to the phone number Raleigh had called from the limo at the end of the run, someone had written a name in blue ink:

Pamela Martin. Written under the name was an address in Santa Monica. Now she had a name and address to go with the phone number.

Mace drove Munch to Digger's house on the Venice canals. Since his father's death, Mace had only been back twice. The place looked different since Caroline had cleared away the thick bramble of ivy and bougainvillea that previously shadowed the front windows. *This place has known too much darkness,* she claimed. *Time to let in some light.*

"Caroline is taking care of the house until we clear probate," Mace explained to Munch, as they pulled up the narrow street.

"How many bedrooms?" she asked.

"Two."

"What are you going to do after it clears probate?" Munch asked.

"We'll put it on the market."

"You should hold on to it," Munch said. "You got a nice little fenced-in yard, parking, you're close to the ocean. Plus the property values have really been going up in this area."

He smiled at her. "Property values?"

"Yeah," she said. "There's like this big boom going on. Even with the high interest rates. You wouldn't believe what they want for a third of a lot in Ghost Town. We looked at one place. They were asking one hundred and thirty thousand, and it wasn't even safe there."

"Maybe this is a good time to sell," he said. "Before everyone comes to their senses."

"And then what?" she asked.

"What do you mean?"

"Are you going to move back to your train car?"

"Probably. I've been there for the last couple of months. It's been all right."

"Doesn't it seem cramped after living in a house?"

"No," he said, and opened the car door. He didn't tell her that instead of cramped, the Bella Donna felt remarkably empty. But none of that made any difference. Letting Caroline keep the house was the obvious choice. She had a small vegetable garden that she'd begun when they moved in with Digger back in December. She was comfortable there, with a bathtub she could soak in, a real kitchen, and her own washer and dryer. There was that, but more importantly, the ghosts of the place didn't haunt her. For him, painful memories lurked around every corner. First his mother, then his father, and finally his marriage.

"There they are," Munch said, pointing to two figures standing by the edge of the canal. She jumped out of the car, called out to them, then headed their way.

Caroline and Asia turned at the same time. Each held chunks of white bread in her hand. A horde of ducks, gulls, and small black birds with yellow eyes surrounded them. Caroline's laugh carried above the clamor of the flock.

"Hey, Mom," Asia yelled. "Come on over here. We're feeding the birds."

"I can see that," Munch said.

Mace followed her to the water's edge. Caroline turned to him. "Hi," she said. "Watch where you step."

Seeing Caroline at play with the little girl filled him with warmth and pain. Was this a glimpse of some sort of alternate life? Should this child have been their own? Would that satisfy in Caroline the emotional connection she claimed to need—a need he failed to meet? Just saying "I love you" was not enough, she said. Nor were flowers, a monthly paycheck, or a diamond ring, he also discovered. What the fuck it would take, he hadn't the energy left to figure out. Hadn't he said he was sorry?

"Where's Derek?" he asked. The question surprised even him. Derek's location was close to the bottom of his list of priorities. Caroline seemed unfazed by his inquiry.

"He needed to go home and take care of his dog," Caroline said. "I told him that we'd be fine without him."

"Good call," Munch said.

Caroline opened her arms to Munch, and said, "How have you been?"

Munch stepped forward and returned the hug, saying, "Really great."

Mace felt his face twitch with the push-pull of longing and sorrow. He folded his lips inside his mouth to stop their quiver and felt a tug on his hand. He looked down to see Asia holding out a piece of bread to him. "Watch out for the big white one over there," she said. "He's a hog."

"Maybe that's how he got so big," Mace said. When he looked up, Caroline was smiling at him. "Did you meet my babies?" he asked Asia.

"Your babies?" she asked, wide-eyed, drawing out the last word.

"Sammy and Nicky."

"Oh. Oh," Asia said, hopping up and down. "Mom, they got dogs. Two of them. The black one is Samantha. She kisses all the time. And if you throw a ball for Nicky, she brings it back to you."

"You'll have to show me that," Munch said.

Asia took her hand. "They're in the house. C'mon."

"You two go ahead," Mace said. "We'll be right in."

He waited until Munch and Asia reached the gate and were out of earshot. "Thanks," he said to Caroline.

"What's going on?" she asked. "Is Munch in some kind of trouble again?"

"I didn't want to take any chances." He filled her in on his case, how the evidence indicated that Munch had inadvertently crossed the path of the Band-Aid Killer. When he told Caroline about the missing registration, she shivered.

"Then they can't go back home until this is resolved," she said. "What about Asia's father? Can he help out?"

"Apparently he's dead. I'm sure there's a whole lot more to that story that she's not telling me."

"Let them stay here," Caroline said. "Maybe I can pry some information out of Munch." Her eyes softened, and he saw a hint of the old tenderness there. "How about you? Can you stay for dinner?"

He wanted more than anything to say yes, to end the drought between them. But he still needed to go back over to the apartment in Hollywood, and he still hadn't heard what Steve Brown had to tell him. "How about I bring back dessert?" he said. "I'll pick up a pie at Polly's."

"Try not to be too late," she said.

Kiss her, you idiot. Tell her you want to change, that you have already. Tell her how sometimes you look at the long days and years ahead without her and you're gripped with such terrible emptiness that you can't believe you're still drawing breath. "Lock everything up," he said. *Gutless, totally gutless, St. John.*

"We'll be okay. We've got the dogs to protect us."

"Oh, right, as long as one of the bad guys doesn't come armed with a tennis ball." He made his mouth smile and felt the rest of his body twitch in confusion as his emotions fought for control of his facial muscles and glands. His mind, always his strongest suit, maintained control.

"I think if someone was really threatening us, they'd do something," she said.

"You like to think the best of everyone," he said, and instantly regretted his words when the smile left her face. Great, he'd done it again, brought up the ghost of one of their arguments. The one where he always accused her of being too liberal. Maybe she was right about the counseling. He'd tell her that when he returned, when the time was right. "Apple all right with you?"

"Whatever looks good to you," she said.

He reached over and gave her arm a squeeze, a tight smile on his face. He wanted to say something else, but couldn't come up with anything, so he just nodded. She stood on the curb and watched him get into his car. He raised his hand once more in farewell and started the engine. It wasn't until he was all the way to the stop sign at the end of the block when it came to him. "You look good to me," he said out loud. How hard was that?

On the way to Hollywood he slammed the steering wheel with his open palm. "Dickhead," he said, addressing himself in the rearview mirror. "Moron." The only thing that comforted him was that at least he had them all together and safe under the same roof. At least he'd done that right.

CHAPTER 18

Mace peeled back the barricade tape at the Hollywood apartment and let himself in with the victim's keys. He went directly to the couch, the one Munch had identified as a hide-a-bed. The SID crew had spent little time in the living room; their main focus had been on the sites where the bodies were discovered, and rightfully so. Everybody's impression had been that the living room was hardly ever used. The only object the techs had dusted for prints was the telephone. He reached down to pull off the couch cushions and stopped. They were now all pointed out the right way.

He lifted the cushions up one at a time and placed them across the room, keeping them in exact order. Then he lifted open the mattress mechanism. The mattress pad was missing. The rest of the hide-a-bed had a faint ammonia odor. He was certain now that he had found the scene of the women's slaughter. The old mattress must have soaked up the blood, making cleanup a simple matter of coming back later and removing the pad and with it such trace evidence as pubic hair and semen. He should have posted guards at the crime scene. But it was too late for that now. The damage had been done. He returned everything as he'd found it and let himself out the way he'd come in.

From a pay phone on the street, he called Cassiletti. "Munch and her kid are going to stay over at Digger's house for now. She's going to need to go back to her house and pick up some clothes. I want you to take her over there. Have a black-and-white unit back you up."

"Sure, Mace. Anything else?"

"Yeah, send the photographers back over to the apartment

on Gower. I want them to shoot another roll of film in the living room. Tell them to bring Luminol. I want the couch taken apart, vacuumed for fibers, and everything sprayed. Carpet, couch, baseboards, the works." If there was any trace of blood left in that living room, the Luminol would find it. It didn't matter how well the place had been cleaned.

He called Steve Brown next and arranged to meet him at Madame Wu's in Santa Monica. Twenty minutes later, the waiter seated them in a private booth under a red-lacquered archway. Mace and Steve had little to say while the tea was brought. They each ordered the special. The waiter beamed at the wisdom of their choice.

Mace glanced around the room at the other diners. He stopped short when he saw a familiar face. "Hey," he whispered excitedly to Steve, "Muhammad Ali is sitting over there."

"Be cool," Steve said.

"Oh, man. Wait till I tell my . . ." Mace stopped mid-sentence. The familiar pall of memories dimmed his pleasure.

"How long has it been?" Steve asked gently.

"March, four months. The worst is watching ball games. Every time the Dodgers score, I keep picking up the phone to call him. We always talked to each other during ball games. Sometimes I'm halfway through dialing his number before I realize he's not there anymore."

Steve poured them both tea.

"What did you find out?" Mace asked.

"I couldn't find any paper trail on Raleigh Ward," Steve said, "and believe me, you won't either. He never existed. The apartment in Culver City was stripped to the baseboards."

"Some kind of spook, right?"

Steve nodded. "Looks like. The way those guys operate is to have three sets of ID. One will be a civilian cover, another as a government employee, and then a third as a CIA or FBI agent and even that one will be under an alias. Now, the other guy. Victor Draicu. He's real."

"That's comforting," Mace said. "What's his deal?"

"He's the third secretary of cultural affairs with the Romanian embassy. He speaks English and was an Olympic gymnast. So maybe he is what he seems. He's been in Los Angeles on and off since December overseeing the accommodations for the Romanian Olympic team."

"Since December?" Mace asked, his pulse quickening.

"Way ahead of you, buddy," Steve said. "I called a Securitate major in Bucharest I know."

"What's the Securitate?" Mace asked. "State police?"

"Yeah, they're controlled by the KGB, though."

"And this guy talked to you?" Mace asked.

"We have an arrangement," Steve said. "Any information that's strictly criminal activity—none of the political bullshit—we share. I asked him about murders fitting your killer's M.O. He found me one. A little gypsy girl in Transylvania. She disappeared from her camp. Two days later, they found her in pieces. First the head, then the rest. My guy remembered the case because it was so weird to him how the killer had taken the time to wash all the body parts and tape the wounds shut."

"How about the hand-over-the-heart thing?"

"He didn't know about that," Steve said.

"Did you ask him if Draicu had any kind of a record?"

"No," Steve said, pouring himself a second cup of tea. "That would have been pushing it. You ask the wrong question or you start naming names, and you don't know what kind of shit you might be stirring up."

The waiter delivered the sweet-and-sour pork. Mace ate without tasting it.

The effects of the dope still lingered in Ellen's system, making her nose itch and her pupils tiny. As soon as she had stuck the needle in her arm, she knew she was making a mistake. She hadn't even enjoyed the rush. The anxiety and fear that the dope was supposed to quiet still raged full blast. Only now her thought processes were too clouded to deal with solutions.

One thing hadn't changed, though. Whenever she shot dope, she had this overwhelming compulsion to wash dishes, clean floors, and put things in order. She did the best she could with Farmer's dungeon given the limited amount of cleaning supplies he kept on hand. After bringing some small degree of organization to her surroundings, she did what she could to clean herself up.

She showered in his tiny bathroom, drying herself off with a small threadbare white towel with Gold's Gym stamped on it. She combed her wet hair straight back. Rummaging though Farmer's drawers, she came across a tube of flesh-colored foundation and dabbed it over the two telltale little pinholes over the veins in the crook of her left arm.

To be caught with fresh tracks was an automatic misdemeanor, especially if coupled with a blood or urine test. And for a person already on parole, it guaranteed an instant return trip to jail. Do not pass Go, do not collect two hundred dollars. Your ass is gone.

God, she thought, *what's wrong with me? I've risked everything: my freedom, my future, and for what?* All she had to show for it was an itchy nose and not even a momentary break from her problems. *Most of which,* she thought miserably, *are really not even my fault.*

She waited two hours before she dared venture out from Farmer's apartment. His telephone, she had discovered, only worked for incoming calls. Her destination, an apartment building on Paloma Avenue, was only two blocks away. It seemed like two miles. She kept to the alleys, hoping that Tommy still lived there and was home.

Tommy was a fiftysomething-year-old guy who had never gotten past adolescent angst. He had greasy hair, one of those complexions that was forever erupting in pimples, and a nervous tic that made his eye flicker whenever a woman addressed him directly. He worked as a bartender at the Oar House and occasionally scored a date at 2 A.M. with some poor hapless female too drunk to realize what she was doing.

Ellen had learned that fact the hard way. She'd tried to forget waking up next to him almost as soon as it happened. After giving him an eight-digit phone number when he kept insisting on some way to reach her, she had stumbled out of his tiny apartment on Paloma and into the bright morning vowing to put as much distance between that night and her memory as possible. Now she was wondering if everything didn't happen for a reason.

"Hey, Tommy," she said, when he came to his door, "you still tending bar over at the Oar House?"

"Sure am, eh—"

"Ellen. You remember me, don't you?"

His eye went into overdrive. "Yeah, sure. Ellen. How you doin'?"

"Fair to middling." She stepped across his threshold. Tommy took a step back, buttoning his shirt. "My car broke down just up the street a ways. I hate to bother you, but I was supposed to pick up my girlfriend, and I don't want her to worry. Think I could use your phone?" she asked, stroking his forearm with the tip of her finger.

Both eyes were going at it now. "You mean now?"

"I haven't come at a bad time, have I?"

"Uh, no," he said, stumbling backwards. "Now is fine. You want a beer?"

"Thanks, darling. I'd just love a beer."

While Tommy went into the kitchen to fetch her drink, she dialed quickly. She crossed her fingers as the phone rang. After the third ring, Munch's voice came over her answering machine. Ellen waited impatiently for the outgoing message to play out. "You there?" she asked. "Please be there. Look, I'm so sorry. The car broke down. But, don't worry"—she patted the money in her pocket—"I've got you covered. I don't know what more to tell you other than I know it looks bad, but believe me, shit got out of control real fast. It wasn't my fault. Those guys were nuts. Oh, God, I wish you were there. I really need to talk to you." She bit her lip. *Think,* she told herself. "I, uh, I'll call you back later. Don't worry."

She hung up. Tommy walked back into the room and handed her a can of Budweiser. She popped it open. He lit a cigarette. "You got another one of those?" she asked.

He handed her the pack. She took a smoke and held his hand while he lit it for her. She smiled encouragingly.

"You mind if I make one more teeny call? My girlfriend wasn't home."

"All right," he said, his hands fluttering about his belt and shirttails as if trying to find a place to roost. He finally jammed them in his pockets.

Ellen placed her second call, taking another long drag of her cigarette.

"Hello," the man answered.

Ellen exhaled quickly. "Dwayne? Is my mom there?"

"Yeah," he said. "Just a minute." He said the words like she was asking him to do her some really big favor. She would have loved to say something like, "If you don't mind moving your fat ass for once," but she knew she couldn't afford to antagonize him.

She heard the phone put down and Dwayne bellow, "Lila Mae, that daughter of yours is on the phone."

A moment later, Ellen's mom picked up. "Where have you been?"

"I've been getting my act together, Mom," Ellen said. "You know, finding an apartment, getting a job."

"Uh-huh. We didn't know what to think. One moment you're here, the next you're gone. And all without so much as a note."

"I did leave you a note," Ellen said.

"Funny that I never saw it. So now what? You're all settled, is that it?"

"Well, I did get a job, but I had to move out of where I was staying." Ellen closed her eyes. "Mom, I ran into some trouble."

"Oh, Gawd," Lila Mae said. "You ain't pregnant." She said it like it was the worst thing that could happen to a person.

"No, nothing like that. I just need a place to stay for a couple of days."

"What about all those great friends of yours? I thought Munch was supposed to help you."

"She did. She was."

"What did you do?"

"Nothing," Ellen said, hating the whining tone that had crept into her voice. "Nothing that was my fault."

"Where have I heard that before? You sound funny."

"I'm just tired."

"Don't give me that crap. What are you on now?"

Ellen took a sip of beer before she answered. This was all so unfair. "Nothing, Mom. Can't you ever believe your own daughter?"

"You stole my sewing machine."

"That was ten years ago," Ellen said. "Could you please just not argue with me?" She exhaled, took a second to collect herself, then began again. "All right, here's the deal. I messed up a little, but now I want to start staying clean again. I just need a little help."

Lila Mae sighed into the phone. "Where are you? I'll send Dwayne to pick you up."

"Can't you come?"

"No, I've got the league tonight."

Oh, well then. That was that. God forbid she should neglect the league or miss a goddamn tournament for once in her life. "You know what, Mom? I think I can get this situation under control myself."

"You sure?"

"Yeah," Ellen said. "Forget I even called." She hung up.

Fuck it. She still had over two hundred bucks left. She had hoped to hand it all over to Munch, but twenty bucks was going to have to go for a motel room.

"Everything all right?" Tommy asked.

"Oh, yeah, hunky-dory. Say, Tommy, you think you could give me a ride over to my friend's house to pick up my stuff?"

CHAPTER 19

He slipped into the dark house without causing a ripple in the neighborhood. The back door was a simple lock, easily picked. He moved like a shadow, not making a sound and wending through the quiet rooms like a wraith of smoke. The power of his daring surged through him, lightening his step and stiffening his cock.

The house had two bedrooms, one of them belonging to a child—a little girl. Pictures of the girl were all over the refrigerator: dressed in a tutu, sitting astride a pony, feeding a cockatiel on some sort of stage. The mother was obviously very pleased to have delivered herself of a girl-child.

He moved to the front bedroom. The noises of the boulevard filtered through to him. At times like these all his senses were extraordinarily acute. That was part of the gift. The curtains of the room were drawn, but a small slit of light from a streetlamp sneaked through where they didn't quite meet. There was enough illumination for him to see that he was in the mother's bedroom. Suddenly the noises from the street grew more personal. He heard the outside gate swing open, footsteps on the path outside the window. He froze, waiting. There was a slight shuffling noise he couldn't identify, and then the scratch of a key entering a lock, the thunk of a dead bolt turning. He took a step deeper into the room's shadows. When the front door opened, he also opened the closet.

Whoever had entered the house did not put on the lights immediately. He listened while the person stumbled in the dark, then entered the child's room. At last a light was put on. He slipped into the open closet, letting the female fabrics hanging there softly caress his face. It was all he could do not to moan out loud. He put a hand over his erection, as if to hold it back.

He reached down and slowly lifted his pant leg. The three-fingered grip of his stinger pleased him. He eased it from the scabbard strapped to his shin.

Noises of objects being moved and dragged across the wooden floor of the child's room masked his own stealthy steps. He heard the intruder murmur. It was a woman. He left the closet to sneak a peek out the bedroom window.

Outside, a man leaned against a yellow Volkswagen Beetle smoking a cigarette. The woman in the house carried a suitcase out to the man with the car. He watched as she stuck out her hand in that splayed two-finger gesture smokers use to indicate they want a drag. The woman inhaled deeply on the cigarette while the Volkswagen man put her bag in his backseat. Then she turned toward the house. He couldn't believe his luck. It was that Ellen creature. Obviously the fates were with him. He saw that she had changed her hair again. Deceptive bitch. She was a blonde now.

She threw down the cigarette. He hated her for her casual littering, her disregard for others. She turned back toward the house, and he lifted his stinger in readiness.

"So what's with him?" Munch asked Caroline as they set the table. Asia was taking a bath before dinner.

"What do you mean?" Caroline asked.

"What's he so mad about all the time?" Munch felt she'd earned the privilege of cutting through the bullshit and getting right to the heart of the matter. Hadn't she been instrumental in the two of them getting together?

Caroline sighed as she smoothed out a place mat. "He's been like that for months."

"Since his dad died?"

"It started even before that." She pulled out a chair and

sat. Munch did the same. "Right after Christmas, Digger stopped eating."

"He told me that," Munch said.

"He did?" Caroline asked, surprise showing on her face.

"Yeah, he said you had to grind everything up in the blender before the old guy would even look at it."

"We tried everything. Small portions, only the freshest ingredients. Sometimes he would eat sweets; mostly he just wanted to be left alone. Mace tried to keep him involved in life, but Digger was just tired. The last few months were the worst."

"Was he in pain?" Munch asked.

"It wasn't so much physical," Caroline said. "Digger thought we were after his money. Once I did my laundry here when the housekeeper took a day off. This was before we moved in full-time. Digger wanted to know why I was using up all his water."

"Sounds like you should have been the one to get pissed off."

"Believe me," Caroline said. "There were times. When I first met Digger, I thought, How cute, this is what Mace will be like in forty years. I loved them both. After living through this last year, I began to look at Mace and think, Now I know what he's going to be like in forty years."

"And you hated them both," Munch said.

Caroline adjusted the salt shaker. "I was tired. Taking care of Digger was like having a newborn. He woke up all hours of the night, needed constant attention, messed his clothes. It got pretty horrendous. But as bad as it was for me, it was that and more for Mace. Once Digger beckoned for Mace from his chair. Mace came to him immediately, as he always did. 'I've got nobody,' Digger said. Mace said, 'What are you talking about, Dad? You've got me, you've got Caroline.' Digger just shook his head, and said, 'I've got nobody.'"

"That's cold," Munch said.

"I wanted to throttle him," Caroline admitted.

"So maybe it wasn't all bad when he died."

"Strangely enough, I was devastated," Caroline said. "As much as I knew it was his time, and that Digger really wanted to go, we still had so much invested in keeping him going on a daily basis. In some ways, it was like losing a child. I cried until I could barely stand. Mace got angry with me—told me he needed me to be strong."

"Tough guy, huh?" Munch said in her best Cagney impression. This brought a small smile to Caroline's lips. "I don't get a big picture of him ever breaking down and crying. Did he?"

"Not in front of me."

"Too bad he couldn't let it out."

Caroline wiped her eyes, and sighed. "I'm tired of knocking at that door."

Munch nodded in understanding, searching her own history for similar experiences. When she thought of Derek, she laughed.

"What?" Caroline asked.

"I'm sorry," Munch said. "I was just thinking it can go too far the other way, too. Take Derek, for instance. Every night when I got home from work, he couldn't wait to share with me all his thoughts and feelings for the day. Right before we broke up, he told me there was some poll on TV about what women wanted most from their spouses. Eighty percent of the woman responded that they wished their mate would open up and talk about his emotions more. Derek was so proud. Then I pointed out that ninety percent of those men probably had jobs and were tired when they got home."

"Did he get the hint?" Caroline asked.

"No," Munch said. "I don't think he's gotten it yet."

"They can be so dense."

"Tell me about it." Munch rubbed a spot on the table. "Is that why you separated?"

"Most of the reason. Starting even before Digger died it

seemed the more I tried to reach Mace, the more hostile and distant he became. Maybe it was mostly subconscious, but it was pretty clear to me he was doing everything he could think of to sabotage us, our love. He finally succeeded. What's really sad is that my giving up on us finally got his attention. Ironic, isn't it? We're both getting what we wanted, and now it's too late."

"So are you guys getting a divorce?" she asked. The question had been on the tip of her tongue all afternoon, but she had been avoiding asking, fearing the answer. She'd been to Mace and Caroline's wedding. Cried when they promised each other their eternal love. Cried because it was such a beautiful, preposterous sentiment.

Caroline's tone was resigned when she answered. "Probably. I keep trying to make allowances for all that he's been through. Then last month I found a condom wrapper in his suit pocket. I confronted him about it. He admitted that he had seen an old girlfriend, they had drinks, one thing led to another—"

"Wait a minute," Munch interrupted. "You're saying he just left it in his pocket?"

"A bit careless, don't you think?" Caroline asked, raising an eyebrow.

"Suicidal," Munch agreed. "Is that when you finally figured, 'Enough already'?"

"He thinks so. The truth is I can get past that. What I can't take any longer is how he refuses to open up to me. How he holds on to all his anger and doesn't leave room for anything else."

"Yeah," Munch said, "I know what you mean. Love only goes so far. You try to give a guy every break, then one day you just reach a point where it's taking you down."

Caroline got up and checked the casserole in the oven. "Enough about me. Tell me about Asia's father," she said. "Mace said he passed away? How long ago was that?"

"Six years." Munch wiped her palms on her pants. She always got nervous when she was about to reveal a secret, especially a big one. "He—"

"Mom," Asia called from the bathroom. "I'm getting all wrinkly."

"All right," Munch said, getting up so quickly that her chair tipped over. "I'll be right there."

The phone rang as Munch entered the bathroom. Caroline picked it up in the living room. Munch opened the bathtub drain, then unfolded a towel for Asia to step into. As she rubbed her daughter dry, Caroline stuck her head into the bathroom. "That was Detective Cassiletti. He's coming by to take you to your house."

"What clothes do you want?" Munch asked Asia.

"Hmmm," she said, looking skyward. "Can't I just go with you?"

"No, I want you to stay here."

"Is Mace coming back?" Asia asked.

"Later."

"Bring my pink dress," Asia said.

"Is that what you want to wear to school tomorrow?"

"I guess."

Munch ruffled the towel over Asia's damp hair, then gathered the girl in her arms and hugged her. "I love you," she said.

"I love you, too," Asia mumbled back.

Munch slipped one of Caroline's T-shirts over the little girl's head.

"You know, when I was your age I used to camp out like this with my mom," Munch said.

"I know," Asia said, rolling her eyes and slumping her small shoulders. "And you used to have to wash your hair in the sinks at the laundromat."

"Oh," Munch said. "I told you that already."

"Yesss," Asia said, her tone long-suffering.

A car horn honked outside. "That's probably Detective Cassiletti now," Munch said. "Be a good girl. Do what Mrs. St. John says. When I get back, we'll all play a game." She turned to Caroline before walking out the door. "When I get back, there's something I need to tell you about."

He entered the hallway connecting the two bedrooms, waiting for the moment when she would cross in front of him.

"You almost ready?" the Volkswagen man's voice called from the open front door.

"Just about," he heard Ellen reply.

He pulled back, controlling his breathing with great difficulty. Sweat dampened his neck and ran down his face. He could taste the saltiness of it already on his lips. Not at all like blood. He retraced his steps backward into the other bedroom. The frustration of unrequited appetite felt like a claw in his chest. He felt the squeeze of repression, so tangible that he had trouble drawing a breath.

"You want some help?" Volkswagen man's voice came from the living room, but judging from the street noise, the front door was still wide-open. *Were these people raised in a barn?* he wondered.

Ellen entered the hallway. "Nah," she said. "I'm all set. Let me just lock the place back up, and we're out of here."

He waited until he heard the door being locked. Then he watched from the bedroom as they loaded a large shopping bag into the man's car. It was an easy matter to take down the license plate, but this did little to ease his frustration. *The next time we meet,* he promised her, *it will be on my terms.*

He still had an erection. Perhaps he was just getting old, but achieving emission was becoming more difficult all the time. He stopped in the kitchen to take one of the child's pictures off of the refrigerator. He chose the one of her in her pink ballet costume with the provocative scooped neck. Then he returned to the child's room and sought the delicate underthings that caressed her young flesh.

Munch let herself into her house. A house that now felt dangerous. She saw a movement in the shadows and grabbed Cassiletti's arm in reflex.

"You want me to go in first?" he asked.

"No, I just got freaked out for a second," she said. "You know how you sometimes see things out of the corner of your eye, but then when you turn real quick there's nothing there and you could have sworn there was an animal in the room or something?"

Cassiletti listened with a growing look of consternation on his face. "No," he said.

"Hmm," she said. "Never mind then." Maybe the phenomenon had more to do with all the psychedelics she'd taken, in which case he wasn't going to get it. She pushed the door open and immediately turned on the light. The house looked the same as she had left it that morning. She walked over to the answering machine and saw that she had a message. She pushed play and listened to Ellen's fumbling apology. Tears of relief filled her eyes.

"Sounds like she made it back to town," she said to Cassiletti.

"Do you have an extra tape you can put into the machine?" he asked.

"Yeah, sure," she said. She made the switch. He held out his hand, and she handed him the tape with Ellen's message on it.

Munch gathered some clothes and went into Asia's room. Cassiletti followed.

"She was here," she told Cassiletti. "She took her stuff."

Munch opened Asia's dresser drawer, the one the little girl kept her socks and underpants in. This month's clothes obsession included her set of new pink underwear. There were seven of them, each had a different day of the week embroidered across the front. Asia would be inconsolable if Munch returned without them. It only took a moment to realize that Monday through Wednesday were gone.

"Huh," she said out loud.

"What?" Cassiletti asked, coming to her side.

"Why would Ellen take Asia's underwear?" Munch spotted several creamy white drops of something fluid on some of Asia's socks. "What's this?" she asked, reaching toward the stuff.

"Hold it right there," Cassiletti said. "Don't touch anything."

"What is it?" she asked.

"I'll know for sure in a minute," he said. "C'mon."

She followed him out to his car, where he retrieved a drop light with a purple bulb.

"What's that for?" she asked.

"Certain body fluids fluoresce under ultraviolet light," he said. They returned to Asia's room. Cassiletti plugged his light in and turned it on, instructing Munch to turn off the overhead lights. When he shined the black light into Asia's drawer, a linear spray pattern of thumbtack-sized spots glowed.

"What kind of body fluids specifically?" she asked, not wanting to believe what she already thought.

"Sperm," he said.

"Oh, God," Munch said. "What kind of a sick fuck . . . ?" Her voice trailed off. She was at a loss for words to adequately describe the murderous rage filling her. She instinctively began collecting sharp and heavy objects, going through the motions of what she would have done to this guy if she had caught him in the act. First she would crush his balls, then she'd smash his face.

Cassiletti stood in the hallway, watching her pace and swear. Hot saliva filled her mouth. She turned into the bathroom, spit into the sink, then ran the cold tap water into a washcloth and held it to her burning face and neck.

"I'm going to use the phone," Cassiletti called to her.

"Go ahead," she said. She heard him go into the living room. She put down the washcloth and stared at her red eyes in the medicine cabinet mirror. Cassiletti was using the phone in the dining room. She heard him ask to speak to Detective St. John. His voice sounded agitated as he described what they'd found. Hearing it all recounted got her upset all over again. She strode into her front room and wrenched the phone from Cassiletti's hand. "Can you believe this mother-fucker?" she asked.

"Go back to Digger's house," Mace said. "I'll meet you there. In fact, I'll spend the night with you guys."

"You'll get no argument from me," Munch said. She looked at her right hand and saw that she was clutching a claw hammer. *That's weird,* she thought. *I don't even remember picking it up.*

CHAPTER 20

At eight o'clock Monday morning, Munch called Ellen's mom.

"Hi, Mrs. Summers," she said, trying to sound upbeat. "It's Munch."

"What time is it?"

"I'm sorry to be calling so early, but I really need to find Ellen. Have you heard from her?"

"Yeah, she called me last night." Lila Mae paused to yawn. "First she wants me to come get her and then before Dwayne can get his shirt on, she says not to bother. That girl can never make up her mind. That's her problem."

"Did she say where she was?"

"We didn't get that far."

"You think she went back to Venice?" Munch asked.

"I hope not, but she always seems to end up there," Lila Mae said. "I heard you were doing real good."

"Yes, ma'am. I have a lot to be grateful for."

"Well, I wish you'd talk some sense into that daughter of mine. She's been nothing but trouble."

"If she calls again, tell her I'm not mad, that I need to talk to her. She can leave me a message at my work. But Mrs. Summers? Tell her not to go to my house. It isn't safe."

"What the hell are you two up to?" Lila Mae asked.

"Please, just give her the message."

"Nothing but trouble," Lila Mae said as she hung up.

"Where were you last night?" Raleigh asked Victor.

"I got hungry," Victor said, lathering his toast with butter and strawberry jam. "Where were you?"

"Never mind about me. You need to keep a low profile until we get this deal wrapped up. The sooner you deliver, the sooner you can get on with your new life."

"I have been thinking about that," Victor said, stuffing another strip of bacon into his mouth. "I will be needing a car. A Cadillac Eldorado."

Raleigh felt the coffee in his throat threaten to reverse direction. "Any particular color?"

"Nothing flashy," Victor said. "Leather upholstery. This is not negotiable."

"My people are getting antsy." Raleigh leaned across the table, lowering his voice to a conspiratorial whisper. "One of our Eastern European analysts is saying that you're full of shit. That you have no product."

Victor raised his fork and knife in agitation. "Who is this analyst? Some Hungarian asshole?"

"You know I can't reveal that."

"This other man is full of shit."

"Make me a believer, Victor," Raleigh said. "Bring me a sample, so I can get my people to relax. And don't forget, you owe me."

The report from Toxicology was waiting for Mace on his desk when he got to Parker Center. A long list of chemicals was printed under the heading: Blood Analysis. Three items jumped out at him: cocaine, chloral hydrate, alcohol. There was also a note for him to call Dr. Sugarman, the chief medical examiner for the city of Los Angeles.

Mace decided to go visit in person and brought along the photographs from the Tijuana morgue. When he got to the coroner's office, he found Sugarman bent over his cluttered desk. The coroner looked up when Mace knocked on the already-open door.

"You look like shit," Sugarman said.

"Compared to what?" Mace asked, looking down the hall.

Sugarman laughed.

"You got something for me on the Gower victims?" Mace prompted.

"Oh, yes, of course. I think I've got your murder weapon identified," Sugarman said. "Fortunately, there were enough bone strikes to give us length." Sugarman picked up a ruler and stared at it. Seconds ticked by.

"Any time you're ready, Doc."

Sugarman set down the ruler and gave his head a little shake. "Sorry, still a little early for me." He took a sip of coffee, then continued, "The weapon, more of a dagger than a knife, is four inches long. The blade is round and pointed at the end, much like an ice pick. The handle is what really gave it away. The bruises were very intriguing, as you know." Sugarman dug through his papers until he found an enlarged photograph of one of the wounds. He placed it on the top of his stack. "The small rectangle of the hilt, very unique. Then the two indentations found in the flesh of wounds when the bone didn't interfere with the plunge of the blade." He pointed to the red oblong bruises next to the punctures. "Here and here. It wasn't until I examined the bone wounds . . ." His voice trailed off as he consulted his notes. "Ah, yes. The punctures in hard tissue were four and five millimeters deep, indicating not only a tremendous force of thrust, but also some sort of mechanism that enabled the user to pull the point from the bone and strike again. I finally realized what we were dealing with."

"Sounds like some sort of custom-made job," Mace said.

"Yes, they were," Sugarman said. "For British commandos operating in North Africa and the Middle East during World War II. Three-finger thrust dagger. Here, I have a picture of one."

Sugarman pushed aside more papers until he uncovered a book, which he opened. The page he had marked was a glossy color plate of all sorts of odd knives. In addition to the thrust dagger, there were thumb blades no bigger than guitar picks, single-edged short swords with brass knuckle grips, even a thin knife that came concealed in specially constructed shoes.

"What is this stuff?" Mace asked. He folded the book closed and read the cover: *The History of Espionage.*

Mace showed Sugarman the Polaroids of the Tijuana victims.

"Yes," Sugarman said. "Quite possibly the same weapon used for the female."

"And the men?"

"Hmm. Single-edged blade. Very sharp. Can I examine the bodies?"

"'Fraid not. We'll just have to make do with the pictures." Mace picked up the espionage book. "Can I use your copying machine?"

"Be my guest," Sugarman said.

After making copies of the picture of the murder weapon and its estimated dimensions, Mace returned to Parker Center. He found Cassiletti hanging up his phone.

"That was the impound lot," Cassiletti said. "They've gone over the limo. Munch can pick it up anytime."

"What did they find?"

"Mud, fibers, assorted vegetation. They were able to lift prints from glasses and bottles, too."

"Any blood?"

"No."

"Great," Mace said, disgusted. "I don't suppose any unaccounted prints were lifted at Munch's house?"

"Not yet. But SID rolled on the Gower apartment early this morning. They sprayed Luminol in the living room and it was just like you thought. They found blood splatter on the hide-a-bed hinges and springs. There was also a faint trail in the back cushions and carpet underneath."

"We got the tox report on the victims."

"I saw that," Cassiletti said. "Looks like our killer drugged the women prior to the assault."

"Which explains how he controlled two victims at once," Mace said.

"Pretty cool customer to take the time to sanitize the bodies."

"You think he was just washing away evidence?" Mace asked.

"Well, yeah," Cassiletti said, not looking very certain at all.

"Then why tape the wounds shut? No, I think we're dealing with one sick pup here. He's intelligent, but mainly he's ruled by his compulsions. Compulsions so overwhelming that he risked being caught to carry out his ritual." Mace threw down the photographs from the Tijuana morgue. He pointed to the pictures of the dead men with the slit throats, and said, "Father, son." He then picked up the photograph of the young girl in the red wig. Holding it in front of Cassiletti's face, he said, "Daughter, sister."

"Same guy did them all?" Cassiletti asked.

"They're connected," Mace said. "I don't think the men were the primary targets. They more likely just got caught in the kill zone."

"The lab did a fiber comparison on the pieces of tape you brought in from the Tijuana victim. They all match up with the tape we took off the Gower victims."

"And the tear marks?" Mace asked.

"Fit together like a jigsaw puzzle."

Mace tapped a pencil on the desk in nervous agitation. Victor Draicu had checked out of the Beverly Wilshire, and his current whereabouts were unknown. Mace had had copies of his photograph made and circulated to patrol officers at morning roll call with a "please advise" request if he was spotted. The APB on Ellen Summers was still in effect.

Mace hated the waiting part of an investigation the worst. Especially when he knew he had a serial situation—one that was obviously escalating. He threw down the pencil and picked up his phone.

"Who are you calling?" Cassiletti asked.

"Caroline." He dialed his father's old number. After the discovery of Asia's soiled and missing panties, his suggestion that the three females stay home had been met with no argument. Caroline had canceled her appointments. Munch had called her boss at the gas station, explained that she had a family emergency, and kept Asia home from school. Caroline answered on the second ring.

"Hello?"

"Hi," he said. "It's me."

"How do you feel?"

"I'm all right."

"Did you get any sleep at all last night?"

"Enough," he said, rubbing his stiff neck. "I don't know how Digger spent so many years in that chair, though."

"Any news?" she asked.

"Nothing of much help." He picked up a pen and poised it over his legal pad. "Munch can pick up her limo. In fact, let me talk to her. I need to ask a few questions."

"She's not here. She went off to try to find her friend."

"What?" he almost shouted. "Why didn't you stop her?"

"How was I supposed to do that? Besides, she's doing what she needs to do. After what you told me last night, I think you're going to need all the help you can get."

Mace threw the pen down. "I don't want her out on the street. You were all supposed to stay put. I can't do my job if I have to worry about everybody."

"You can't do anything if you have to worry about everybody. For once in your life, have some faith."

Faith. Sometimes it was like they lived in separate universes. Could they ever find their way back to each other? He sucked in a large breath and blew it out. "All right, all right." He forced his voice to sound calm. "Tell her to call me as soon as you hear from her. It's very important we talk to Ellen, and I don't think we're the only ones looking for her."

"Have you set up a task force?"

"There is no task force," he said.

"On a case this important?"

"Times are tough," he said. He took another deep breath and rolled his head side to side, feeling the stiff muscles, hearing his neck crack. "What's Asia doing?"

"We're making cookies," Caroline said. She dropped her voice to a whisper. "She wanted to know what your favorite kind was. I think I have some competition here."

"Not in a million years, babe," Mace said.

"I'll call you as soon as I hear from Munch," Caroline said. "I'm sure she'll be checking in."

Munch drove through Venice noting the abundance of liquor stores. Every corner seemed to have a building with WINE AND SPIRITS painted on a stuccoed wall. She parked in a lot on Market Street that was a half block up from the boardwalk. Venice Beach had changed little from the time she used to hang out there. Tattooed gang members still walked their pit bulls. Even that crazy tall black guy on roller skates with the guitar was still there, singing Jimi Hendrix songs. He nodded to her and smiled as he rolled past.

She walked until she came to the semicircle of benches they called the pagoda because of the Japanese-style awning sheltering them. The pagoda was a favorite hangout of the local winos, who drank their spirits from brown paper bags. If anyone knew who was around, it would be one of them. She looked for a familiar face.

"Thirteen cents," a red-faced man yelled at Munch. He held out his palm and pointed to the change already there. "I'm just thirteen cents short," he said.

Munch lifted her arms out from her sides as she made an

exaggerated shrug. "Sorry," she said. In good conscience, there was no way she could give them change, not for their poison of choice. Helping an addict/alcoholic was a tricky business. The line was often very thin between helping and enabling.

"Willie around?" she asked.

"Who wants to know?" a large, surly black man asked.

"He's a friend of a friend," she said.

"What friend is that?" the man asked, crossing his arms over his chest.

"White girl named Ellen," Munch said. "You seen her?"

"I ain't even seen you," the man said, and turned his back on her.

Munch realized that the winos weren't going to be any help after all. She headed back up the boardwalk. Across from Small World Books, she spotted a skeletal woman sitting cross-legged on the grass. As Munch drew closer, she realized she knew this woman. It was Pat, looking thinner but much the same as she had when Munch last saw her. Pat had been a junkie so long that there was no telling her real age. One thing about smack, it retarded the aging process. It was rare to find a using junkie with wrinkles or all their teeth for that matter. Personal hygiene tended to fall by the wayside. Munch was glad to see that Pat had hers in today.

Pat had a blanket spread out before her. On it she had a ragtag assortment of costume jewelry, kitchenware, and used paperbacks. Munch kicked a string of wooden beads with her toe. "How much?" she asked.

Pat looked up, her eyes quick and calculating. Munch realized Pat hadn't recognized her. The woman was too busy sizing up a potential mark, taking in Munch's clothes, posture, age, anything that would give her a clue how much to charge for her collection of knickknacked goods.

Munch crouched down so that they were eye level. "Hello, Pat."

Pat regarded her suspiciously, and Munch knew her dope-addled mind was flooded with a new set of decisions. The first being if she would acknowledge her own name. Then something clicked in her tired eyes.

"Munch?"

"What's up?" Munch asked.

"Nothing," Pat said.

Now she's trying to remember how happy she should be to see me, Munch thought. *She's asking herself if she ripped me off the last time we met or if maybe I owe her.*

"Yeah, I see," Munch said, looking at the junk on the blanket. "Nothing's changed at all."

"Where you been?" Pat asked.

Munch spread out her grease-stained fingers. "I've got a job working on cars. I put down. I haven't used in seven years."

"You on methadone? I never see you at the clinic."

"No, I don't do that shit. I don't do anything."

Pat regarded her with fresh suspicion. "What brings you here?"

"I'm trying to find Ellen."

"Who's Ellen?" Pat asked.

"You know, Crazy Ellen. Wears those wigs all the time? Southern accent?"

"Big tits?"

Munch smiled. She hadn't thought to mention those. "Yeah, that's her."

"Why you looking for her? She rip you off or something?"

"She's in danger." Munch studied the gaunt face across from her. "Are you hungry?"

"What?"

"Can I buy you something to eat?"

"If you got a buck or two to spare," Pat said, scratching her arm. "Maybe I could buy some groceries later, you know."

"That's not the offer," Munch said.

"I can't leave my stuff," Pat said.

"I'll bring it to you." Munch walked across the boardwalk to the pizza stand and bought Pat a slice of pepperoni pizza and a Coke.

"So this danger Ellen's in—how bad is it?" Pat asked, biting into the pizza.

"Pretty serious."

"You might want to check with Farmer."

"He still on Brooks?"

"Yeah, he's still there."

Munch started to leave, but then stopped. She crouched once more so that their faces were level. "You know, it doesn't have to be like this. There's another way to go."

"Which way is that?"

"I can get you a bed at the detox in West L.A. We can hit some meetings together."

"And then what?" Pat asked. "I get clean. I get a job. I walk around in panty hose, working myself to death for minimum fucking wage. Then I die. What's the difference? At least this way I get high every once in a while."

Munch stood. "As long as you're still having fun."

"Munch?"

"Yeah?"

"Thanks for the pizza."

"Sure." Munch walked back to her car and paid the ransom to get it back. It only took five minutes to reach Farmer's place. She parked in an adjacent lot, then walked back to pound on his door. She tried to turn the knob but found it locked. Yelling his name also brought no response. She was about to give up when, from around the corner of the building, she heard the familiar roar of a Harley with straight pipes. Farmer appeared seconds later and pulled up on the sidewalk astride his ratty Panhead. She waited as he put down his kickstand. While the motorcycle idled uncertainly, Farmer swung his leg over the Fat Bob tanks and took two steps to his door.

"You want something?" he asked as he unlocked his door and swung it open. The naked fingers protruding from his cut-off gloves were almost as dark as the leather.

"Hey, Farmer," she said.

He raised his cheap black sunglasses and blinked once. "Munch?"

"Yeah. Long time."

He returned to his bike, remounted it, and kicked it into gear. Before he let out the clutch, he asked, "You looking for Ellen?"

Her pulse quickened. "Yeah. I sure am. You know where she is?"

He revved the throttle a few times, causing a loud backfire. When the bike returned to idle he looked at her, and said, "Nope." With that he let out the clutch and drove into his dark apartment.

She stood in his doorway and waited for him to shut the bike off. "But you saw her?"

"Not since yesterday."

"Any idea where she went?"

"To find a phone. You want to shut the door?" he said.

Wouldn't want to let in any fresh air, she thought. "Was she all right?" Munch asked.

Farmer slicked back his hair with one hand and hunched his shoulders. "I don't know. She was crying about something."

"Think she's coming back?"

"Fuck, I don't know. Maybe."

"If you see her again, would you tell her that I came by? There's some serious shit going down. Tell her that guy is looking for her. He already came to my house once."

"So you're saying she should split town?"

"I'd like to talk to her first. Tell her to leave word at my work. I'll keep checking."

CHAPTER 21

"Captain Earl called," Cassiletti told Mace.

"Now what?" Mace asked, hanging his sports coat on the back of his chair. "Oh, shit, I promised him my report."

"I already took care of that," Cassiletti said. "Although I couldn't be too detailed about what went on in Tijuana."

Mace didn't miss the tone. There were times when having a partner was as bad as being married. He put a smile on his face and spoke with a tone he hoped would mollify. "Yeah? Way to go, Tiger."

"Don't get too happy. He wants to see both of us."

"Don't tell me. Code two, right?"

"Well, yeah."

Mace picked up his phone and dialed Earl's extension. Brenda answered, "Captain Earl's office."

"Hi," Mace said. "Does he have time for us now?"

"Let me check," she said. A moment later she came back on the phone. "He said to come right over."

Mace hung up the phone and let out a resigned sigh. He turned to Cassiletti with raised eyebrows and a shrug. "Let's go see whose dick we stepped on this time."

Mace and Cassiletti walked the long hallway to the captain's office. Two command audiences in as many days was not good. The captain didn't hold private face-to-face meetings so he could pass out doughnuts. He only acted this way when he wanted to issue a reprimand or give not-to-be-misinterpreted, not-to-be-ignored orders.

They reached the outer office. Brenda looked up from her paperwork to say, "Go right in." Another bad sign. She didn't even use the intercom.

Earl was standing, gazing out his window when the two detectives entered his office. Cassiletti's report of the most recent activity in the Band-Aid case sat open on Earl's desk. Another man was also in the room, leaning against the low bookshelves, his back to the picture of Captain Earl shaking hands with Mayor Bradley. Mace recognized him immediately. It was Deputy Chief Tumpane.

"You wanted to see us, Captain?" Mace said.

"Close the door," Earl said.

Cassiletti held the knob twisted open as he closed the door, making no noise as he carried out the captain's request. Mace was always surprised at his partner's capacity for gentleness.

"I've read your report," Earl said. "This man, Victor Draicu." Earl pointed to a line on the paper in front of him. "You know he's a Romanian diplomat."

"Yes, sir," Mace said. "He's also been placed at a crime scene." Mace looked at the deputy chief, who in turn was regarding him. "Do you want me to ignore that?"

Captain Earl deferred to his superior with a nod.

Tumpane straightened from his casual pose. "As you may or may not know," he said, "the '84 Olympics has a record number of countries competing. One hundred and four, even with the Eastern Bloc boycott."

"Yes, sir," Mace said, wondering how this bit of politics was going to screw up his investigation.

"Romania's participation is something we're especially pleased about."

"I just want to interview the guy," Mace said.

"And that's all very proper," Tumpane said. "Just not at this time."

"And what time would be convenient for everybody?" Mace asked, feeling his blood pressure rise. The first hours after a crime were crucial. After that memories faded, evidence grew tainted.

"July twentieth."

"You're kidding, right?" Mace asked. "That's six weeks away."

"By then the games will be safely under way. There's a bigger picture to consider. We need you on the antiterrorist squad. It hasn't been reported in the papers, but threats have been made."

"You already have a competent antiterrorist unit," Mace said. "I need to stay after this guy. He's going to strike again. He's already accelerated."

"You have your orders," Tumpane said. "I'm not in the habit of repeating myself."

"Six weeks, my ass," Mace said, cold with rage.

"Detective," Earl warned.

"No," Mace said. "Fuck this." He pulled out the pictures of the murder victims. "She didn't get the bigger picture." He threw the Polaroid of the young Mexican girl on Earl's desk.

"Let me put it another way, Detectives," Earl said, without looking at the image of the dead girl. "You're off this case. I want all your notes on my desk in one hour."

Cassiletti opened the door. Mace gathered his photographs and stormed out. His shoulder grazed Tumpane's chest in passing. Cassiletti pulled the door shut behind him. Mace paused at Brenda's desk and put a finger to his lips. She watched wide-eyed as he pushed the interoffice intercom button. Earl's voice came across loud and clear.

"I told you he wouldn't like it."

Tumpane responded with, "He doesn't have to like it."

"I'm just saying they don't call him the Hound Dog for nothing."

"Well maybe," Tumpane replied, "we'll have to throw him a bone."

Brenda and Cassiletti exchanged worried glances. Mace let go of the intercom button. "Let's get out of here."

As usual, Cassiletti followed.

■ ■ ■

Back at his desk, Mace dumped his notes, sketches, and photographs related to the Band-Aid Killer into a cardboard file box. He withheld copies of the photographs from Tijuana since officially they were not part of the murder book of events. He also withheld copies of the videotapes from the Bank of America and the Gower apartment building's surveillance cameras.

When the phone rang, Cassiletti answered. He listened a moment, then said, "Yeah, here he is."

Mace took the receiver. "Yeah?"

"It's Steve. You want to catch some lunch?"

"Uh, yeah. How about an early one? I have some extra time on my hands."

"Wing Fu's in twenty?"

"That'll work. I'm bringing my partner," Mace said, casting a sidelong glance at Cassiletti. Cassiletti's expression reminded Mace of a schoolyard wallflower who'd been picked for the team.

Wing Fu's Bar-b-que was located on North Broadway in the heart of Chinatown, five minutes away from Parker Center. When Mace had first come to work downtown, he'd been having lunch one day when three boys no older than fifteen came in to shake down the owner. Mace followed the kids into the parking lot, where he and Cassiletti were fully prepared to knock some respect into the punks. To his surprise, it was Wing Fu himself who came to the boys' rescue. Later Wing Fu explained that although he appreciated the effort, the tong's levies were duly factored into his cost of doing business. And besides, where would Mace be when they burned his place down at three in the morning?

The restaurant was nestled between the Best Western

Dragon Gate Inn and the Friendly Hair Salon, with its pictures of Caucasian hairstyles in the window. They parked in front of the Hualuan Book Company. The sign on the door indicated that tax services were also offered there.

Because the day was already promising to be hot, Mace pulled the car under one of the large blossoming coral trees that lined the block. He liked how the tree's persimmon-colored flowers and intricate branch patterns harmonized with the neighborhood architecture. Even the Methodist Church across the street had gambrel rooflines with upswept eaves and was painted lacquer red.

The smell of seafood and steamed bok choy overwhelmed him when he stepped out of the car. Chinese women holding black umbrellas strolled the busy sidewalk. He and Cassiletti gave them right of way, then walked the short half block to Wing Fu's. Colorful tasseled paper lamps hung over the opaque storefront window of the restaurant. A life-size gilded lion, to the left of the front door, raised a paw in welcome.

Steve was already inside, seated at a table for four beside a small Buddhist shrine adorned with fresh fruit and flower offerings.

Mace and Cassiletti took the seats on either side of him. The three men had the place to themselves. After the waiter took their order, Steve showed Mace a blue folder with a State Department logo on it and beneath that the word: SECRET.

"You can keep a secret, right?" Steve asked.

Mace looked at his partner. "We're both good." Cassiletti sat a little straighter in his chair.

"I did some more asking around about your guy, Victor Draicu," Steve said. "Much to my surprise, I received some answers." Steve passed them the folder. "Open it," he said.

"How did you get this?" Mace asked.

"I know a guy who knows a guy," Steve said.

Mace folded back the cover. The first thing he saw was a photograph of a red Folger's coffee can—one pound.

Underneath the photo was an assayer's form. PLUTONIUM-239 had been highlighted. There was also what appeared to be some sort of bill of lading. The words on this document were written in Cyrillic script. The letterhead included an address in Chernobyl, Russia. The shipping destination was an address in Kozlodvy, Bulgaria. On the right-hand sides of the papers, there were columns which listed weights in kilograms.

"What am I looking at?" Mace asked.

"An inventory of weapons-grade plutonium ingots, salvaged from nuclear weapons. Approximately twenty tons of the stuff are produced annually—a sight more than needed for use in weapons. In Eastern Europe, they're experimenting with conversion facilities to reprocess plutonium-239 into reactor-grade plutonium. Four kilograms of this shipment never reached its intended destination. Just to give you an idea of what we're talking about, one kilogram would be enough to create a bomb half the power of the bomb that destroyed Nagasaki."

"All right," Mace said. "You've got my attention." He passed the folder to Cassiletti, who studied it for a moment and then handed it back.

"Have you ever heard of Operation Courtship?" Steve asked.

"No," Mace said.

"It was formed in 1980 after President Reagan was elected. The Carter administration ran the intelligence community down to nothing. Operation Courtship is a combined effort between the FBI and the CIA to bring us back up to snuff."

"How are they doing that?" Mace asked.

"The main focus domestically is to recruit assets: foreign ambassadors, embassy staff. Courtship agents spend months observing. Then psychiatrists review all available information on the prospect for signs of receptivity: how they dress, how well they speak English, how interested they seem in American customs and society."

"Blackmail?" Mace asked.

"No, I think that's generally accepted as nonviable. But vices are always useful: sex, gambling, booze, drugs. Your basic food groups."

"Is this where the two women from the Gower apartment come in?"

"Bingo. But there's more." Steve held up the photograph of the Folger's coffee can. "Three months ago, this container was found in the trash inside the stadium where the Romanian Olympic track-and-field team drills. The coffee can had been filled with sawdust, and in that sawdust traces of weapons-grade plutonium-239 were detected, most probably part of the above missing shipment."

"Not good," Mace said.

"This is where Victor Draicu enters the picture. Which reminds me . . ." Steve said, reaching into his coat pocket for an envelope. "Victor's brother is Bela Draicu, the First Deputy Atomic Energy Minister of Romania." He opened the envelope and removed a photograph, which he handed over to Mace. The picture was of a large room with comfortable-looking sofas, dramatic flower arrangements, and a fireplace large enough to roast a pig in. "American embassy in Romania. The brothers Draicu are standing together by the fireplace."

"Who are these other guys?"

"Americans, other diplomats, probably half of them spooks."

"Can I keep this?" Mace asked.

Steve looked at the picture for a few seconds.

"I'll make a copy and bring you back the original."

"All right," he finally said. "But I can't give you any of this other stuff."

"No problem," Mace said, sliding the photograph into his pocket. "I'm sure I'll remember all the pertinent details. So you think this guy Victor might know where the plutonium is?"

"I think it's only logical to assume that he's here to market his goods. I don't think I need to mention how dangerous the plutonium would be in the wrong hands."

"Which would be anybody's but ours?" Mace asked. Suddenly, another piece of the puzzle fell into place. What the voice on Munch's limo tape had said that didn't make any sense until now: *Pakistan has come in at three hundred and twenty thousand.*

"The feds want to know who's buying and when and where the product will be shipped. Victor Draicu is their best and only ticket in to those proceedings."

"So they need him on the streets," Mace said. *I think we can push Iran to three thirty.*

"They have him under around-the-clock surveillance," Steve said.

"Well, their surveillance ain't worth a shit," Mace said. "I've got seven dead that I know of."

"I don't mean to sound cold," Steve said, "but it's the law of large numbers." He hunched forward, spreading his hands out to either side. His voice dropped. "When you think about it, seven isn't that many. If you exposed this guy now, he would be declared persona non grata and sent back home. Sure, he'd be out of your yard."

"You think that's all I want?" Mace asked, his voice tight.

"Hey, I'm not the enemy here," Steve said, raising his hands in mock surrender.

"What are you?" Mace asked.

"We're off the case," Cassiletti suddenly said. Up until then, he had been silent, observing the exchange between the two men like a fan at a tennis match.

Mace glared at his partner.

"Until July twentieth," Cassiletti added.

The food arrived. They stopped talking to eat. The waiter hovered over them and asked if everything was all right. They nodded with full mouths, and the waiter retreated.

"So they want you to do nothing, huh?" Steve asked.

"That's right," Mace said.

"Who gave the order?"

"Tumpane," Cassiletti said.

"Pogue," Steve muttered. He sipped his tea and took another bite of fried rice. "I don't suppose knowing what's at stake makes this any easier for you."

"You mean easier to do nothing about this asshole? Easier to sit back while he kills again?"

"What choice do you have?"

Cassiletti's head swiveled back to Mace.

Mace pushed back his plate. "I think you've gotten too used to sitting on the sidelines, Steve."

"What the fuck does that mean?" Steve asked.

"Nothing. Maybe you're happy playing messenger boy."

"You're out of line," Steve said. "And you're out of your league."

Mace reached into his sports-coat pocket for the photographs of the murder victims.

"What's this?" Steve asked.

Mace said nothing. He just closed his eyes as if in pain and clasped his hands behind his head. "Um-hmm," he said, almost to himself. He let another moment of silence pass, then let out a long sigh, and opened his eyes. "Tell me again how this law of large numbers works." Cassiletti's expression betrayed nothing, but it was obvious he was waiting.

Steve finally broke the impasse. He dabbed his mouth with his napkin, then threw it down on his empty plate. "All right, so what do you want me to do?"

"What you do best, buddy," Mace said, grinning. "Keep your eyes and ears open, be there if I need backup."

"You're going to owe me big-time," Steve said.

"Just think how well you're going to sleep at night."

Steve pulled out his notepad. "Tell me who and where, and don't worry about how well I sleep."

"I don't think the guy is stupid enough to go back to

Munch's house, but we should probably keep a unit there anyway. The boyfriend lives across the street. We can set up there." Mace handed him the picture of Victor Draicu taken outside the Gower apartment building. "I've had some duplicates made."

"What about the spook?"

"I'm working on that."

When the check arrived, Steve picked it up.

"You sure?" Mace asked.

"Yeah," Steve said. "I'll just put it on my expense account."

"C'mon, Tiger," Mace told Cassiletti. "Let's hit it."

"Where are we going?" Cassiletti asked when they got to the car.

"El Segundo."

"Where the sewer meets the sea?"

"We're going to go see a guy I know," Mace said. "He works at the Aerospace Corporation, and what he can do with a computer and a videotape will flat blow your mind."

Ellen stared at the mirror above the bed. After Tommy had brought her to the motel she'd unpacked, taken a bath, and fallen into a deep, dreamless sleep. Now it was morning. Time to get to work.

She dug out her book and flipped through the names. Her finger stopped on a guy she called John Z. He was also Mr. Reliable. John was a quiet black guy. He always paid promptly, came in five minutes, and never talked much—just a sweet, shy smile when he finished. Perfect.

She dialed his number.

"Hello," he said.

"Is this John?" she asked.

"Yes, it is."

"This is Ellen, been a while."

"Yeah, it sure has. How are you?"

"I was wondering if you'd like to get together."

"Um, yeah. When?"

"Well, how about now?" she asked.

"Yeah, all right," he said. "Where are you?"

She named the motel. "Room Three."

"I'll be there in an hour," he said.

"Great," she said, wondering why she didn't feel more pleased at the prospect of making some easy money. She took a long time applying her makeup, washing it off and reapplying it three times before she gave up. *Must be these damn lights,* she thought. *They're too goddamn harsh.* When John knocked on the door at eleven, she about jumped out of her skin. That's when she realized she'd been hoping he wouldn't show.

"Showtime," she told herself in the mirror. "Just get it over with." She answered the door and let him in.

"Hi," he said, his head tilted downward, raising his eyes just enough to meet hers. There was that shy, almost reluctant smile of his. She took his hand, led him to the bed, and started to undo his belt.

"Oh, here, wait a minute," he said, blushing and backing up. He reached in his back pocket, pulled out his wallet, and took out two twenties. She accepted the money and laid it on the nightstand.

"I know you like to get paid first," he said.

"Yeah, thanks," she said, unbuttoning her blouse. She hoped he didn't notice how she avoided touching his skin as she took the bills. He wasn't unpleasant, far from it. He always showered first, never tried to get her to kiss him. No, John understood all the rules and abided by them faithfully. It wasn't him. It was her.

He slid off his slacks and folded them over the back of a chair.

It's the goddamn sobriety, she realized. Munch and all her A.A., Higher Power, there's-another-way-to-go bullshit had totally infected her system and ruined her for the life. She didn't enjoy the dope. Drinking was a disaster, and now turning a simple trick wasn't going to fly either. *Jesus, what a predicament.*

She pulled her blouse shut, reached behind her, and grabbed the money.

"Here," she said, holding it out to John. She saw that he already had a hard-on, bless his heart.

"What's wrong?" he asked.

"I'm sorry," she said. "I just can't. I'm truly sorry."

John pressed the money back to her. "That's okay," he said. "Keep it. It was good just to see you again."

She felt slow hot tears roll down her cheeks. Wasn't he just the nicest man? She was tempted to do him anyway, but why spoil the moment?

"Thanks," she said as he pulled his clothes back on. "I'll pay you back one day."

"Don't worry about it." Before he walked out the door he paused and turned around. "Good luck," he said.

She watched him pull away in his brown 280Z and, for the first time ever, wondered what his life was beyond their encounters. *That's the problem,* she realized. *Everybody's becoming real people around me.*

After she shut the door, she picked up the phone book and looked up Alcoholics Anonymous. She dialed the number and told the woman who answered that she needed a meeting.

"Where are you?" the woman asked.

"Venice."

"There's an Alano Clubhouse on Centinela and Washington. They have a meeting at noon. You need someone to come pick you up?"

"You'd do that?" Ellen asked.

"Sure. Give me your address."

"The Rose Motel on Lincoln Boulevard."

"Oh, yeah," the woman said, chuckling. "I know right where that is."

"Room Three," Ellen said.

"The corner unit?" the woman asked.

"My," Ellen said, "you do know your way around."

"I paid my dues. Listen, the only way this is going to work is if you don't drink or use until they get there."

"Don't worry," Ellen said. "I'm all through with that."

"Right," the woman said. "I've heard that before, too."

Ellen hung up the phone thinking she'd just show her what she was capable of once she set her mind to something. Then she laughed. Did that reverse psychology shit work with most people?

CHAPTER 22

Traffic control reported an accident on the 405 near the airport, so Mace and Cassiletti drove to El Segundo by an alternate route that took them in the back way through Playa Del Rey.

El Segundo—also referred to as El Stinko—was a coastal community with relatively low housing costs. The reason for the exceptional values was the town's proximity to the Hyperion Treatment Plant on the north and the Chevron refinery directly south. In fact, the town was named for the refinery. Originally it was La Segunda, meaning "the Second" because it was Standard Oil's second refinery in California. Over time, the name switched to the male gender: El Segundo. Mace had learned all this from a talkative real-estate agent he and Caroline had spent a long weekend with back in January. The idea had been to buy a home big enough for all of them. Caroline, himself, his dad, and the dogs.

At the top of Pershing, the domed roof of Hyperion Treatment Plant could be seen. The factory lay on the water's edge to the north, separating solids from outgoing sewage. The foul cesspool smell assaulted them as they turned on Imperial Highway and headed east.

"Jeez," Cassiletti said, wrinkling his nose. "Can you imagine working with that all day?"

"Someone's got to do it," Mace said.

The detectives' destination was the massive Aerospace Corporation complex at the edge of town. Mace turned down Main Street, driving past the high school and city hall. Banners celebrating the Olympics were strung across the street. At El Segundo Boulevard he turned left. The Erector set structure of the Chevron refinery loomed in the background. Odious gray smoke poured from the stacks of derrick-encased cokers, making their own foul contribution to the city's bouquet of methane, hydrogen sulfates, and petroleum by-products. The refinery also provided fifteen hundred jobs, built parks, maintained the civic center, and made generous donations to the local schools.

Actually, Mace knew that despite the occasional assault on the olfactory senses, El Segundo was a decent place to live, to raise a family. He'd learned that from the city's chief of police, who owned one of the two-story Spanish-style homes in town. In fact, the majority of the department chose to live nearby. That sold him more than the agent with the bright green blazer and nonstop pitch. The woman had given even Caroline a headache. Then he'd picked a stupid argument about nothing important, and the house hunt had been called off. He'd give anything to recall half the hurtful words he'd thrown at her. She knew Digger hurt him, but he should have been man enough to keep his feelings to himself. People died. No one knew that better than he.

"So what does this guy do?" Cassiletti asked while they waited for the light to change.

"I'll have him give you a demonstration," Mace said.

They turned down Douglas and stopped at Gatehouse C. A uniformed guard emerged from the booth. "Can I help you, sirs?" he asked.

Mace handed over his badge and identification. "We're here to see Dr. Rudy Roberts. Building 107."

"Just a minute, sir." The guard returned to his booth with Mace's ID. They watched him make a call, nod, then reemerge with a clipboard. The guard returned Mace's badge and walked to the rear of the detective's unmarked car, where he wrote down the license plate number. Then he consulted his watch and made yet another notation.

"Pretty intense security," Cassiletti said.

Mace smiled. "Just wait."

The guard lifted the barrier gate. Mace pulled into the parking lot, finding a space marked VISITOR. Before leaving the car, he folded his police ID over his front pocket so that the badge was clearly visible. Cassiletti followed suit.

Mace opened the trunk and retrieved three boxes of videotapes, which he transferred into a brown-paper lunch sack. They walked over to the building marked 107. The door was locked. Mace rang the buzzer. A tall, good-looking man wearing a suit came to the foyer. When he saw Mace, he smiled and opened the door for them.

"Hey, Dr. Rudy," Mace said, extending his hand. "Thanks for seeing us. This is my partner, Tony Cassiletti."

"Detective," the man said, sizing Cassiletti up with friendly, but intense blue eyes.

"Call him Tiger." Mace clapped the big man on the back. "This here is Dr. Rudy Roberts. The Department of Justice's answer to that guy in the James Bond movies who makes all the gadgets for 007."

"Q?" Cassiletti said.

"Please," Roberts said, "I'm basically an engineer."

"Yeah," Mace said, "that's right. Like George Foreman is basically a boxer."

"What do you do here?" Cassiletti asked.

Roberts hesitated for a moment before answering. "We do support research for various federal agencies." He turned to Mace. "So, you have some videotapes you want me to look at?"

Mace handed over the brown-paper sack. Roberts pulled out the three videotape boxes. "Are these the originals?" he asked.

"No," Mace said. "But these haven't been played since I made the copies."

"All right," Roberts said. "We'll see what we can do. What are you looking for?"

"The first two videos are from surveillance cameras mounted on fifteen-foot poles at the entrance of an apartment building. I've got some people in the back of a limo that I want to identify."

"And the other?" Roberts asked, seemingly weighing the third videotape in his hand.

"Pretty poor quality on that one, I'm afraid," Mace said. "It's from a Bank of America roof camera. It was pointed down a dark alley behind the apartment building where some homicides occurred. The other videos are from that building's security cameras."

"Time-lapse?" Roberts asked.

"Yeah, but then it switched to real-time when the gate's keypad was operated. The cameras were positioned at either side of the entrance driveway."

"Okay, good. What about the bank video?"

"Time-lapse and like I said, the alley was dark. You can just make out a figure hopping the back wall. According to the time line of events, it was after the homicide. Anything you can give me on that guy would be great."

"We'll see what we can do," Roberts said. He handed each of the detectives plastic clip-on visitor badges. "Let's go to the lab. I'll load these on to the computer and we'll see if we can find you any valuable information."

They followed Roberts out of Building 107 and deeper into the complex. The concrete paths were all clean and the landscaping well maintained. None of the buildings they passed had any identification on it other than a numerical designation.

"It's pretty amazing what a computer can do with a blurry picture," Mace told Cassiletti. "Just like you see in the spy movies. All that CIA stuff."

Roberts slowed his pace and turned to face the two detectives. "We taught them everything they know," he said.

Mace winked at Cassiletti.

"Rudy," he said. "You ever hear about an operation called Southern Air Transport?"

Again, the engineer's pace faltered, but this time he didn't turn around. "I can neither confirm nor deny knowledge of that operation," he said.

"So it's like that," Mace said.

"Like I said," Roberts repeated, "we do support research for various federal entities." They were crossing an immaculate courtyard. Concrete benches sat between planters full of maple and oak trees.

Mace directed Cassiletti's attention to a three-story building surrounded by an electric fence. Then he nodded to the louvered air vents beneath the benches. "That's actually a five-story building," he whispered.

Cassiletti nodded, his eyes wide.

A Chevy Suburban pulled in front of the building. Two beefy men emerged and studied their surroundings with somber faces. Mace would have pointed out the gun turrets in the Suburban, but the men were staring at him and Cassiletti.

"How's it going?" Mace said.

"Just great," the man who had been driving answered. His tone was courteous, but his expression was grim. They faced off for another few seconds. *God,* Mace wondered, *do these guys ever blink?*

When they were out of earshot, Cassiletti asked, "Spooks?"

"I'd say so," Mace answered dryly.

They arrived at another group of buildings. An armed guard checked their badges, then opened the door for them. The hallway they entered was something out of a futuristic novel. Steel casing, eight inches wide and two inches deep ran down the center of the ceiling. Fuse-box-looking steel boxes were attached at various junctions.

"What's all this?" Cassiletti asked.

"Cable," Roberts said.

"And these?" Cassiletti asked, pointing to an overhead shower nozzle.

"In case of chemical spill," Roberts said. "We also have eye-wash stations, and self-contained breathing apparatus."

Mace stared through the thick glass window at the laboratory on his right. Technicians were loading petri dishes into some sort of oven. They wore protective gear over their eyes, face masks, and heavy gloves. He didn't want to know. He was just grateful for the airlock separating them.

Roberts turned into a room full of computer equipment, several large television monitors, and stacked audio equipment. He stuck the Gower apartment building video into a VCR and turned on his computer. "This won't take very long," he said. "First I need to load the tapes into my computer system. Once they're there I can play around with the images."

"Like a TV, right?" Cassiletti asked. "You adjust the tint and contrast."

"A little more than that," Roberts said, his eyes brighter now that he was back in his environment of choice. "You know what a pixel is?"

"Yeah, it's like a little dot that's part of a picture."

"Yes. A typical broadcast television picture has six hundred and forty by four hundred and eighty pixels. With videotape surveillance video, you have even less resolution. However, we have ways to improve on that. Every pixel stores information. When you have a series of pictures of the same object—a vehicle, for instance, driving down the road—each frame has its own pixels, and each of those pixels has slightly different information. By superimposing the pixels of the same vehicle from a series of frames, we come up with a much more detailed image."

"You see?" Mace asked, nudging his partner.

The beginning of the surveillance video appeared on Roberts's screen. He rolled his mouse on its pad and the video played.

"Where do you want me to start?"

Mace consulted his notes. "Eleven twenty-nine."

Roberts split the image on his screen and advanced both videos to the specified time. The picture of the limo appeared.

"It's pretty murky," he said. "I don't know how much I can do with this." They watched and listened as he demonstrated how he could eliminate shadows, suppress glints, adjust contrasts and tones, and eliminate background. The face in the limo refused to materialize. After thirty minutes, he had to admit defeat.

"All right," he said. "Let's try the bank tape." He repeated his earlier procedure, and soon the footage of the dark alley appeared on the screen.

"There," Mace said, pointing. A dark figure had appeared at the top of the apartment complex's cinder-block rear wall. The next frame showed the figure on the ground.

"Is that your guy?" Roberts asked, his fingers busy on his controls.

"Yeah, pretty poor image."

"There's a few more things we can try here. The bank uses infrared cameras on their rooftop jobs. I've created a few image-contrasting algorithms that will bring out thermal characteristics not visible to the naked eye."

"In English?" Mace said.

"The CCD array collects in the infrared spectrum . . ." Roberts paused, looked from one detective to the other, and said, "Uh, heat registers as a color."

"How does that help us?" Mace asked.

"Let's find out." Roberts worked his magic and soon the same scene had color. The face and hands of the figure took on a reddish hue. "We're reading skin temperature. This guy must have been pretty worked up." He used his pointer on the screen to advance the time-lapse photos.

"What are we looking at now?" Mace asked.

"The guy moved his hand to his mouth," Roberts said, studying the screen intently. "Isn't your suspect bald?"

"Yeah, you saw his picture in the other tape."

"What we're looking at here," Roberts said, pointing to the red man's head, "is not a bald head, or it would be the same color as the face. Hair acts as insulation."

"Maybe he's got a hat on," Cassiletti said.

"I don't think so," Roberts said. "See the scalp line? The ears? No, this is hair."

"We've got another suspect—possible accomplice," Mace said. "He might be a CIA operative."

"Hmm," Roberts said, rolling his mouse again. "Now what would a mostly hollow head look like?"

Raleigh used a pay phone to call in. That day's code was a beep and screech that sounded like a fax line. Raleigh pressed 8, 5, 6, then the star key. A woman's voice came on asking what extension he wanted.

"Two bravo echo six," Raleigh replied.

"Confirmed," she said. "Please hold."

Seconds later another voice took over—this time a man's. "We've been unable to locate the woman," he said. "Her full name is Ellen Summers. Hard copy to follow. The LAPD is also looking for her."

Raleigh's stomach muscles contracted painfully. She could blow everything. "What else have they got?" He popped an Altoid in his mouth and followed that with an amphetamine.

"The lead detective has been ordered to stand down from his investigation. His reports will be in the packet. Frankly, his case is very damaging. He knows about the business in Mexico. He recovered pieces of medical tape off of a murder victim that they've conclusively linked to the Band-Aid Killer."

"Son of a bitch," Raleigh said.

"You've been sloppy. This can't go on."

"I'll take care of it," Raleigh said.

"We've already confiscated the physical evidence," the man said. "But you better hope we find that witness before the cops do."

"Any leads?"

"She's back in town. It's all in the reports."

"I'll pick them up now," Raleigh said.

"What about Gameboy?"

"He's going to bring me a sample. I told him to make it happen, and it will. You've got my personal guarantee on that."

"His compensation requests have been approved."

"I'll pass that on." Raleigh looked at his own dilapidated Vega and felt a fresh surge of resentment. Where was the justice in this world?

The plan was that when the deal finally went down, Victor would be keeping the monies paid for the plutonium. Which was only fair, the Romanian had reasoned, and no skin off of America's vast back. Victor's participation in the international sting operation ensured that the United States government would be able to confiscate the radioactive contraband, thereby preventing it from falling into the hands of terrorists or fanatics.

Raleigh knew Victor's motives were far from altruistic. After slipping Victor an opiate/amphetamine cocktail back in December, the Romanian had let slip all the other extenuating circumstances that would make his return to his homeland once the Olympics had concluded a most unpleasant one.

But that wasn't going to happen. The United States was going to provide him with a new identity and history, and he would quietly slip away under the cover of his new life.

After hanging up, Raleigh let his head rest on the Plexiglas half wall of the pay phone. What happened to the good old days, when a mission involved a simple in and out? Target, assignment, execution. Bing, bang, boom. Now you had to play cutesy with every mom-and-pop organization, fucking keystone cops. Fucking Democrats—that's when it started. He should have quit then. Seen the writing on the wall when that goddamn peanut farmer took the helm. Jimmy Carter and his cutbacks sent the intelligence community back to the Stone Age. Two and a half years of Reagan was only just starting to repair the damage. A leader needed to be strong, like Bismarck. Power is not achieved with speeches. It is bought with "Blood and Iron" warfare and military. Great leaders take whatever action is necessary whether or not it might be considered legal or ethical by the day's standards.

And now the supreme irony. Wasn't it always a woman who ultimately fucked up everything? Ellen, fucking Ellen. He tightened his fist into a ball. She was like a bad memory, popping up at the worst possible moments. There was only one thing for it—he would have to find her himself before some hotshot prosecutor got hold of her and turned the whole world inside out.

Raleigh climbed back into his Vega and headed for the dead drop. He cruised an underpass in Westwood, seeing the chalk mark recently placed there. This informed him that his documents would be found inside the hollow trunk of a tree in the VA cemetery. Stone crypts sheltered his movements as he retrieved the packet.

He waited until he was miles away before he unwrapped the plastic cover and devoured the contents.

First, there were the police reports. Detective Tony Cassiletti's neat print carefully cataloged all the known information relating to the case of the Band-Aid Killer. Raleigh skimmed through the affidavits of witnesses—or rather nonwitnesses. People who had been in the Westwood apartment building at the time of the homicides, yet had reported not noticing anything amiss until the police and coroner arrived. He lingered over the photographs of the dead woman.

The report on the Hollywood slaying had more details. The weapon had been tentatively identified and toxicology reports showed that the women had been drugged—it was assumed unwillingly. In addition to the crime-scene photographs of the victims and the apartment, there were also three videotapes recovered from surveillance cameras. None of this came as any surprise to Raleigh. He studied the photographs derived from the video footage. The resolution was poor, but that fool Victor was easily recognizable. He even smiled into the camera. Amateur.

The connection between Mace St. John and Munch Mancini surfaced several times. The two of them had gone to Mexico together, ostensibly to retrieve the limousine. Obviously there was some personal connection going on there. Which meant that he might not so easily abandon his investigation.

St. John had also visited the Tijuana morgue. He had absolutely no legal business there, not that that would help anybody now. Forensics on the tape recovered from the body of a teenage Mexican girl backed up St. John's theory that he'd found yet another victim of the Band-Aid Killer. He'd probably already made the connection between the dead girl and her family. This cop was proving quite troublesome.

Raleigh also read with interest the police records of Miranda "Munch" Mancini and Ellen Summers. The report on Ellen was believable. He'd seen the bitch in action. Munch's priors surprised him. Went to show you how well some people could blend in. The FBI file on her would come in especially useful. The people in disinformation would shred their credibility, but hopefully the situation would be contained without its coming to that. The country didn't need another "conspiracy theory" debacle.

Raleigh stifled an exclamation of surprise when he read about the semen Detective Cassiletti had discovered at the Mancini residence. It was just as his mother always said, idle hands were the devil's plaything.

He checked his watch. Victor was meeting him at the Olympic Village at UCLA. Raleigh was tired of messing around with this guy. It was time to make America safe.

CHAPTER 23

The couple who came to pick Ellen up for the meeting drove a sixties-vintage Dodge Dart. A rainbow-hued bumper sticker pasted to the back window read HIGHER POWERED. The man and woman were much like the car, not much to look at but clean, Ellen thought as she opened the door to greet them.

The woman stuck out her hand, and said, "Hi, I'm Diane, and this is Danny."

Isn't that just too cute? Ellen thought. *It's a wonder they don't have matching shirts.* She shook the woman's hand while smiling at the man. "I'm Ellen."

"So, Ellen," Diane said, casting glances at Danny as if needing his approval for every word, "what prompted you to make the call?"

"Call?"

"To Central Office."

"Well," Ellen said, wondering if this were this woman's first time out the chute, "everything was going so great I just had a thought that I'd check y'all out. Just for fun."

Diane shot a perplexed look at Danny, who at least had the what-with-all to smile. "You ever been to a meeting before?" he asked.

"Yeah," Ellen said. "They had groups of you guys come see us up at CIW." In fact, it was at that meeting that she'd seen Munch again after five years of not hearing a peep. She'd even wondered if that little pistol had gone and gotten herself killed. But then there she was, sitting up on that panel of reformed drug addicts and telling her story. If Ellen had not seen and heard firsthand, she wouldn't have believed it. Munch on the straight and narrow. Who would have dreamed? She was so proud of her she almost cried on the spot.

"CIW?" Diane asked.

"California Institution for Women at Frontera," Ellen said.

"Oh."

"You never heard of it?" Ellen asked. *Jesus, where has this one been?*

"No," Diane answered, her mouth losing that happy-to-have-you-with-us smile. "I'm fortunate that my disease never progressed that far." Danny-boy put a hand on her shoulder. She stopped talking.

"Shall we go?" he asked. He opened the car door for Ellen. She took a deep breath before stepping into the backseat, wondering at her need for courage just then. She had dressed for the occasion in jeans, sandals with two-inch heels, and a white serving-wench-style shirt with billowing sleeves and a ruffled front that revealed a generous peek of cleavage. She went with the brunette wig and dark red lipstick, topping the outfit off with silver loop earrings.

Danny-boy wore jeans and a T-shirt, but then ruined everything with sandals. Guys who wore sandals gave her the creeps. Diane had on fish-tank-algae green corduroys, a polyester shirt buttoned all the way to the top, and a crocheted vest.

Lord, Ellen thought, *if that's what it takes to get sober, I might have to give this whole business a good second think.*

"So how long y'all been going to these meetings?" she asked.

"I have sixteen months," Diane said proudly, "and Danny is coming up on three years."

"Three, huh?" Ellen said. "I've got a friend with seven years."

"Who's that?" Diane asked.

"Isn't this supposed to be an anonymous program?" Ellen asked.

"Not to each other," Diane said.

"Well, still," Ellen said.

"Is he married?" Danny asked.

"Oh, you," Ellen said, playfully pushing the back of Danny's head with her hand and letting her fingertips linger at the back of his neck. She was gratified to see the skin there flush red. "It's not like that at all. What you must think."

Diane looked like her own neck was giving her problems. Ellen gave Danny a little pat on the shoulder, then settled back into her seat.

Danny rolled down his window a few inches, Ellen noted with satisfaction. *Getting a little warm, is he?* "So," she said, catching Diane's eye in the rearview mirror, "is all this A.A. stuff worth the trouble?"

"Our worst day sober is better than our best day using," Diane said.

Where had this one partied? Ellen wondered, starting to feel a little sorry for the broad. "Is that right?" she asked.

Diane nodded like one of those spring-necked dogs that you put in the back window of your car. "All you have to worry about is today," she said, and looked over at Danny, who responded by patting her hand.

Pathetic, Ellen thought. *This girl really needs my help.*

"So, Diane," Ellen asked, "what do you do when you really want to cut loose?"

Diane licked her lips and cast a nervous glance at Danny. "I'm very content," she said.

"That's not what I asked you," Ellen said.

"What about you, Ellen?" Danny asked. "What have you done for yourself lately?"

Ellen knew a trick question when she heard one. "Why, I called y'all. Isn't that the first step?"

They arrived at the clubhouse. Diane drove the Dodge down a narrow driveway and parked in the rear lot. Ellen's escorts held hands all the way inside. Chairs were arranged around a long cafeteria-style table. Ellen excused herself to use the bathroom. Five minutes later someone knocked on the door. The lights flicked on and off.

"Meeting's starting," a voice yelled in to her.

"I'll be there directly," she said. She splashed cold water on her face and went out to join them.

The room had filled up some. There were maybe twelve people seated around the table. *Wasn't that the number at the Last Supper?* she wondered. Diane gave her hand a little squeeze as she sat down.

"This is going to be a little different than the meeting you went to before," Diane said. "Instead of speakers on a panel, this will be a participation meeting. All you have to do is listen."

"And what if I want to say something?" Ellen asked. *Isn't that what they all do at these meetings? Spill their guts.*

"You can't share at the meeting unless you have twenty-four hours of consecutive sobriety."

Ellen mentally calculated. She'd gotten loaded about mid-day yesterday. Well, maybe a teensy bit later, but considering the lack of effect she was perfectly justified in docking a few hours. "I qualify," she said.

Diane looked at her uncertainly. "You do?"

Ellen started to get pissed off. If they were going to question her integrity first off . . .

The guy sitting at the head of the table read a bunch of stuff, then he called on someone else to read the Twelve Steps and some other stuff. They'd done all that in the jailhouse meetings, too, so she tuned out, waited for them to get it over with. Finally, the meeting got under way. Some guy told a story about trying to install his own toilet over the weekend and how everything went wrong. "Self will run riot," he said. Everybody laughed. Ellen didn't see what that had to do with anything. When he finished, she raised her hand. The leader looked at her with that same uncertain expression on his face, then called on Diane. Ellen had trained herself early in life not to react, to stay unaffected by others' power trips and efforts to control. If you let people's disapproval get to you, you'd never have any fun at all.

Diane told some sad-sack tale about how her mother didn't understand her and her father ignored her and she was learning to set boundaries. Ellen tapped her foot impatiently. Boy, could she teach these people a thing or two. Who gave a shit what her mother did or didn't understand? Today was what was important. That was another thing. Diane could do a whole lot better than that Danny fellow, sitting there so smug with his personalized ceramic mug. Mr. No Socks, Mr. Sandals. What kind of a real man wears sandals anyway? That's what she should be noticing—not the way his eyes walked all over Ellen. Hell, she should be glad he was red-blooded enough for that. That was the real compliment. If he was some low-testosterone wimp who never looked at another woman, that said nothing. But if he kept coming back to her after his eye wandered. Well, that was something else again. What that girl needed was some confidence. A makeover. Like the one Ellen did for that little gal in Mexico. Giovanna. In fact that little interlude with Giovanna was one of the few things Ellen did remember of her activities before she passed out. She laughed to herself, shaking her head. Munch was right. What good was partying if you couldn't remember any of it?

"Did you want to share?" the leader asked her, breaking her reverie.

"Do what now?" Ellen asked.

"Didn't you have your hand up?"

"Oh, you mean talk. Sure. My name's Ellen," she said, copying how the others had begun.

"What are you?" the leader asked.

"I'm a Scorpio," she said. To her consternation, everybody laughed.

"No," the leader said, putting on a tone of voice as if he were speaking to some idiot child. "Identify your disease."

"Say you're an alcoholic and a drug addict," Diane said sotto voce.

"I'm an alcoholic and a drug addict," Ellen said.

"HI, ELLEN," the people around the table responded.

Diane beamed. "Now, don't you feel better?" she asked.

"Oh, yeah," Ellen said. "I'm just pounds lighter."

Diane's face fought a smile. Ellen winked at her. "I think y'all are doing a wonderful thing for yourselves here."

"Is that all?" the leader asked.

"Yeah," she said. "I'm done." She leaned over to Diane, and whispered, "You got some time after the meeting?"

"Sure."

Munch drove around Venice. Up and down Main and Pacific. She checked out the foot traffic on Windward, cruised the narrow alleys of the canal streets. Ellen was nowhere. She stopped at a bank of pay phones bolted to the wall of a liquor store on South Venice Boulevard and Main Street.

A Monte Carlo with tinted windows and wide, low-profile tires on chrome rims cruised past. The bass of its radio vibrated the storefront window in front of her. The driver, a young Hispanic kid with a bandanna tied over his head pirate fashion, sat slumped behind the wheel, his eyes just level with the dashboard.

Munch called Caroline.

"How's Asia?" she asked after they exchanged greetings.

"We made cookies."

"Chocolate chip?" Munch asked. A car cruised by slowly, the man leaning over in his seat to get a look at Munch.

"Are you working?" his hopeful expression asked. She turned her back on him.

"She ate more dough than we baked," Caroline said.

"That's my kid," Munch said.

"What are your plans now?" Caroline asked.

"I thought I'd pick us up some lunch at McDonald's."

"Mace called. He said you can pick up your limo anytime."

"Great."

"He wants you to call him right away."

"Does he have any other news?"

"Something to do with Ellen, I think. Did you find her?"

"Not yet. She's around though. People have seen her."

"Do you have Mace's number?"

"No, hang on a minute." Munch reached for her shirt pocket for a pen, then remembered she wasn't in uniform. She rummaged in her purse and came up with a crayon and a napkin. "Go ahead."

Caroline read off two numbers, his office and his beeper. Munch thanked her and hung up. She got an answering machine at Parker Center and didn't leave a message. She decided to wait and call the beeper number after she got back to the house. She called her work. Lou had no messages for her and sounded harried. She checked her answering machine at home, but there had been no activity there since last night. The last number she called was Derek. He was home.

"What was going on at your house last night?" he asked. "I saw all the cops."

"Did you see Ellen?"

"No, they already asked me."

"Who asked you?"

"The cops," he said.

"You mean last night?"

"Last night, this morning. What did she do?"

"It's not what she did," Munch said. "More like what she saw."

"A murder?"

"That's what it's looking like. Keep an eye out for her."

"What should I do if I see her?" he asked.

"Tell her to lie low until the cops find the killer."

"Do they know who he is?" Derek asked.

"I think it's a short list," Munch said. "You'd be better off staying clear of my house for the next couple of days, until this thing plays out. Some creep broke into my house and jerked off on Asia's underwear."

"When was this?"

"Sometime last night. Ellen came by, too, and picked up her shit. You didn't see anything?"

"No. Sorry. Christ, what next?"

"Hopefully they'll catch this guy before he kills again."

"Are you in danger?" he asked.

"No, I'm fine."

"Where are you now? I tried you at work."

"I took the day off."

"I don't blame you," he said. "Where did you stay last night?"

"Derek."

"I'm just concerned," he said.

Not jealous. Derek didn't expend that kind of energy. Still, it was nice he cared enough to ask, no matter what his reasons. "You know that cop?" she said. "Mace St. John? He put us up at his dad's old house in Venice."

"Well, that's good. Kinda fucked up to not be able to go to your own house."

"Yeah, it is," she said.

"If you do find Ellen or anything else happens, will you call me?"

Maybe she didn't give Derek enough credit sometimes. "I'll do that."

Derek hung up the phone.

The man sitting next to him nodded his approval. "You did great."

"I don't want her to get hurt," Derek said.

"Nobody does," the man assured him. "Your cooperation will ensure that."

CHAPTER 24

After the A.A. meeting, Ellen went with Diane to drop Danny-boy off at his apartment. She promised to pick him up at eight for the evening meeting.

"Will I see you then?" he asked Ellen.

"I'm counting on it, sugar," Ellen said, not giving a hint of the surprise she had in mind for him. Wipe that smug look right off his face.

"So you two don't live together?" Ellen asked, as they drove away.

"No, he's got two roommates, and my apartment is very small."

"Why doesn't he drive?"

"He doesn't have a car."

"Oh, please," Ellen said, more exasperated than ever. "No wheels even? What do you see in him?"

"He's very spiritual."

"That may be so, but I wouldn't date Gandhi either."

Diane fought off another smile, but she was weakening. They pulled up to the motel.

"You got a minute?" Ellen asked.

"Sure," Diane said, putting the Dodge into park and shutting off the engine. "You feel like talking now?"

"Let me just ask you one question," Ellen said. "Have you ever thought about thinning those eyebrows?"

"My eyebrows?" Diane asked, her hand reaching up to touch them.

"Yeah, it would really bring out your eyes. I could show you how."

"I never learned about that stuff," Diane said, her eyes filling with tears. "My mother—"

"Yeah, yeah. I know," Ellen said, cutting her off. "You gotta let that shit go."

They both got out of the car. Ellen took out her motel key and opened the door.

"From the mouths of babes," Diane said.

"What are you talking about?" Ellen asked.

"They always say you can learn so much from newcomers."

"Yeah," Ellen said, ushering Diane into her room. "I'm sure this is exactly what they meant by that. Sit down over here." Ellen turned a chair so that it faced away from the mirror over the vanity table. After Diane sat, Ellen opened her large makeup case and found her tweezers. "This is gonna sting a mite, but it's worth it."

She switched on the radio and thought back to that drunken night in the bar. The alcohol was hitting her hard, so she had gone into the bathroom to make herself throw up. That's when she'd met Giovanna. Boy did that little gal seem young, Ellen had thought through her drunken haze. Too young to be selling blow jobs for twelve dollars. She struck up a conversation and learned that Giovanna was saving her money to go to America. "First off," Ellen told her, "you have got to raise your prices."

"Almost done?" Diane asked, wincing.

"I'm just getting started," Ellen said. "You just hold on." She rummaged through her makeup arsenal, finding shadow and blush, liner and lipstick. She had tried to do the same for Giovanna, only she'd been drunk, with only minimal supplies. So she improvised, even taking the wig off her own head and leaving herself with just a scrawny topknot. Sometimes when she was on a roll she couldn't stop herself. Maybe that was that self-will-run-riot thing the guy with the toilet had been talking about. One improvement she had been able to make was to wipe off the pale white lip gloss Giovanna had on. "That shade went out with the sixties," Ellen told her. The girl's own natural color was ten times better.

The song "Still Crazy after All These Years" came on the radio. Ellen turned up the volume. She had always considered the tune her personal theme song. She and Diane sang along. Diane turned out to have a decent voice and knew all the words.

"Well, you're just full of surprises, aren't you?" Ellen said.

Diane tried to turn around and see herself in the mirror.

"Not yet," Ellen said. She lifted the blond wig from its stand, placed it over Diane's own lank hair, and pinned it into place. Using a styling pick, she fluffed the curls over Diane's forehead. The mouse was becoming a tiger.

"We've gotta do something about those clothes," she said. "Lose the vest, and unbutton your blouse—the top three buttons anyway. Show some wares, girl. You don't get to keep them forever."

Diane blushed but did as she was told.

"What size waist do you have?" Ellen asked.

"I usually wear thirty-two-inch jeans," Diane said.

Ellen dug in her drawer until she came up with a pair of thirty-inch Levi's. "Try these."

She watched Diane shyly pull down her fish-tank-shit green cords. Her shirttails covered her underpants, but Ellen didn't have to see them to know they'd be cotton and not bikini style. As Diane dressed, she balanced her head like she had a basket on it.

"Go ahead and move," Ellen said. "It won't fall off. I put enough pins in that thing to withstand a hurricane."

"Can I look now?" Diane asked.

"Just about." Ellen dug a pair of high-heeled sandals out of her suitcase and took the pair of big hoop earrings out of her own ears. "Put these on."

Diane did, and finally Ellen allowed her to turn and see the results of her labor. Diane made a funny yelping noise that was halfway between a choke and a scream. Giovanna had also been amazed at her transformation. It had been uncanny really. Giovanna had somehow taken on Ellen's looks as a teenager. It was too weird, seeing herself again with so many less miles on her. To thank her, Giovanna had pulled out a pouch of pills and offered them to Ellen. Ellen had sorted through the pharmaceuticals, picking out her favorites. Then she came to some white capsules.

"Is this what I think it is?" she'd asked.

"You put it in the drink," Giovanna had said, miming the action. "And night-night sailor boy."

"Give me a couple of those, too," Ellen had said. And hadn't that turned out to be a fortunate choice?

Diane was still standing speechless in front of the mirror. "I bet you didn't dream in a million years you had it in you," Ellen said proudly.

Diane nodded dumbly, then said, "I don't even look like me." When she talked, she barely moved her lips. Ellen wondered if this were the first time she'd ever had lipstick on. Poor thing.

"Come on," she said. "Let's take you out for a test drive."

"Oh, I don't know," Diane said, balking, as Ellen took her arm and steered her for the door. The phone rang. Ellen looked at it in surprise. Who had this number? It rang again.

She picked it up and said, "Hello?" No one answered her, but it seemed like someone was there. "Hello?" she said again. Whoever it was hung up. She tried to shrug off her creeping paranoia as she put the receiver down. No one knew to look for her there.

"Where will we go?" Diane asked. She was turning in front of the mirror and apparently getting used to herself.

"Let's go listen to some music," Ellen said, feeling an increasingly urgent need to be gone already. "I know a coffee shop over in Marina Del Rey."

"All right." Diane opened the door and stepped out into the sunlight.

"Just a minute," Ellen said. "I want to get another pair of earrings." She knelt beside the bed to retrieve her jewelry case. Outside she heard squealing tires and the wop wop of a helicopter. It sounded like it was landing on the roof. Men shouted. She heard one of them say, "Ellen Summers," and peeked out the motel room's curtain in time to see a man handcuffing Diane. Diane started to scream, and then another man put something over her face and she slumped to the ground. Ellen scrambled into the bathroom, picking up Diane's discarded clothes as she went. She locked the door behind her, threw open the window, pushed out the screen, and climbed out. It was a wonder she managed to have the presence of mind to take her makeup case with her.

Munch brought the bag of hamburgers to the house. Asia was playing some involved game with the dogs. She'd tied scarves around their necks. "Now, kids," she was saying in a falsetto voice, "you must learn to behave or no cookies."

Sam responded by leaning forward and licking the girl's face. Asia looked up and saw her mother. "She keeps licking the inside of my mouth," she complained.

Munch suppressed a smile. "Go wash your hands. I brought lunch."

From the bathroom Munch heard Asia exclaim in the same falsetto, "Shut the door. Can't I get any privacy around here?"

Nicky's tail could be seen waving out the door.

Munch called her work.

"Bel Air Texaco," Lou answered.

"Hi," she said. "How's it going?"

"You better get in here," he said.

"Why? What's up?"

"Here, I'll let her tell you herself."

Munch heard some scuffling noises as the phone was laid down, then Lou came back on. "I don't know what's going on here. She won't come to the phone."

"That's all right," Munch said. "I'm on my way."

She grabbed a hamburger out of the bag. Asia walked into the kitchen. "Let me see your hands," Munch said.

Asia held out her hands, palms up. They passed inspection. Caroline had heard Munch's end of the telephone conversation and looked at her quizzically. "I need to run by my work real quick," Munch said.

"Did you call Mace?"

"He wasn't in. I'll try again as soon as I get back."

Munch drove to the Texaco station. Lou was talking to a customer when she pulled in. He saw her and pointed to the rear of the shop, circling his finger to indicate that he meant around the back. A six-foot ivy-covered berm separated the rear of the lube bay from a neighboring apartment building. The shop used the space to store broken equipment and used body parts. Munch pushed past an unreliable tranny jack and the fender off a Toyota pickup truck.

A woman stepped out from behind a fifty-gallon drum. Despite the clothes and short straight hair, Munch recognized her immediately. "I oughta kick your ass," she said.

"What did I do?" Ellen said.

"Why don't you tell me," Munch said, not knowing whether to punch or hug her friend. "And where did you get those clothes?"

Ellen tugged at the crocheted vest. "Can you believe people wear this kind of thing when they don't have to?"

Munch held up her hand, hoping to ward off a side trip into bullshit. "C'mon, let's get out of here. You can tell me on the way."

"Where are we going?" Ellen asked. "Back to your house?"

"No, my house isn't safe anymore. Asia and I are staying at a friend's place in Venice."

"What happened at your house?" Ellen asked.

"No," Munch said. "You go first. What happened in Mexico, and what the fuck were you thinking, taking my limo down there in the first place?" Now she felt like hitting her again.

"I was trying to help you out," Ellen said, sounding affronted. Tears formed in her eyes.

"You're dangerous when you think," Munch said, trying to remain indifferent to her friend's tears even though she suspected they were sincere for a change.

They reached Munch's car. Ellen put her head down and slunk into the front seat. "I'm sorry," she said.

Munch came around to the driver's seat. Instead of starting the engine, she said, "I thought you were dead." And then she was crying, too. They hugged. Then laughed, then cried some more. Ellen broke it off first.

"Will you look at the two of us?" she said, laughing and wiping her face with a corner of the crocheted vest. She lifted the corners of the vest with both hands. "Are we a sight or what?" This got them both laughing so hard that they stopped making noise.

Lou walked over to the car and bent down so that he was looking in at them through the driver's window. "What's so funny?" he asked.

Munch composed herself enough to say, "Lou, you remember my friend—"

"Diane," Ellen said, cutting her off. "And no, I don't think we've met."

Ellen's accent was completely absent. She also seemed to have undergone a complete physical transformation. It was just a trick of body language, Munch realized, how Ellen scrunched her nose as she spoke and showed a lot of teeth. She also rounded her shoulders and used her hands a lot.

"I've got to take Diane to—"

"a shelter," Ellen said, finishing her sentence.

"Her—"

"Son of a bitch husband," Ellen said, "has hit me for the last time."

Munch nodded. Had she thought of this before or was this story an inspiration of the moment? Either way, Ellen was good. "I told you that guy was an asshole," Munch said. "So Lou, this guy is dangerous. If anyone comes by asking questions . . ."

"Don't worry," Lou said. "I won't say a thing. When are you coming back to work?"

"As soon as I can," Munch said. "I can't wait for things to get back to normal." She looked at Ellen as she said the last sentence.

Lou patted the window frame, and said, "You do what you need to do."

"Thanks," she said.

As they drove away, Ellen said, "He seems like a nice fellow."

"Forget him," Munch said. "What happened in Mexico?"

"How did you find out about Mexico?" Ellen asked.

"A cop friend of mine found out you crossed the border."

"Why did you think I was dead?"

"That same cop also had a tip that the police had an unidentified murder victim—a young woman wearing nothing but a red wig."

Ellen's face drained of color. "How young?"

"Maybe thirteen. I went to identify her, thinking it was going to be you."

"How was she killed?" Ellen asked.

"She was stabbed with some kind of pointed tool. When the killer was done, he taped white crosses over the wounds. The cop didn't say, but I'm sure the killer was this guy they're calling the Band-Aid Killer."

"What kind of tape?" Ellen asked.

"White medical tape, like the kind they use to hold gauze in place." Munch also told Ellen about the murders in Hollywood and Mexico and finally about the sperm trail in Asia's underwear drawer. "Mace St. John, the detective I know, thinks it must be one of the guys you took down to Mexico."

"I am not surprised. They were not very nice men." Then Ellen told Munch what she had found when she went through each of the unconscious men's pockets.

"That's why we've been so worried about you," Munch said, not missing the fact that Ellen omitted that she had relieved the men of their cash. "I have microphones in the back of the limo that come on whenever the privacy partition goes up. On the tape, they were talking about you. Wondering if you'd seen anything."

"Good," Ellen said. "I hope they are losing sleep over it."

"I wouldn't count on that. These guys are really connected. I heard Mace talking last night. He said every time he gets a lead, his boss tells him to back off. I heard him tell his wife that this guy was probably going to get away with it if they didn't get some kind of break."

"What can we do?"

"I have a plan," Munch said, feeling the delicious thrill of fear mixed with excitement. Being a passive victim had never been her style.

"Hot damn," Ellen said, letting out a hoot. "It's about time we got us a dog in this hunt."

CHAPTER 25

Raleigh couldn't take his eyes off the pictures of the dead women. He had moved his base of operations to a small condo on Barrington in Brentwood. Because of the heat generated by first the Hollywood incident, and then the fiasco in Mexico, many plans had to be changed. Victor was too much of a wild card. The Romanian needed to be brought under control, and if *he* couldn't do it, who was going to?

He spread the photographs of the dead women out before him on his kitchen table. It was clear he needed to take charge of the situation and do the right thing. As usual, the burden fell on his shoulders to act in the best interests of everyone, with or without official sanction.

He lifted the one-pound Folger's coffee can out of his bag of groceries. At least Victor had come through with his promised sample.

Raleigh handled the can with great respect, knowing that nestled within the sawdust inside this can were two buttons of plutonium-239, each weighing a quarter of a kilogram. The reports he read assured him that this particular plutonium isotope had a half-life of more than twenty-four thousand years, meaning that it gave off very few radioactive particles. The most prominent form of radiation it did emit was alpha radiation, which was incapable of even penetrating a sheet of paper, much less a layer of human skin, or the stainless steel of a Folger's coffee can. Still, he was gentle when he removed the can from his bag of groceries.

Cassandra meowed and rubbed against his leg.

"All right," he said, reaching for a can of tuna fish.

"Daddy's taking care of you." He opened the can, separated the chunks on a small ceramic dish, then lifted the cat onto the counter to eat.

He would return the merchandise to Victor in time for the man to complete his transaction. The Libyans had won the bidding war. They would receive the shipment in exchange for $380,000, to be delivered in bundles of hundred-dollar bills. God bless America.

Munch drove to her neighborhood, but didn't make the turn down her street. A quick glance told her that no police cars were parked in front, but who knew who else was watching? She turned down the next street and stopped at the house of the neighbor whose backyard connected to hers.

"Come on," she told Ellen.

Munch knocked on the door. A minute later, she tried the bell.

"It looks like no one is home," Ellen said.

"Yeah, I know the couple who lives here, and they both work," Munch said. "I just wanted to make sure." Munch led the way. They walked casually around to the side of the property where an eight-foot cyclone fence extended from the exterior wall of the garage. On the other side of the fence, there was a narrow dog run that ran the depth of the house and yard. Munch climbed the fence and dropped down into the dirt on the other side. Ellen followed.

An old golden retriever with a white muzzle and rheumy eyes lifted his head. Munch reached down and petted him. "Hey, Rocky," she said. "It's okay, boy." The dog wagged his tail feebly. The two women crossed the neighbor's yard. Munch lifted a loose plank in the fence separating the two yards and slid through. Ellen did the same.

"Let's just do what we came to do," Munch said, as they

entered the house by the back door, "and then get the hell out of here."

"Fine by me," Ellen said.

They both dropped to their hands and knees and crawled across the kitchen floor until they reached the limo office. Munch reached into a filing cabinet and retrieved her log-book. The paperwork from the Saturday night limo booking was right on top. She circled the number Raleigh had called from the limousine.

"Hand me that phone," Ellen whispered.

Thirty minutes later, Munch and Ellen arrived at the house on Carroll Canal. Mace was already there and looking grim. *No surprise there,* Munch thought, feeling herself bristling in the presence of his perpetual anger. *No wonder Caroline is bailing on the relationship.*

Mace stood on the front porch and watched as the two women emerged from the car.

"Hey," Munch said.

"You must be Ellen," Mace said, regarding Munch's pas-senger with a cop's eye for detail.

On the ride over Ellen had ditched the vest and opened the collar of her shirt. Then she'd opened up her hat-box-size cosmetic case and applied eyeliner, three shades of shadow, copious mascara, and a fresh coat of lipstick. Now as she left the car, she raked her eyes over Mace, giving him the full ben-efit of her artwork, and said, "And you must be the man who's going to straighten this whole mess out."

Mace looked up and down the street, then said, "You bet-ter come inside."

The house smelled of freshly baked cookies. Caroline emerged from the bedroom, a worried look on her face. She relaxed visibly when she spotted Munch. "Oh, good," she said. "You're back."

"Anything wrong?" Munch asked. "Where's Asia?"

"She's asleep on my bed," Caroline said.

The bathroom door opened, and Cassiletti stepped out. Ellen brightened. "And who might you be?"

"This is Detective Cassiletti," Munch said.

Ellen extended her hand, all eyes. "Now a girl would feel real safe with you," she said.

"Why don't we all go in the kitchen," Caroline said, casting a nervous glance down the hallway at the open bedroom door. "I'll make some coffee."

After they were all seated around the kitchen table, Munch turned to Ellen. "Tell them what you saw," she said.

"Where would you like me to start?" Ellen asked.

"Pick it up from the bar," Munch said. She noticed the stack of official-looking police documents in the center of the table.

"What bar is this?" Mace asked.

"Some miserable little hole in the wall in Tijuana," Ellen said. "I was going to wait in the car, but Raleigh insisted I come inside."

"Raleigh Ward?" Mace asked.

"Yes, and that other fellow, Victor."

"Victor Draicu?" Mace asked.

"Just Victor. I never got the last name," Ellen answered, casting a look at Munch as if to ask, Does this man want to hear me out, or not? Munch shrugged an answer.

"This man?" Mace asked, holding up the photograph Steve had given him.

"Yes, that's him," Ellen said, then pointed a second man out. "And Raleigh here."

Mace took the picture back and stared at it. "One of these men is Raleigh Ward?"

Munch looked at the picture, too. "Yep, he's the guy right here. With the drink in his hand."

Mace took a pen and circled the image of Raleigh Ward. "Go on," he said.

"Finally," Munch muttered.

"Well, I wasn't going to have anything to drink," Ellen began, shooting an apologetic glance at Munch. Munch raised her hand and shook her head. They'd been through all that in the car. Whatever her intentions had been, she'd blown it. Now all she could do was start over, hopefully that much wiser.

"There was another little gal who joined our party," Ellen continued. "A working girl. Victor took a shine to her."

"How old a girl?" Mace asked, exchanging looks with Munch. She nodded affirmation.

"Same one," she said.

Mace sorted through his papers until he found a photograph. "Is this the same girl?" he asked, showing it to Ellen.

She gasped.

Munch was pretty sure her reaction was genuine. Even though Munch had told her about it all, there was nothing like staring violent death in the face. She looked up at Caroline, whose eyes were moist, rimmed in red.

"Bastards," Caroline hissed.

Mace took her hand in his.

"Her name was Giovanna," Ellen said. "And we're going to get the bastard that did it."

"I'm not so sure about that," Mace said. "Victor Draicu has diplomatic immunity, and Raleigh Ward has disappeared."

"Oh," Ellen said, smiling sideways at Munch, "we might be able to turn over the rock he's hiding under."

"What are you talking about?" Mace said.

"Tell them about—" Munch's words were cut off by the thunder of helicopter blades.

"Oh, shit," Ellen said. "Here we go again." Her words were followed by a pounding on the door that woke up Asia and set the dogs to barking with all their teeth showing.

"FBI," a man's voice boomed from the other side of the door. "Open up."

Mace and Cassiletti took out their badges. Mace pointed

for the women to stand in a corner of the kitchen, then strode to the front of the house. He opened the front door with his badge prominently displayed.

"What's this about?" he asked.

"We have arrest warrants for Ellen Summers and Miranda Mancini," a sandy-haired agent said.

"Can I see them and your identification?" Mace asked.

Asia emerged sleepy-eyed from the bedroom and went to stand at Munch's legs. A sharp rap was heard at the back door, and Munch saw the faces of two more men clothed in SWAT gear.

"Mom?" Asia asked.

Munch bent down and picked her up. "It's okay, honey," she said, smoothing a hand over the girl's sleep-damp curls. Asia snuggled her cheek into the hollow at the base of Munch's neck.

Mace frowned as he looked over the paperwork the FBI agent had handed him.

"What are the charges?" Caroline asked.

"Parole violation, crossing interstate lines to avoid prosecution." Munch looked at her friend with true sympathy. Would she be going back to prison so soon?

"What about Munch?" Caroline said.

Mace looked at her, puzzled. "Kidnapping."

Munch felt the floor lurch, then she realized it was her knees collapsing. She caught herself before she went all the way down. Asia's hands clutched her arms.

"We'll be taking the child, too," the agent said. Another woman entered the room.

"I'm Mrs. Flamm," she said. "I'm with Social Services."

"Wait," Caroline said. "I'm an officer of the court. I work with social services all the time. Leave the child with me until this misunderstanding is straightened out."

"I'm afraid those aren't my orders, ma'am," the sandy-haired agent said.

"Mommy?" Asia asked.

Mrs. Flamm reached for her. The FBI agent produced a set of handcuffs.

Munch blocked out everything and everyone else in the room as she sought the eyes of the child she loved more than anything or anybody in the world. "Don't listen to them," she said. "It's not true. Remember, I love you."

CHAPTER 26

Raleigh picked Victor up in his wheezing Vega. Victor eyed the car with disdain. "Get in," Raleigh said. "This is it."

Victor threw his suitcase into the backseat, cast one more disparaging look at the faded upholstery, then lowered himself into the passenger seat. "This is the best you could do?" he asked.

"Low-profile," Raleigh said. "You've gotta slam the door or it doesn't latch."

Victor pulled his door shut with a resounding crunch. Even though he was ready for it, Raleigh still winced as the vibration and sound played off his bones. He was always extra sensitive like this when the end of a mission was at hand.

"Where to?"

"The bus station in Santa Monica," Victor said. "It's in a locker."

Raleigh waited in the parking lot of the bus station while Victor went inside to retrieve his goods. After ten anxious minutes of breathing diesel exhaust fumes, Raleigh was ready to go in after the guy. But then Victor emerged, carrying a cardboard box and smiling.

"You want to put it in the trunk?" Raleigh asked, slipping a mint into his mouth and wishing he had something stronger.

"No. Where is the sixth can?" Victor asked. "I cannot make the delivery short."

Raleigh reached into the bag of groceries in the backseat and removed the plutonium-laden coffee can that would complete the case. Victor inspected the seams carefully. He would find nothing amiss, Raleigh knew. The engineers who secreted the miniature homing device into the welds at the base of the can didn't make mistakes. They knew lives depended on their work being flawless.

Victor placed this can with the rest of the case and got into the car with the cardboard box balanced on his lap. The exchange was to be made at crowded Pauley Pavilion. It was the perfect venue for this sort of intrigue. The Olympic Committee had voted to have no metal detectors or bomb-sniffing dogs there. The thinking was that Los Angeles was not going to appear to the world to be a police state.

Raleigh handed Victor a green press badge. Victor clipped the badge to his collar.

"So this is it," Victor said.

"Are you okay?" Raleigh asked.

"What is it they call this?" Victor said. "The first day of the rest of my life."

Raleigh couldn't help but smile. He didn't know how right he was.

Ellen and Munch were handcuffed and taken away in separate gray sedans.

"Where are we going?" Munch asked. She had lost sight of the car Ellen was in.

"Downtown," the agent in the passenger seat said.

"I want to talk to whoever's in charge," Munch said. She twisted so that the handcuffs weren't digging into her back.

The two men in the front seat exchanged amused looks. "You do, huh?" the agent in the passenger seat said. "Why don't you tell me whatever it is you want to say, and I'll deliver the message."

"I'll wait," she said. She looked out the window, thinking how long it had been since she'd had her hands bound behind her and her freedom in the control of another. She'd hoped all this stuff was behind her. Someone had told her once that she would have to repeat sober everything she'd done drinking and using. She'd thought they were speaking more metaphorically.

They took her to a sprawling three-story building made of concrete and glass with the California state and American flags flanking the entrance. Her captors drove around to the side of the building, to where an electronic gate slid open. The driveway leading down to the underground parking lot was dark and angled steeply. A yellow sign above the entrance designated the building as a fallout shelter. Inside the black circle with the three inverted yellow triangles was another smaller yellow ring and the words CAPACITY 1730 also printed in yellow.

The garage smelled of exhaust fumes. If the radiation didn't get you, the carbon dioxide would. The passenger agent came around to her door and opened it.

"Let's go," he said, grabbing her arm to help her out of the car.

She shrugged him off and stood on her own. They led her to a small interrogation room and sat her in a straight-backed chair. The walls were lined with acoustical board. Were they keeping sounds in or out? she wondered uneasily. There was no wall of two-way mirror, nothing as obvious as that. She read the graffiti scratched into the metal desk in front of her and waited for her interrogators to return.

After what seemed like an hour—the room had no clock— two different agents unlocked and entered the door.

The first fed, a thin blond man, showed her a birth certificate. It was for a live birth of one Asia Garillo. The mother was listed as Karen Parker, the father Jonathan Garillo.

"I don't see your name anywhere on this document, Ms. Mancini," Blondie said.

"It's bogus," Munch answered, knowing that Karen had given birth at home and never registered Asia's entry into the world.

"There are tests now," the other agent said, stroking his small goatee.

"DNA," Blondie said. He rested his knuckles on the desk top between them. "Ever hear of it?"

Munch remained silent. She was sure one of these guys was going to tell her.

"Every living thing has distinctive markers in its cellular construction," Whiskers said. "Those markers come from two sources, the mother and the father. What do you suppose we'll find if we test you and your so-called daughter?"

"The deal was," Munch said through gritted teeth, "I keep my mouth shut about how a certain situation was handled, and in exchange everybody lives their own lives."

"Don't forget the money," Whiskers said.

The money they referred to was from an FBI fund earmarked for confidential informants. Jonathan Garillo, known to his friends as Sleaze John, had been killed in an FBI scheme to catch a group of dope-smuggling bikers. Asia had been only six months old. Karen Parker, Asia's birth mother, preceded Sleaze in death by two months from a drug overdose.

Munch had helped bring the case against the bikers to a successful close. All she wanted out of the deal originally was to ensure Asia's safety. But the more she learned about how things had gone down, how reckless the feds could be with the lives of others, the angrier she'd become. "You make it sound like I was the one to do something dirty," she said. "The money was for Asia."

"And you used that money to buy a limousine," Blondie said, showing her a copy of the DMV receipt.

"I've got some damaging information on you guys, too," she said, in one last-ditch attempt to gain some footing.

"I don't think blackmailing the government will help you win any custody battles," Whiskers said.

"What do you want?" she asked, feeling her eyes shut with sudden, overwhelming exhaustion.

"Your cooperation," Blondie said. "You and your friend have managed to get yourself in the middle of a matter that involves national, indeed worldwide, security."

"Maybe we can find a way to avoid a lot of grief for all of us," she said.

"That's more of the attitude we like to see," Whiskers said. "What did Ellen tell you about her trip to Mexico?"

"Just that everybody got drunk. She wandered away from the car and got lost. The next morning she hitched back up to Los Angeles, and I had to go down to Mexico to get my car back."

"That's it?" Blondie asked.

"Ask her yourself," Munch said.

"We're polygraphing her now," he said.

Munch relaxed back into the chair and fought back a smile. Ellen ate lie-detector tests for breakfast. "Do what you have to do."

CHAPTER 27

After Victor left the car, Raleigh went to a pay phone and dialed the day's number. When he heard the call go through, he said, "Echo, bravo, two, niner."

"Confirmed."

Several beeps sounded, then another man came on the line. "What's the status with Gameboy?"

"He's making the exchange right now."

"We've begun tracking. Good job."

"Any word on our bogies?" Raleigh asked.

"The two women were apprehended."

"Have they been debriefed?" he asked.

"Yeah, you can relax. The Summers woman remembers nothing from the time she left the bar until she woke up in the bushes the next day."

"You confirmed that with a polygraph?" Raleigh asked, wiping his hands on his pants.

"She came across one hundred percent truthful."

Raleigh knew the news should have given him some sense of relief, yet it didn't. The way this mission had gone to date, he knew it was much too soon to start celebrating. Nothing in this world was ever one hundred percent. That was one of the reasons people like him were needed.

Victor entered the small kitchen off the pressroom and set his case of coffee on the counter. A swarthy man wearing a head scarf approached Victor with a canvas athletic bag in one hand and a cumbersome aluminum briefcase in the other.

Victor took the bag. The Libyan locked the door behind

himself. Victor pointed to the case of coffee cans next to the sink. The Libyan nodded curtly and set his valise down next to the cardboard box. He opened the briefcase, and Victor saw delicate and expensive-looking test equipment nestled in foam rubber.

While Victor unloaded and then stacked the cash on the counter, the Libyan made a small puncture in one of the cans and placed a small piece of what looked like gum foil over the opening. He then took the foil and placed it inside a device that was approximately the size of a portable typewriter. That would be a neutron detector, Victor knew. As much as he understood the process, plutonium's neutron-emitting properties were what split atoms and created fission. The Libyan studied the screen on his machine, then brought out a second device. This piece of equipment was slightly smaller than a shoe box with an L-shaped handle. Two dial-faced gauges protruded from the end. One was labeled ALPHA RADIATION, the other BETA RADIATION. Along the side in neat black letters were the words: SCINTILLATION COUNTER. Victor returned his attention to the bundles of cash, while the quiet man in the head garb did his thing.

Some minutes passed. Then, apparently satisfied with what his instruments had detected, the Libyan resealed the opening he had made in the can with a lead-colored paste.

Throughout the exchange, the two men said nothing. Victor finally broke the silence with, "Are you satisfied?"

The Libyan nodded. Victor clapped him on the back. "Very good," he said. Satisfaction was always good.

Raleigh watched Victor approach the car clutching a canvas bag to his chest.

"How did it go?" Raleigh asked.

"No problem."

They got on the 405 freeway and drove north. Victor asked

no questions, which suited Raleigh just fine. The sooner he was shed of this guy the better. Once again, it had all come down to him.

"We had to make some adjustments to the plan. Seems there was a witness to what happened in Mexico."

"Ellen?"

"That's right, and she's threatening to go public."

"This is bad," Victor said. He smiled. "Bad for you."

"We're going to turn it around."

"Turn what around?"

"You're really going to disappear, Victor," Raleigh said. They had crested the Sepulveda pass. Raleigh stayed in the right lane, the one that fed into the Ventura freeways. They passed under the sign that read VENTURA FREEWAY WEST.

Victor nodded at the passing scenery, smiling. "At last."

They got off the freeway at Sherman Way and followed signs to the Van Nuys airport. "We're going to go one better than you simply dropping out of sight. We're going to make sure that nobody ever looks for you."

Raleigh reached behind him and grabbed a valise. He hoisted it between the seat and dropped it in Victor's lap. "Open it."

Victor did. "This is just blank paper," he said. "Hotel stationery."

"Take the pen and write your suicide note."

"My . . . ? Oh, I see. Very clever."

They stopped at a padlocked gate. Raleigh got out of the car. Shielding his activities from Victor, he picked the lock and swung the gate open. When he got back into the car, Victor was still staring over the blank page.

"What should I say?" Victor asked.

"Just write that you can't go on living this double life. Apologize to your family and country. Say that this was the only way out for you."

Victor nodded as Raleigh spoke. The hotel pen moved

quickly across the page. "This is a good idea. Make sure a copy of this note gets to my brother's superiors."

Raleigh was gratified that Victor was thinking of someone else besides himself for a change. He knew the Romanian had left his brother holding the bag for the missing shipment of uranium. If Raleigh had had a brother, he would never have done such a thing. If he had had a brother, the two of them would have stood together against their mother.

"Say that what happened in Mexico was unavoidable," Raleigh told Victor. "That someone must answer for the tragic way those three people died."

"Three?" Victor asked, his pen stopping.

"Work with me, Vic," Raleigh said.

"Only in America," the Romanian mumbled, as Raleigh jumped out of the Vega to open the door of an abandoned hangar. He pulled the car inside.

"Where's my Cadillac?" Victor asked.

"It's coming."

Raleigh opened the trunk and pulled out a wad of pastel fabric. From a brown paper sack he withdrew a 9mm automatic.

"Victor," he called as he squeezed clumps of swimmer's wax into each ear. "Come on over here."

Victor walked to the back of the car.

"No, over here," Raleigh said, moving toward a low steel cart covered with a canvas tarp. He handed Victor the gun. "Hold this like you're going to shoot it. We need your prints on the gun."

"Is it loaded?" Victor asked.

"Now, how safe would that be?" Raleigh said.

Victor wrapped his hand around the butt of the gun and slipped his finger into the trigger guard. Raleigh grabbed Victor's hand and with one deft move was standing behind him. The gun now pointed at Victor's temple. Raleigh angled the muzzle away from himself and slipped his own finger over

Victor's. The trick was to find the temporal lobe. He favored eye sockets, but those entries were rarely seen in suicides, and it was important this look authentic.

Victor's body bucked in his arms. For all his excesses, Victor was still strong.

"Time to pledge allegiance," Raleigh whispered into the man's ear, then he squeezed the trigger. The pop of the gunshot resounded sharply off the hangar walls. Victor jolted backward, nearly butting Raleigh's head. And then he was still. Raleigh allowed the body to drop, holding the gun hand so that Victor's grip stayed intact.

Raleigh placed the hand with the gun still in it to the dead man's side and removed the wax from his ears. The finishing touch was the wad of pink fabric. Raleigh ran a finger lovingly over the embroidery, feeling a surge of his juices at the sight of the delicate little crotch panel between the seams of white elastic. He pressed that sweet spot of the panties briefly to his lips, regretting the need to give them up.

"So be it." He sighed, stuffing them into Victor's pocket. "You're it, Vic. As my mother would say, you've been wicked. A very wicked boy."

He brought up the edges of the tarp so that they covered the body, then wheeled it over to a door that connected to the next hangar. There was a brand-new taupe-colored Cadillac Eldorado with leather upholstery parked there already. He threw the canvas bag full of cash behind the driver's seat, then went back to mop up the trail of blood.

He used industrial-strength floor cleaner and a high-powered hose, humming as he worked. This was the last time he would be cleaning up after this asshole.

Twenty minutes later there was nothing to identify the hangar as a crime scene. He removed the Vega's license plates and brought them over to a neighboring hangar. The facility had been vacant for months, the lease and prepaid rent seized by the government when the former tenants had been caught smuggling drugs. The Vega, whenever it was found, would be untraceable.

Raleigh let himself into a smaller room that had once served as an office for the former tenants. He sat down behind the desk and studied the posters lining the walls. Bikini-clad women sunned themselves on virgin beaches while cerulean blue waters lapped at their toes. He was due for an extended vacation. Lord knew, he had it coming.

He looked at the phone for a minute before picking it up. Might as well make a clean sweep of things. He dialed his estranged wife's number.

"Pam?" he asked when she answered the phone. "Please don't hang up."

"What do you want?" she asked.

"I was hoping we could spend some time together."

"Oh, yeah? Who's Ellen?" she asked.

"Ellen?" he echoed, his hand gripping the phone.

"Yeah, she called this morning. She said she had some tape you left behind in her limousine. Some kind of bandage stuff. When were you in a limousine?"

"It was part of a job."

"Oh, I see," she said, the familiar coldness slipping back into her voice.

"Did Ellen mention where I could pick up the tape?" he asked.

"I don't know why I have to be involved in this. How did she even have my number? What's going on?"

"Please, Pam," he said, feeling the blood pounding behind his eyes. "What exactly did she say?"

"She said you owed her for damages. I told her we were legally separated and that I wasn't responsible for your debts."

"You have no idea how much you're responsible for," he said. "None of you women ever think you have to pay." He slammed down the phone. That was going to change.

CHAPTER 28

"Did you know about this?" Mace asked Caroline, still feeling the devastation of watching Asia and Munch wrenched from each other. Goddamn her and her complicated life. The child had cried and screamed for her mother as she was led away, even beseeched Mace to do something, anything. The agents had at least had the sensitivity not to handcuff Munch in front of the kid.

"I knew she wasn't the birth mother," Caroline said, hanging up the phone after leaving a message for her friend who worked for the Dependency Court system as a children's advocate.

"Were you going to tell me?" Mace asked.

"Where are the parents?" Cassiletti asked.

"They're dead," Caroline said. "The mother died of a drug overdose when Asia was four months old. The father was killed in a shooting two months after that."

"Munch said that he got on the wrong end of a dope deal with some bikers," Mace said. "She left out the part about not being the real mother."

"The birth mother," Caroline corrected. "She's raised that child as her own for the last six years."

"Sounds like the kidnapping charge is a stretch," he said.

"It's complicated," Caroline said. "But I'm sure we can help her."

We, Mace thought. *She said, We.*

"Sir?" Cassiletti said. Caroline and Mace both shifted their attention to the big man. "What do you suppose Ellen meant about turning over the rock he was lying under?"

"I don't know," he said. "Why would they even want to draw the guy out?"

"Perhaps she's angry," Caroline said. "That's always a powerful motivator."

"Look where it's got them," Mace said, choosing to ignore Caroline's irony. He was in no mood for another character lesson.

"Can you help them?" Caroline asked.

"I doubt if the feds will let me get near them. They'll probably slap a forty-eight-hour hold on them without filing charges. And you can be pretty damn sure they won't be allowing any phone calls or interviews." Mace picked up the phone and called Steve's pager. Two minutes later the phone rang.

"St. John," Mace answered. It was Steve Brown returning his call.

"We went out to the boyfriend's apartment," Steve said. "He's gone. A note on the door says he's taken a week's vacation."

"Just ducky," Mace said. "Suddenly everyone inconvenient is out of the way. You know that picture you lent me?"

"Yeah," Steve said.

"My witness identified one of the men in it as Raleigh Ward."

"That's not surprising. Ward and Draicu probably go back a long way together."

Mace felt a dull thudding in his temples. A kaleidoscope of thoughts tumbled through his brain, each theory uglier than the last. He felt his case spinning out of his control.

"Hey," Steve said. "Hold on a minute. Something's coming over the radio." Mace waited, hearing the sounds of air chatter, call numbers. Steve came back on the phone. "Your troubles might all be over, buddy."

"Yeah, why's that?" Mace asked.

"Victor Draicu has turned up. He blew his brains out."

"Oh, really?" Mace said.

"Yep, suicide—the sincerest form of apology."

"How convenient."

"What's it take to make you happy?" Steve asked.

"Now you sound like my"—he looked over and saw Caroline watching him—"doctor," he finished. "I'll roll out there, now. Thanks for the heads-up."

"What's going on?" Caroline asked.

"Victor Draicu has apparently killed himself. I'm going to go check it out."

"Be careful," she said.

"What do I have to worry about?" he said. "The bad guy is dead."

Cassiletti's expression was that of a man trying very hard to figure out if what he'd just heard was a joke and, if so, what the punch line was.

The body was in a remote stretch of Balboa Park on the Encino-Reseda border. Two boys on bicycles had discovered it and called the police. When Mace and Cassiletti got there, the area was cordoned off with sawhorses, police cars, and yellow crime-scene tape. Channels 2, 4, and 7 all had sent satellite vans and their top reporters. Another news helicopter hovered overhead. Deputy Chief Tumpane was there, as was Captain Earl.

"Looks like you were right," Tumpane said, as Mace approached the scene.

"Thank you, sir," Mace said.

The body was lying on a bed of leaves, under a canopy of morning glory vines. Apparently the sprinkler system had come on recently. The ground cover underfoot squished as they approached. Mace noticed something pink protruding from Victor Draicu's pocket. Using his pen, he extracted the object. It was a pair of little girl's panties. Monday, the script writing read.

"There's a note, too," Earl said.

"Confessing to everything?" Mace asked. He noticed the positioning of Victor's hand over his heart.

"I'll be recommending a commendation," Earl said. "The mayor is going to be very pleased."

"That's great," Mace said. "Just great."

"How's the dog?" the FBI agent captaining the boat asked.

Derek lifted his head and mumbled, "I think she's over the worst of it." He sighed and rolled over, taking a sip of his Diet Coke. They had been cruising the bay for the last few hours. The forty-foot ketch had formerly belonged to a Colombian drug lord, he was told. Now it was the property of the United States government, and Derek was their guest. The arrangements had been hurried, barely giving him time to grab a pair of swim trunks, a few changes of clothes, and leave a note on his door.

They couldn't tell him how long his stay would last. Derek told them not to worry. He could get used to this. He was nothing if not accommodating. "Just keep the Diet Coke and Alpo flowing," he said.

He looked now into the box where Violet lay whining miserably. Her long ears were matted with vomit. She turned sad eyes on her master and started to heave again. Derek dipped the edge of his towel overboard and used the damp corners to bring whatever comfort he could to the dog.

Idly, he wondered what Munch was doing.

CHAPTER 29

Munch was released from the U.S. Marshal's temporary holding facility the following morning. Charges weren't going to be filed, after all. She was not surprised. Nobody apologized throughout the long release procedure. Not the deputy who fetched her bag of street clothes, or the cop in property who had her sign for her keys and pocket change that had been scrupulously inventoried and held for safekeeping in a manila envelope.

Mace and Cassiletti were there in the lobby when she emerged.

"Asia's fine," Mace said.

"Where is she?" Munch asked, striding past them, anxious to be away from that place.

"We took her over to the Bella Donna. Caroline was able to convince the court to let her stay with us until this is all straightened out."

"I guess it's time to do that," Munch said, glad to hear they had had the sense to get away from the house. The train car was much more defensible, set out in the open, and girded with inches of steel. She stepped out into the bright sunlight and blinked. The next thing she did was rip off the plastic wristband and throw it at the building behind her.

"You know," Mace said, "that's what I like about you. You never go for the easy way. You can't just have a kid. It's got to be somebody else's kid."

"Mace—" Cassiletti said, looking nervously at Munch. "She's been through a lot."

"Excuse me," he said. "Was I being insensitive? Where are my manners?"

"What are you pissed off at me for?" Munch asked.

"I'm sick of having to waste my time worrying about everybody," he said.

She ran her hands through her hair, wishing she had a brush. Her mouth tasted like old coffee. She stopped at the stairs to bend down and tie her shoes.

"Where's Ellen?"

"Still in custody."

"Where?"

"I think you should be worrying about you," Mace said.

She straightened and stared at him. "You got some kind of personal rule about not letting people think for themselves?"

Mace looked surprised. Cassiletti, she noted, was almost smiling.

"Your friend is still in federal custody pending transfer to county and a parole hearing. Feel better now?"

"Yeah, tons." She sniffed.

The three of them walked out to the parking lot, Munch and Mace side by side, Cassiletti bringing up the rear.

"It's over," Mace said. "Victor Draicu killed himself."

"I'm sure he did the right thing," Munch said. "But it's far from over. Ellen saw him kill one of those men in Mexico. The younger guy went first, she said. Then Raleigh slit the older guy's throat. They didn't know she saw. The first chance she got, she slipped them a Mickey, then dumped their bodies by the side of the road."

"We figured that much out," Mace said.

"But what you didn't know was that when she went through their pockets she found a roll of Johnson & Johnson medical tape on Raleigh. He also had some weird kind of knife strapped to his shin. It was long and pointy and had some kind of modified brass-knuckles-looking thing for a grip."

"Three-fingered thrust dagger," Mace said, nodding. "What did she mean," he asked, "about not hearing the last from Raleigh Ward?" He unlocked the car and opened the passenger door for Munch. She got in the front; Cassiletti slid into the back.

"We called his ex," Munch said after Mace had come around to the driver's side and gotten in.

"You did what?"

"You know that woman he called from the limo at the end of the run? Ellen told her that he owed us for damages and that for a price she'd sell him back the roll of tape."

"Do you have any idea what you've done?" Mace's eyes turned cold and hard. He slammed his hand on the dashboard. "Forget how much you've jeopardized the case. You put yourselves in danger. Why didn't you call me? Fuck!" He hit the steering wheel, took a deep breath, and gave her a look that would peel chrome. "Where is it now?"

"You'd have to ask her that." His anger scared her, but she wasn't about to deprive Ellen of her hard-earned bargaining chip. Her little excursion to Mexico was a parole violation. Enough of a violation to put her back in prison for six months. Another stretch of CIW would not help her on the road to recovery.

"Did his ex say she knew where he was?" Mace maneuvered his sedan out of the parking lot.

"No, she was pretty hostile. She said they were almost divorced and had been legally separated since December."

"What did you hope to accomplish?" Mace asked. His tone was quiet, low. It bothered her worse than his shouting.

"I'm trying to help you grab this guy, in case you hadn't noticed." She tucked her hair behind her ears.

"That's my job," he said.

"I know," she answered. She realized she was close to tears. Tears she didn't want him to see. Out of reflex, she had begun braiding her hair. In the bad old days, when part of the evening's entertainment usually involved a fistfight, she always tied her hair back first. Glasses off, hair back. Those were the indicators that she was ready to get down to it. Tears had no place in the equation. Tears were for later. She turned to Mace with resolve in her voice, and asked, "You got an elastic band or something for my hair?"

"Look in the glove box," Mace said, casting her a half-amused smile.

Munch rummaged in the glove box, finding a packet of maps bound together. She liberated the red rubber band holding them together and used it to secure her braid.

"You know you've set yourself up as a target now," Mace said.

"Better me than my kid," Munch said.

"I'm not letting you out of my sight," Mace said.

"I was sort of counting on that," Munch said. "Let's go pick up my limo. And then we'll go get Ellen. Don't worry. She'll corroborate the evidence. No way will this guy walk. We've got him cold."

"We got nothing yet," Mace said.

"We will," she said, squinting out the window.

Raleigh didn't get back home until four in the morning. Cassandra made a point of ignoring him until he made her her favorite treat of scrambled eggs with lots of butter. After seeing to the cat's needs, he fell into the deep, untroubled sleep of the righteous.

It was nearly 9 A.M. when he woke up. He listened to the radio as he got dressed, putting on his black track suit. The top news story was the suicide found in Balboa Park. Police were attributing a string of murder/rapes to the as-yet-unidentified white male.

Raleigh reached into his pocket and pulled out a vial of pills. Who knew when he'd be sleeping again? He fortified himself with the last of his uppers. Another trip across the border was obviously in order.

He grabbed his new gym bag by its straps and slung it over his shoulder. He actually whistled as he took the stairs down to the underground parking. He'd forgotten the simple pleasure of driving a fine automobile. The Cadillac handled like a dream. One thing he had to say about Victor, the guy had good taste in cars.

If only Raleigh had known last night what he knew now, Victor would very probably still be among the living. Raleigh had at least five more victims in mind to credit to Victor's account. He'd start with Ellen Summers, Munch Mancini, and the little girl-child. He'd never had three at once. He'd like to take them somewhere where their screams wouldn't be heard. Where they'd be conscious to watch and let their fear build. He would take his time with them.

On his way out of town, he'd make time for his ex-wives. He was unstoppable. He could feel the power running through him. Perhaps he was finally on his way to running the world.

Even Victor was still helping from beyond the grave. Raleigh was grateful that old Vic hadn't requested a Porsche or a Corvette. No, he wanted a Cadillac. And wouldn't the car's big trunk come in handy? It had already.

Raleigh chuckled as he unlocked the door of the Eldorado, threw the canvas bag full of money behind the driver's seat, and slipped behind the wheel.

"Ah, me," he said out loud, rubbing his hand across the seat. Nothing like the feel and smell of leather. He reached over into the glove compartment and pulled out his FBI identification. Just a few more loose ends to take care of, and then he would be on his way.

He thought about the money in the backseat. A man could live like a king in Mexico with that kind of money. Hot- and cold-running señoritas. Well, forget the running part. He laughed. He'd learned so much about himself in the six months. The denial was over. It was time he stopped worrying about everyone else and do a little something special for himself. A third-world country was the ticket. Somewhere where the value of life was cheap and all ages of female flesh plentiful.

Ellen was not surprised when she saw the face of the man who had come to take her out of federal custody. She also knew they weren't heading for county lockup.

"I see you got my message," she said as they left the Federal Building.

"Where is it?" he asked. He led her over to a new-looking Cadillac parked at the curb.

"Did you bring my money?" she countered.

"How much do you want?" he asked.

"Five thousand dollars," she said. "And that is not negotiable."

"I wouldn't dream of it," he said, taking her arm and helping her into the car. "Where is it?"

Raleigh's quick acceptance of her terms disquieted Ellen. Either she had asked for too little, or the sucker had no intention of paying. "You sure you can get the money?" she asked.

He reached behind him and unzipped a bag stashed behind the front seat. Her eyes widened when she saw the bundles of hundreds revealed. He zipped it back shut and started the car. "Where's the tape?"

"I'll have to go get it," she said.

"I'll take you," he answered, pulling away from the curb.

"No," she said. "That is not the way it is going to happen. I will go get it. You bring the money. We'll meet at, uh, Mr. J's on Lincoln. You know it?" Raleigh had stopped responding to her. In fact, his whole manner toward her had changed from the moment the car got in motion. Without even asking her what direction to go in, he got on the freeway. "It's somewhere very safe. Your prints are all over it. Anything happens to me, and my friend makes sure the D.A. gets it."

"You've been very clever, haven't you?" Raleigh said.

"Why don't you pull off up here?" she said, pointing at the next off-ramp. "Let me out, and I'll meet you in an hour."

He made no move to get over into the right lane. She started to say something else when his fist shot out at her. She felt her lip split like a ripe plum. Hot blood filled her mouth. He hit her again, this time above the bridge of her nose. The world around her receded into echoes and blackness.

Steve Brown radioed Mace as soon as he saw Raleigh Ward escort Ellen out from the federal courthouse. She wasn't hand-cuffed and didn't look distressed. The two got into a taupe-col-ored Cadillac Eldorado and jumped on the Hollywood freeway. Steve took up a cautious pursuit. He read off the plate number to Mace as they maneuvered through the crush of morning traf-fic. The situation quickly got out of control as six lanes of com-muter traffic converged and merged. He knew that up ahead were several options. Raleigh could stay on the 101, or he might break off and take the Harbor or the Pasadena freeway.

Just then a bus pulled in front of Steve, temporarily block-ing his view. By the time he was clear of it, the Cadillac was nowhere in sight.

"Fuck," he said out loud, and then relayed the bad news to Mace.

Mace was waiting for Munch as she rolled out of the driveway of the Parker Center Print Shed, where her limo had been kept while criminalists searched for fibers and prints. The Print Shed was located just behind Parker Center and adja-cent to the employee parking lot. She'd signed all the requi-site release forms, noting with resignation the black powder all over the bar, the television, and the passenger control pan-els for all the car's various bells and whistles.

As soon as she cleared the gate, Mace jumped in beside her. "Raleigh has Ellen," he said. "Turn right up here and jump on the freeway."

Munch floored the accelerator and followed his directions. "Which way?" she asked.

"Stay on the Hollywood," Mace said. "He's in a late-model light beige Caddy Eldorado. Last seen heading north."

"Last seen?" Munch asked, running a red light and swerving to avoid a Honda.

"We lost him at the merge. Cassiletti took the Pasadena, and we have another unit heading south on the Harbor."

Munch turned onto the on-ramp, ignoring the twenty-mile-per-hour sign, making the tires scream as she took the sharp curve at forty miles per hour. Mace clutched the hand-hold above the door with one hand while he worked the mouthpiece of his radio with the other. She steered onto the emergency shoulder lane of the freeway and floored it. The limo jumped over the roadside debris. The remains of a tire thumped the undercarriage. She heard glass break as she rolled over an orange plastic bag full of garbage.

"I see him," she said. She started trying to merge into traffic. The shoulder up ahead was occupied by a pickup truck full of plywood. As she got closer, she saw that the truck's driveshaft was hanging loose.

"Possible suspect sighted," Mace said into his mouthpiece. "He's on the Hollywood northbound."

"He's getting off," Munch said. She rolled down her window and signaled desperately with her arm. None of the parallel traffic gave any indication of allowing her in. "Hold on," she said, and cut the wheel hard. Horns blared. Brakes shrieked in the fashion that usually precedes the sound of scrunching metal. The limo jolted as it pushed aside a Volkswagen Rabbit. The rest of the traffic magically cleared a place for her. "We're losing him," she yelled.

Mace continued to relay their position. Munch fought her way over to the two-lane Glendale off-ramp. She was just in time to see the rear of the Caddy making the curve at the top of the overpass. "I don't see Ellen," she said.

She kept her foot on the accelerator and quickly closed on the Cadillac. They pulled alongside, and she saw what looked like blood smeared on the inside of the passenger window.

"Wait for backup," Mace said. "Just stay with him."

Raleigh looked over then, and their eyes met. His expression didn't change as he swerved toward the limo, knocking his right fender into the driver's side of the limo. Both cars jerked. Munch looked over in time to see Ellen's head flop backward. Her face was bloody. Munch couldn't tell if she was just unconscious or—Bam! He swerved into her again. Munch fought for control. The limo was knocked over into the guardrail of the overpass. She pumped the brakes and fought all survival instincts telling her to steer away from the edge of the road. Instead she turned into the skid, an action that made her feel as if she were heading for the edge and a thirty-foot drop. Which indeed she was. But her action was also the only way she could hope to regain control. She was only vaguely aware that she was screaming. Mace also yelled. Then they hit a large concrete stanchion, and the big car caromed back into the lane.

Mace started to speak into his radio, then threw it down.

"What?" she asked, her throat feeling raw.

"It broke," he said, holding up the severed cord.

Up ahead, Raleigh took the first available off-ramp, heading for the sleepy town of Eagle Rock. Munch again took up pursuit. "The phone's in the back," she said. "In the armrest."

Mace climbed over the driver's seat to get to it.

She took the same off-ramp Raleigh had disappeared down, looking desperately for some glimpse of him. At the intersection at the bottom of the ramp, she spotted a hubcap still wobbling on the side of the road to their right. She followed in the direction he must have gone.

"How do I get this thing to work?" Mace asked from the backseat.

She spotted the Caddy making a left up ahead. She had a clean shot at the driver's side. "Hold on," she yelled again to Mace.

She aimed for the Caddy's front wheel well, thinking that she would disable the other vehicle by wiping out the steering linkage. Later, if it came to that, she would say that she must have miscalculated the speed of the other car, she would swear to it if she had to. The truth was that the last few seconds before contact seemed to happen in slow motion. Just before the two cars collided she saw two hands to the right of Raleigh's head. One was his, something glinted long and silvery in the second. Raleigh's Cadillac swerved left. The front fender of the limo plowed right through the wide driver's door of the Eldorado.

Both cars threw up showers of tempered window glass. Steel screamed in protest as it was ripped from its bolted moorings. She didn't hear the tires popping. Her chest hit the steering wheel, and then the side of her head smashed against the window post. She felt the thud of Mace's body being knocked around in the back. Then all was still.

A minute, maybe more, passed before she was able to make sense of the world.

"You okay?" she asked Mace in the backseat.

"Yeah, yeah," he said. He let himself out the back door as she shakily emerged from her side. They stumbled over to the wreckage and looked in through the window of the Eldorado. Ellen groaned. She was holding a bloody hand to her mouth. Her eyes were glazed over. Raleigh seemed worse off. A gash had opened on his throat. The blood leaking out was a dark bright red.

"Call for help," Mace said as he went around to Ellen's side of the car.

Munch went back to the limo and used the mobile phone to call the police. Within minutes, fire trucks and police cars reached the scene of the accident. Cassiletti arrived just as the first ambulance got there. Ellen managed to find a damaged smile for the fireman who lifted her from the wrecked car.

"Would you just be a dear," Ellen asked him, "and grab my bag from the backseat?"

The Jaws of Life had to be used to remove Raleigh from the wreckage. The rescue workers did what they could to stop the flow of blood streaming from Raleigh's neck wound. They loaded him onto a gurney and rushed to the waiting ambulance.

As they passed by her, Munch made a quick assessment. He was still alive. His skin looked extremely pale, but she could see his chest rise and fall. He made slight snoring noises as he exhaled.

One of his pant legs was ripped, and the sheath for his odd knife that Ellen had described was plainly visible. Munch noticed it was empty. She pictured the wound on Raleigh's neck—how it had looked before the paramedics covered it. It looked just like the wound she had seen on the Mexican woman's body in the Tijuana morgue. Munch looked for her friend and saw her sitting on the curb. Beside her was a storm drain. Ellen was wiping her hands on the grass beside her.

Fucking Ellen. You have to love her.

"Take him to County," Mace told the ambulance driver.

Munch looked at Mace. So did Cassiletti. Then they looked at each other, and knew they were all of the same mind. How could it ever be proved that any of them remembered Glendale Memorial, less than five minutes away, whereas USC County was easily three times the distance and twice the traffic? The bleeding man would never make it.

Mace walked over to where Ellen was being ministered to at the side of the road. "How are you?" he asked.

"I believe I'll be just fine," she said.

"I'll have an officer take you to the hospital just to make sure."

Ellen winked at Munch. Munch could only wonder what she had up her sleeve.

CHAPTER 30

After the limo was towed away, Cassiletti gave Munch and Mace a ride over to the Bella Donna.

"You want to come in?" Mace asked Cassiletti.

Caroline and Asia came out to the platform. "Mommy!" Asia yelled. Munch waved and opened the car door before the car came to a complete stop.

"No, you go on," Cassiletti said. "I'll start writing up our report."

Munch jumped from the car and ran over to the steps of the train car. She gathered Asia in her arms and hugged her until the little girl squirmed and begged to be released.

Caroline watched with tears running freely. Even Mace was seen scratching the corner of his eye.

"C'mon," he said, shooing them all inside. "I need a drink."

They entered the parlor.

"Mom," Asia said, "you should see this place." She grabbed Munch's hand and showed her the brass lamps with the Tiffany shades bolted to the small wooden tables. She demonstrated how the green-satin shades pulled down over the leaded-glass windows.

"Hey, easy with that," Mace said.

"Watch this," Asia said. She sat in an armchair next to the door and pushed one of the white buttons set in brass on the wall. A slight clunk was heard in the kitchen. Asia led Munch in there and showed her where a number 1 had dropped into a slot. "That's so the potter knows who wants something."

"The porter, dear," Caroline said.

"Cool," Munch said.

"And the piano," Asia said. "It really works."

"Wow," Munch said, memorizing every nuance of expression on her beloved little girl's face. She bent down until they were at eye level. "Honey, you know how we talked about how some mommies grow babies in their tummies and some get their babies from other ladies' tummies?"

"It's okay, Mom," Asia said. "I love you no matter where you come from."

"I spoke to an attorney friend," Caroline said. "She's going to pave the way for you to resolve your custody issue."

"Thanks," Munch said. Had ever the word felt more inadequate?

Mace set Asia on one of the barstools and lifted the bar top to let himself in behind the bar. "What can I get you, ma'am?" he asked her.

Asia grinned, clearly in heaven. "A martini," she said.

"One Shirley Temple coming right up," Mace said.

Munch moved closer to Caroline and spoke in a tone keyed out of Asia's hearing range. "So what's next?"

"For now the court has granted you guardianship. The judge is convinced it would be detrimental to the minor involved to break custody. They'll want to do a home study and a background check. We'll write you letters of recommendation. Everything will work out."

"Anything I should be doing to get ready?" Munch asked.

"Do you have anything in writing that indicates that you have the consent of the parents?"

"You mean like a will or something?" Munch asked.

"Social Services would accept a letter in Jonathan Garillo's or Karen Parker's handwriting in lieu of a formally witnessed document."

"I think I have something like that," Munch said. "It just needs to say that me having Asia is what he wanted, right?" Finding such a document should be no trouble at all.

Caroline's mouth formed a half smile. "Yes, that should do it." The two women embraced.

"All right, all right," Mace called out from behind the bar top. "Enough with all that. I'm still taking orders here." He addressed Munch. "What'll be? A Coke?"

"Coffee," she said, moving to the small porter's kitchen. "I'll get it." The cabinets were lined with snug-fitting shelves, reminding her of the setup in her limo. She imagined that when a train was in motion, it was much like a boat, and everything needed to be secured to handle the sway and bumps of the track. She found a kettle and filled it with water, then opened other cabinets until she found instant coffee, creamer, sugar, and mugs.

"How about you, Caroline?" Munch asked.

Caroline was sitting on the piano bench, watching the play between Mace and Asia. "I'm fine," she said.

Munch filled a mug and brought it into the front room of the Bella Donna. Mace turned to say something to her, and then his face went ashen.

"What?" Munch asked, looking down at her clothes, her chest, wondering what had caused his reaction. Then she looked at the mug in her hand, noticing for the first time the name printed across it: Digger. "Oh," she said. "I'm sorry. I didn't mean to—"

But Mace cut her off with an upturned palm. "It's all right," he said. "I, uh. I, just, uh." He clamped his mouth shut and shook his head. When he spoke, his voice was strangled. "Excuse me a minute." He stumbled out from behind the bar, down the hallway toward the rear bedroom.

The women watched him stop, turn, then sink to his knees in an upright fetal position. He covered his face, and a moment later they heard the unmistakable sounds of a grown man sobbing.

"Mommy?" Asia asked.

"Don't worry," Munch said. "It's okay."

Caroline was already up and moving down the hallway. Then she was beside her husband, cradling him, rocking him. After a minute, Mace's arms opened to accept her.

Munch heard her murmur, "Finally."

EPILOGUE

That evening Munch saw a green four-door Buick sedan drop Derek and Violet off in front of his building. Derek waved good-bye with the sheaf of papers in his hand.

"Where have you been?" she asked.

"I cannot comment on that," he said.

"What's got into you?"

"I've had an epiphany," he said. "I'm going to become an FBI agent." He crossed the street to show her the papers. They were application forms. "I'm going to need a reference from someone in law enforcement. Do you think Mace St. John would help me out?"

"I don't know. I think he's planning on taking a week off from work. Maybe you can ask him when he gets back."

"Hey," Derek said, "where's the limo?"

"At the body shop." She didn't tell him about the bundle of hundred-dollar bills Ellen had pressed on her at the hospital. She hadn't asked Ellen where they came from. With Ellen, it was sometimes better just not to know.

"What happened?" he asked.

"Got in a little fender bender."

"What about your friend?"

"She needs a little work, too."

"But everything turned out okay, right?" he asked.

"Yeah, I guess it did." From inside the house, Munch heard the phone ringing. She ran inside to catch it. She was trying to get Ellen a bed in a women's recovery house. They said they would call if a space for Ellen opened. Whether she would stay there was up to her.

ABOUT THE AUTHOR

Barbara Seranella was born in Santa Monica and grew up in Pacific Palisades. After a restless childhood that included running away from home at fourteen, joining a hippie commune in the Haight, and riding with outlaw motorcycle clubs, she decided to settle down and do something normal, so she became an auto mechanic.

She worked at an Arco station in Sherman Oaks for five years and then a Texaco station in Brentwood for another twelve. At the Texaco station, she rose to the rank of service manager before retiring in 1993 to pursue the writing life.

When working on her novels, she spends many hours doing on-location research. She has toured crime labs and crime scenes, gone on ride-alongs, and interviewed homicide detectives as well as criminals or anyone else who figures in her stories. She reports that ride-alongs are much more fun when you are sitting in the front seat.

Seranella is a member of the Orange County Sisters in Crime and the Mystery Writers of America. She's the First Vice President of the Palm Springs Branch of the League of American Pen Women as well as the Palm Springs Writers Guild.

Other novels by Seranella include *No Human Involved* (which debuted at number five on the *LA Times* best seller list, made Amazon.com's list of best ten mysteries of 1997, and went into four printings), and *No Offense Intended*. Both novels feature lady mechanic with a past, Munch Mancini.

Mrs. Seranella divides her time between her homes in Laguna Beach and La Quinta, California, where she lives with her husband, Ron, and their three dogs.